UNLUCKY CHARMS

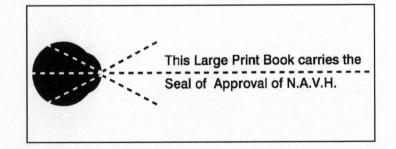

This Large Print Book carries the
Seal of Approval of N.A.V.H.

A SUPERSTITION MYSTERY

UNLUCKY CHARMS

LINDA O. JOHNSTON

WHEELER PUBLISHING
A part of Gale, Cengage Learning

GALE
CENGAGE Learning·

Farmington Hills, Mich • San Francisco • New York • Waterville, Maine
Meriden, Conn • Mason, Ohio • Chicago

GALE
CENGAGE Learning·

LIBRARY OF CONGRESS CATALOGING-IN-PUBLICATION DATA

Names: Johnston, Linda O., author.
Title: Unlucky charms / Linda O. Johnston.
Description: Large print edition. | Waterville, Maine : Wheeler Publishing Large Print, 2017. | Series: A superstition mystery | Series: Wheeler Publishing Large Print cozy mystery
Identifiers: LCCN 2016045204| ISBN 9781410494634 (paperback) | ISBN 1410494632 (softcover)
Subjects: LCSH: Murder—Investigation—Fiction. | Superstition—Fiction. | BISAC: FICTION / Mystery & Detective / Women Sleuths. | GSAFD: Mystery fiction.
Classification: LCC PS3610.O387 U55 2017 | DDC 813/.6—dc23
LC record available at https://lccn.loc.gov/2016045204

Published in 2017 by arrangement with Midnight Ink, an imprint of Llewellyn Publications, Woodbury, MN 55125-2989

Printed in the United States of America
1 2 3 4 5 6 7 21 20 19 18 17

To all people who believe in superstitions, and to those who claim they don't but follow one or two — or more — just in case. May you have lots of luck, and may all of it be good!

And again, to my readers, particularly those who enjoy cozy mysteries with fun-to-write themes . . . like superstitions. Unlimited luck to all of you, too — and keep on reading!

And as always, to my husband Fred.

ACKNOWLEDGMENTS

Repetitious? Perhaps. But definitely true! I again thank my wonderful agent Paige Wheeler as well as my delightful editor Terri Bischoff, great production editor Sandy Sullivan, amazing publicist Katie Mickschl, and all the other fantastic Midnight Ink folks — as well as the other MI authors who are all so wonderful and supportive.

Thanks again, too, to those who read and critiqued and helped me polish the *Unlucky Charms* manuscript.

ONE

This was far from my first "Black Dogs and Black Cats" presentation at the Break-a-Leg Theater. What was it — the eighth? Ninth? I'd lost count even though I gave these talks fairly often. Maybe because I was rather nervous this time.

At the moment, my dog Pluckie and I stood off to one side of the dimly lit stage listening to the noisy crowd take their seats, waiting till it was time for us to walk out in front of them. The curtains, though partially pulled back, interfered with my ability to see anyone, which was probably a good thing.

Why was I so edgy tonight? Had I actually become superstitious? After all, despite the pet superstition theme of my talk this evening, a lot of it was about me, personally. My ideas. My hopes to increase sales exponentially at the Lucky Dog Boutique, the very special shop I managed, even though the store was already doing just fine.

Tonight I was going to talk about our newest products — superstition-related items for pets I had dreamed up and designed. I'd recently gotten a company to manufacture them for us.

Was this good luck? My shop had built up its reputation for canine delights long before I started working there, offering everything from plush black-cat toys and specialty dog foods to rhine-stone-studded collars and leashes and amulets with smiling animal faces. Would it be bad luck to change or add to things that were already working?

I, Rory Chasen, was about to find out.

"What do you think, Pluckie?" I whispered to my dog. "This is kind of a business meeting, so you'll give me lots of good luck tonight, right?"

After all, black dogs were often said to be lucky, and black and white ones like my adorable spaniel-terrier mix were particularly lucky at business meetings. I'd learned that on my very first day here in Destiny, when Pluckie had pretty much saved the life of Martha Jallopia, the owner of the Lucky Dog Boutique, by finding her unconscious in the back room.

Martha would be here tonight, too, sitting in her wheelchair near the front row as she always did for my presentations at the Destiny Welcome show. The angle was such that I couldn't see that area, but she probably had already arrived.

Pluckie now stood on her hind legs, her front paws on my thighs and her nose in the air, staring me straight in the eye for comfort. Reassurance. And lots of doggy love. She'd obviously heard me talking to her. I doubted she understood exactly what I said, but I knew she read my uneasy mood and was responding.

"You're right." I bent down to grasp her in my arms and give her a big hug.

That made me let go of the handle I was holding. At its end was the small black suitcase containing all the items I'd talk about and show off that night. My creations that represented what Destiny was all about.

"Hi, Rory," boomed a familiar voice from behind me. I turned.

Mayor Bevin Dermot stood there, beaming. As usual, he wore what I considered to be his leprechaun outfit: dark pants with a dressy green jacket over them, adorned with a pin depicting — what else? — a leprechaun. He was chubby, and his hair and beard were both silver.

"Hi, Bevin," I said softly. I knew my expression must look quizzical. He had sometimes come to my talks but not always, and when he did, he generally sat in the audience.

"Would you like me to introduce you tonight?" he asked.

I didn't really have time to ponder it. I saw Phil, a young guy who worked at the theater, gesture to me from across the stage. He apparently wanted to know if I was ready.

Well, I was as ready as I was going to get that evening, so I nodded and waved. The stage lights got brighter, while the house lights dimmed.

It was time for someone to go out there. And why shouldn't it be the town's mayor? His presence wouldn't hurt my talk — or my shop's sales. It was more likely to help both.

"That would be wonderful," I told him. "Thanks."

With no further ado, Bevin strode out to the microphone. He introduced himself first and got a loud round of applause. Then he introduced me.

"You are about to hear from Rory Chasen, manager of one of our best local stores, the Lucky Dog Boutique. She's a relative newcomer to our town, but she's a real winner — and I hope she stays that way." He crossed the fingers on his right hand and waved them in an arc before him. And then he turned toward me. "Rory?"

I smiled at him despite still feeling uneasy, and his compliment didn't make me feel any better. Right now, my own creativity and ingenuity — and luck — were on the line. Maybe I had a right to be nervous.

For reassurance and luck, I bent to pat Pluckie again. Then I stood, holding her leash in one hand and the handle of my bag on wheels in the other. I strode onto the stage, hoping I looked okay in the new black dress I'd bought at the Right Side Out clothing shop; I usually just wore a Lucky Dog T-shirt when I gave these talks. I wanted to reach up and check my straight blond hair, or at least fluff my bangs — but I did neither. I looked how I looked.

I stopped at the microphone, which had already been adjusted to my height, and glanced briefly at the auditorium's tall ceiling, ornate chandeliers, and plain walls that I assumed were the result of renovations in this lovely, aging place. "Thank you, Mayor Dermot," I said with a smile I hoped appeared genuine. "And hi, everyone. I'm Rory Chasen, manager of the Lucky Dog Boutique, and, as our mayor said, a relatively new Destiny resident. I'm here to talk

13

to you about animals and superstitions."

I managed to glance around at the audience as people began clapping, which made me all the more uncomfortable even though I wasn't a shy and retiring person — or at least I hadn't been before. Bevin clapped, too, as he backed off the stage, leaving me alone there with Pluckie. I hadn't said anything special for the audience to acknowledge. Not yet, at least.

But one of the most exuberant clappers was Martha, who indeed was in her wheelchair off to the side of the front row. One of my shop assistants, Millie Weedin, was with her, as I'd anticipated, sitting in the end seat. Off to the other side of the theater was my very good friend Gemma Grayfield, who'd followed me to Destiny and now lived here as well, managing the Broken Mirror Bookstore.

I also noticed some fellow shop managers and owners, who gave talks now and then about their stores and luck-related products. One of them was Kiara Mardeer from the Heads-Up Penny Gift Shop. Her daughter, Jeri, another of my part-time assistants at the Lucky Dog, was with her. Brad Nereida, one of the owners of the Wish-on-a-Star children's shop, was also there. I glanced around but didn't see his wife,

Lorraine. I recognized quite a few other people, but the audience was mostly composed of strangers who were probably tourists.

But I was really only looking for one person: Justin Halbertson, chief of the Destiny Police Department. His presence, here and otherwise, was becoming very important to me.

I didn't see him, though. A good number of people filled the auditorium, so maybe I had somehow overlooked him — but I doubted it.

As I continued to smile and look around, the clapping wound down. Time for me to dive into my speech.

"As I said, I'm here tonight to talk about dogs and cats and other pets, as I generally do in my talks called 'Black Dogs and Black Cats.' I'll bet you're not surprised about that."

A few small laughs permeated the audience, but I didn't wait to listen to them.

"What I intend to mostly discuss tonight, however, is the store I currently manage here in Destiny, the Lucky Dog Boutique. Its owner, Martha Jallopia, is in the audience to listen to me and scold me if I don't do a good job, so I'd better excel. Say hi, Martha." I waved my arm toward her.

15

My boss rose from her wheelchair, turned, and grinned. "You bet I'll scold you if you blow this, Rory," she yelled, and even though she didn't have a microphone, I believed she was audible all over the room. "Hi, everyone."

"What Martha doesn't know," I said, speaking into the microphone in a loud whisper, "is that my intent tonight is to promote myself and my ideas for some very special products that I came up with to sell at the Lucky Dog — ones related to superstitions, of course — which I hope will provide the customers who buy them, and their pets, with good luck."

Part of what I said wasn't true. Martha knew what my talk was about; we were good friends as well as business associates, and I had no intention of doing anything at the store without her knowledge and okay. We'd discussed this dramatic approach to introducing my new products, and she had been fine with it.

I bent down and unzipped my bag, pulling back the top and extracting a few of the items — including my very favorite one. Once I was at the microphone again, I hugged all the objects to me except for my favorite, which I held in one hand and waved in the air.

It was a white rabbit that resembled a children's toy — somewhat large and stuffed, and sturdily made to resist tearing apart even when a dog chomped down and worried it. The materials were faux fur and other fabrics that would run through a dog's system without causing harm in the event they were swallowed. I'd done careful research on the materials, even getting in touch with some of my contacts from when I'd been assistant manager at a MegaPets major chain store before moving to Destiny. They'd helped me to find the right manufacturer to put my new products together safely, although the labels encouraged owners not to allow the toys or their contents to be eaten.

The most fun thing about the toy rabbits was their link to Destiny and superstitions. Each had one disproportionately large and lucky rabbit's foot!

"Here we are," I said. "This is Richy the Rabbit. He can be nearly any dog's best friend, and he will eventually come in several sizes. And you know what?" I didn't wait for anyone to respond. "He'll bring both you and your dog lots of luck. That's why he's named Richy. His big rabbit's foot will help you and your dog get rich with whatever it is that makes you feel that way.

No guarantees, of course, but maybe that means money for you, or a better career. And treats for your best friend." I paused, but only for a few seconds. Then I stuffed Richy into the arm that held the other toys and raised my right hand. I crossed my fingers and said into the microphone, "At least I, and everyone at the Lucky Dog, will cross our fingers to help ensure it."

At my words, Martha rose again, and this time both Millie and Jeri stood too, raising their arms and crossing their fingers.

The audience laughed, cheered, and applauded.

Most of the other toys I'd designed and manufactured so far also had lucky connotations, like . . . well, black dogs and black cats, deemed good luck in some cultures if not here, and ladybugs and woodpeckers, each with a smiley face. They had personalities. They were cartoonish. Many of them squeaked when squeezed.

They were hopefully lucky for dogs and their humans alike.

And they were potentially lucrative if they sold well.

I'd even added a toy Dalmatian — a lucky black and white dog, of course. It had been one of my first ideas for a new dog toy when I'd started working at the Lucky Dog.

I held each toy up individually and explained its superstitious significance and why I'd chosen that particular theme — which mostly had to do with providing good luck, or so truly superstitious people said.

I didn't mention that I wasn't sure if I was one of those people. I happened to remain a superstition agnostic. I'd come to Destiny to learn whether my dear fiancé Warren's death had really occurred because he'd walked under a ladder just prior to being hit by a car, and I wound up staying for many reasons.

But becoming a true believer wasn't among those reasons.

I continued my presentation for maybe another ten minutes, also describing some superstitions relating to dogs, particularly those who were black or black and white, like Pluckie. And I of course discussed black cats, who might be unfairly maligned when considered bad luck when they cross your path — or not.

Eventually, I was done. I thanked everyone for coming and invited them all to visit the Lucky Dog — and perhaps buy some of the things I had shown off.

I wasn't surprised when Mayor Bevin wound up striding back onto the stage and retaking the microphone, thanking everyone for coming to Destiny and inviting them to visit all our shops and restaurants, take our tours, and just have a fantastic, superstitious, and lucky time here.

While he talked, I wheeled my bag off to the side and put the toys back in, with Pluckie at my side. Then we exited the stage and went to the theater's entry area to wait and greet the audience as they left.

I was soon surrounded by people who thanked me and said how much they'd enjoyed my program. Some tourists promised to come visit my shop.

Jostling the group nearest me aside, Flora Curtival was suddenly in front of me. "Great talk!" she said.

I'd first met Flora about a month ago, when she'd stayed at the Rainbow Bed and Breakfast after arriving in town. She'd moved out a week or so later — into an apartment, I'd heard — after getting a job in real estate. Then she started approaching people she'd met in Destiny as potential clients, including me — which wasn't a bad idea, since I'd finally started to seriously consider living someplace other than the Rainbow B&B. I liked the inn, but I'd now decided to stay in Destiny indefinitely. I'd even been the one who'd arranged for Gemma to manage the Broken Mirror. I wasn't sure yet whether I wanted to buy a house or condo, or find a nice apartment to rent, but either way, I knew it would be fun to work out something where Gemma and I could be roommates.

But not necessarily right this moment. Despite our interest in the town, we weren't in a hurry to move.

Flora was tall and thin. She dressed almost professionally, in a slender brown dress and heels I'd never dare donning without incurring a lot of bad luck for my legs and muscles. Her makeup was model perfect, and her short brown hair provided a nice frame to her attractive face.

In short, she appeared to be someone who had something she hoped to sell to everyone she met. Which was fine with me, as long as she wasn't too pushy about it.

"Thanks," I responded, then looked away as Gemma approached, along with the Lucky Dog contingent, including Millie pushing Martha in her chair.

"So who's up for a drink at the Clinking Glass Saloon tonight to celebrate Rory's talk?" Gemma called.

I wasn't surprised when Jeri and her mother said yes, as did my good friend Carolyn Innes of the Buttons of Fortune shop and a couple of others, including Martha's nephew Arlen, who I hadn't noticed earlier.

Flora said yes, too. Maybe she'd buy me a drink to cultivate my business.

"It'll be good luck," I declared. "I'll be there."

Two

It was mid-November, and tonight was cool — not as cold, of course, as in many parts of the country, but still noticeable to me, since I'd grown up in Pasadena. Destiny was just south of California's Los Padres National Forest. The daytime temperatures here were fairly moderate, but it often got chilly at night, sometimes going down to the 30s or 40s.

Even so, the weather was dry, so I had no problem sitting outside on the patio of the Clinking Glass Saloon to ensure that Pluckie would be welcome. In fact, I usually preferred the patio, since the bar inside was dark, often crowded, and always noisy. Since I generally came here to chat with friends, some of whom had dogs too, the outside area fulfilled my needs more.

Now I was sitting at one of the small round tables under a patio heater, waiting for more people to join us before ordering drinks. Only Gemma was there with Pluckie and me so far. Despite the chill, it was crowded on the patio, and not only with people who'd been at my talk. Pluckie nestled down on the cement near my feet, snuggling up to me.

A lot of noise emanated from the bar inside, where some kind of ballgame — most likely football — was playing on the television. There were conversations out here, too, that ramped up the decibels, although not right next to us.

"Great talk," Gemma said, probably for the fifth time since we'd headed toward the saloon.

If I was the kind of person who got jealous of women who were prettier than me, I'd have hated Gemma, but I've always liked her a lot. She's lovely. She wears her brunette hair short, which helps to emphasize the dark loveliness of her cinnamon-brown eyes with their long lashes. She always seems to wear the perfect outfit for the occasion. Tonight it was a short and slinky beige dress with long sleeves.

One sign that Gemma was a close friend was the fact that I hadn't had to tell her before my speech that I was nervous. Nor did I have to tell her, now, that although my nervousness was not so acute, it hadn't left me completely. Did people enjoy my talk? Would the new products I'd created sell well? Was I just acting superstitious, worried that saying something good about a thing would mean everything about it would turn bad? She knew me so well.

Plus, not long ago, I'd helped to ensure that Gemma wasn't arrested for a murder she hadn't committed. That had helped to bolster our friendship even more.

I could order a drink either at the patio or at the bar — and despite my talk being over, I needed one now. I glanced around. Some of the people Gemma had invited to join us were finally arriving — Jeri Mardeer and Kiara, Millie and Martha, and also Mayor Bevin and Brad Nereida. As long as we stayed out here and Millie didn't order anything alcoholic, I believed she'd be allowed to stay, even though she was only twenty, not yet drinking age. They all found nearby tables and sat down under the heaters.

Martha's nephew Arlen arrived then too, as did Carolyn Innes. Most everyone stopped to say hi to Gemma and me, which I appreciated. Most also said something nice about my talk.

Had Gemma told them I was nervous — or was it so apparent that everyone felt they had to compliment me? I supposed they could actually have enjoyed it . . . at least I hoped so.

A few people I hadn't noticed at the Destiny Welcome joined us as well, including Celia Vardox, who, with her brother Derek, owned the local newspaper, the *Destiny Star.* Would my talk and my new products be mentioned in the paper? Keeping my hand under the table, I crossed my fingers.

No Justin, though. I'd managed to text him on our walk here, just a friendly invitation to join us. His response had come fairly quickly — that he was involved in a police matter but would get there as soon as he could.

If he could, was what I read into it. But at least he hadn't said no.

I noticed a server entering the patio from the bar and motioned toward him. There were a bunch of other patrons out here, too, and I wasn't sure our group was first on his list. Fortunately, the server saw my gesture and was at our table in seconds. I didn't recognize him, although he wore the usual outfit here at the Clinking Glass: a white button-down shirt and a short white apron over his dark trousers. Most of the servers were men, but the women all wore something similar.

I ordered a glass of wine, figuring I would most likely follow it up with a second one later. Maybe more.

Was it my imagination, or did the group who had joined Gemma and me appear sort of quiet and not especially happy? Were they all just here to humor me? If so . . . well, I wasn't close friends with all of them, only some.

What was going on?

As the server took Gemma's order — also wine — I looked around. Carolyn had been standing at the table where Brad Nereida sat. He was maybe my age, and he and Lorraine had several children — which may have been why they ran the Wish-on-a-Star children's shop. Was Lorraine's absence a result of them being unable to get a sitter that night, or had Lorraine simply decided she wasn't interested in my talk?

If so, I wouldn't hold it against her. But she and Brad had presented a couple of talks since I'd been in Destiny. I'd attended them out of friendliness and politeness, since I didn't have children or any likelihood of children in the near future.

Maybe I'd skip the next one.

"Hey, Rory," Carolyn said. "And Gemma." She looked concerned, and her voice was so low I could barely hear her. Was something wrong? "Have you heard about —"

She didn't finish, just stared forward. I turned to see what she was looking at. No, *who* she was looking at. It was Justin, who'd come out the doorway from the bar to the patio.

"Have we heard what?" Gemma prompted, as I'd have done if I hadn't been staring at Justin.

He'd joined us after all, and much sooner than I'd anticipated. My heart rate accelerated a bit, as if I'd just been touched by the best good luck symbol in Destiny — although I wasn't sure what it might be. Maybe it was one of the toys I'd designed, which remained in the bag-on-wheels at my feet under the table.

"I'll talk to you about it later," Carolyn finished.

I looked at her and saw that her gaze remained on Justin. Whatever it was she had to say, she obviously didn't want him to hear it. Why? Was bad luck involved? And did the fact I was even wondering such a thing mean I was really settling down as a Destiny resident, with superstitions edging their way into my sense of being?

"Hi, ladies," Justin said as he reached the

table. His greeting took all of us in, but his eyes met mine before he looked around and smiled at Gemma, sitting beside me, and then at Carolyn, who'd taken the other seat.

"Please join us," Gemma said, preempting the same invitation I'd been about to issue.

"Yes, please do." I looked around and saw a few empty chairs at nearby tables. Justin did the same and went to fetch one.

I used the brief opportunity to look at Carolyn. "What's wrong?" I asked softly.

"Someone's stealing things and more," she said, so fast and so quietly that I had to replay her words in my mind before they sank in. But as Justin pulled his chair up to the table — between Carolyn and me, as it turned out — and sat down, she just gave me a small smile, shrugged, and turned away. "So how have you been, Justin?" she asked. "I didn't see you at Rory's talk."

"No, unfortunately something came up and I wasn't able to get there."

Justin was one good-looking guy. The hair on his head was thick and dark, and the dusting of facial hair at this hour emphasized it. He had gorgeous blue eyes and sharp, angular features, and a smile that generally made me feel happy — and more — in return. In fact, he was a very special guy to me. Inside, I kept apologizing to

Warren, especially at times when Justin and I found ourselves getting close. Very close.

As usual, instead of an official-looking uniform, he wore a light blue shirt over dark trousers. And, in keeping with Destiny tradition, he wore an amulet — a bronzed acorn, which meant good luck, and also supposedly kept the wearer young. Not that Justin, who at age thirty-five was only a year older than I was, needed the latter just yet.

Right now, he was responding to Carolyn but looking at me, as if in apology.

What could I do but accept it?

Though I could still joke about it. "So you mean that a case was so important to the Destiny police chief that you had to work instead of coming to hear me speak?" I punctuated the words with a scowl that I purposely made look false. Of course he had stuff come up that was important — a lot more important to him than I was. I got it.

I only hoped that this time it wasn't another murder. There had been a couple in Destiny since my arrival, which had only been about five months ago.

"Yep, that happens sometimes, no matter what I'd rather do." He kept his voice light, but I did see what appeared to be regret in his eyes.

That made me feel a little better. "Well,

see that it doesn't happen again," I said lightly. Then it dawned on me. Carolyn had mentioned some sort of a theft. Justin had had to work. Could these things be related?

Apparently, neither was going to give more detail about what was on their minds, so I'd have to wait and ask them separately, later. I felt confident that Carolyn would continue with what she'd been about to say. With Justin, though, he might be bound up in some kind of confidentiality requirement, so I might never learn what had kept him away from my talk.

Well, he was here now, at least. And I was glad.

"So how did your presentation go?" he asked, but before I could start describing it our server came over. I got my wine, as did Gemma. Carolyn received her beer, and Justin ordered a Scotch and soda.

When the server left, I raised my glass, as did the other women at the table. "Time to clink glasses for luck here at the Clinking Glass Saloon," I quipped. Or it would have been a quip, anywhere but in Destiny. We all toasted, and then I took a sip of a delightfully dry Cabernet and smiled. "I think it all went fine," I finally said, in response to Justin. "Ladies?"

Both Gemma and Carolyn began expounding on how well I'd done — not that I'd expected them to do otherwise. But they both genuinely had nice things to say, not only about my presentation but also about the new doggy toys I'd introduced.

"I'll have to get some of those for Killer," Justin said with a smile when they were through. "You'll need to recommend which ones would be best for a Doberman."

"I think any of them would be fine," I said. "I designed them to be strong and safe enough for any dog, and Killer — despite his name — is one sweet pup."

"I'll drink to that." Justin raised a glass that was imaginary, but only for a minute since our server returned just then with his drink.

I took another healthy sip of my wine. "To Killer. And Pluckie." My dog, lying near my chair, sat up at hearing her name.

"And to your toys and talk," Justin added.

All of us drank to that.

I pondered for a second what to say that everyone at the table would be interested in — despite my desire to quiz Justin about whatever he'd been involved with during my talk.

Before I said anything, though, I noticed a couple of people approaching our table: Flora Curtival and her boss, Brie Timons, who was the owner of Rising Moon Realty. I'd learned that the company's name was based on the idea that it's good luck to move into a new home when the moon is waxing, not waning.

"Hi, Rory, Gemma," Brie said. She appeared fiftyish and wore pantsuits rather than dresses, but she always appeared professional despite how untamed her graying-black hair looked. "Carolyn and Justin, too. Do you know everyone here?" She turned toward Flora, at her side.

"Sorry, no." Flora seemed quite pleased by Brie's introduction to Justin and Carolyn. And why not? Real estate agents lived to know people — and relocate them, with generous commissions, into new homes, condos, and apartments. Not a bad way to make a living.

"Flora and I have been talking over some ideas I had," Brie was saying. Justin had risen and moved around the patio till he found a couple of now-rare empty chairs and brought them back so that the real estate ladies could sit down and join us.

"That's good." I tried to keep the dubiousness out of my voice.

"We're really here for two reasons," Flora said. She was sitting on Justin's other side, and I had to look past his buff body to see her. "Good reasons," she continued, and her face lit up with an enormous smile.

"What reasons?" I asked, as I knew I was supposed to.

"Flora just closed a deal with one of our clients today to buy a house in a nice area east of town," Brie said, also grinning. "She did it this morning so she could go to your talk later. I helped with the paperwork this afternoon."

"Thanks," I said, again realizing what was expected. "And the second reason?"

"Well, it's connected to the first one," Flora said. "Now that this deal has been completed, I can concentrate more on finding the two of you the ideal living situation. Isn't that great?"

"Sure," said Gemma, although her smile indicated that she felt as hesitant as I did.

"Right," I said. "I'm interested, but I've got a lot going on, and I don't want to take on additional pressures."

"I understand," Brie said. "But I'm sure Flora will find you something perfect."

She was sure? I wasn't.

On the other hand, I knew I was staying in Destiny. And I'd been living in the B&B long enough.

And I could always say no to whatever she showed me. So could Gemma.

I looked toward Flora and caught Justin's eye. There was something unreadable in his gaze. Was he glad about what I'd said? Sorry? Off in his own world, considering whatever had kept him from attending my presentation?

"Okay, maybe," I said. "As long as we have good luck in this situation" — as always these days, I feigned like I really bought into superstitions — "let's give it a try."

THREE

I felt a bit irritated, though, when Flora insisted on accompanying me to the restroom. Gemma stayed at the table, watching Pluckie for me, or I'd have left it to her to talk down this overly enthusiastic real estate lady. When I'd agreed to let Flora search for us, Gemma had shot me a look, then rolled her eyes, demonstrating to me that she was equally irritated but willing to go along with it.

Yes, we'd agreed to start looking for a new place — but only sort of. Some advice or assistance might be helpful, *might* being the operative word. We'd still take our time. And if this woman and her boss wound up with a commission eventually, fine.

As long as they didn't overdo their pushiness with us.

"So here are some of the most recent ideas I've had," Flora shouted as we stepped through the door into the barely lighted bar.

Unfortunately, she was loud enough that I could hear her over the many conversations and blaring TV. "Some of the most charming places in this town are either from the Gold Rush days or have been built to look like that, including some absolutely wonderful condo developments south of downtown. And —"

We'd reached the hallway that led to the restrooms, and I preceded her down it. I soon pushed open the door to the bathroom. It was a lot quieter in here, but the doors to all three stalls were closed. Darn. I couldn't escape her presence quite yet.

"You know, Flora, I really appreciate your help and ideas." A fib or two was in order, to soften what I was about to say. "The thing is, if the perfect location were to show up right away, Gemma and I would jump right in. But we're not sure what's perfect for us, and I'd hate for you to spend a lot of time on the search when we're still not in a huge hurry to move."

Good timing. A senior lady with an embarrassed smile opened the door to one of the stalls and walked out. I waved to Flora and hurried inside.

I heard another toilet flush soon after that, so I figured Flora would soon be settled in that stall and I could hurry back to the table outside. But she was a lot quicker than me, maybe intentionally, and exited that other stall about the same time I left mine.

Standing at the sink as we washed our hands, I tried to concentrate more on soap and water than on Flora, but that wasn't what she wanted. "I really thought you were serious about a new place to live, Rory. I've talked to other people in Destiny, and everyone thinks you're ready to settle down here for the long haul. That doesn't mean living in a bed and breakfast forever."

"They're right, and you're right," I said. I'd pulled a paper towel from the dispenser near the sink and turned to face her. "But I hate to do anything under pressure. And finding a new place to live, especially if it means buying a house or condo — well, that's a large financial commitment as well as a lifestyle commitment. We'd be glad to look at listings you come up with, of course, and if something seems to fit we'll take it. But don't spend all your time trying to help us when we're simply not primed to hurry."

A few minutes later I was seated once more at our table. After we'd returned, Brie's expression had been puzzled, but she'd obeyed the summons when Flora had motioned for her to join her at another table

— one far across the patio.

Good.

"Everything okay?" Gemma asked.

"Sure. I told her we'd appreciate her help but not to focus on just us right now." That was close enough, and I could discuss it more with Gemma later.

"So you're actually looking for another place to live?" Justin asked.

"Maybe," I said. "I've probably been in a temporary living situation long enough. I'm not committing to stay in Destiny forever, but a B&B has its limitations. And I do intend to run the Lucky Dog for the foreseeable future, at least." Maybe even forever, despite what I'd just said.

Justin's look was again indecipherable, but I guessed he was attempting to see what was in my mind the same way I tried to read his.

Did he want me to stay here indefinitely? If so, why?

And did I want to stay here indefinitely? To spend more time with Justin?

To finally get over losing my beloved Warren?

I surreptitiously crossed my fingers under the table at that thought. I'd never forget Warren, of course. But I'd recognized before that I needed to get on with my life —

which was largely why I'd come to Destiny in the first place. I'd made progress. I recognized that.

And of course I was attracted to Justin. But where were we going? Anywhere? Nowhere?

Did I want our growing closeness to increase?

I took a last gulp of my wine and glanced at my tablemates. They'd both finished their drinks. "Are we ready to leave?" I asked.

"If you are," Gemma said.

We stood and I settled Pluckie's leash over my wrist, but then I picked my girl up, since the place was so crowded — and people who'd been drinking might not be too careful about a dog making her way along the patio. Gemma was kind enough to grab the handle of my wheeled bag and tow it out with us.

Outside the gate, I glanced at Justin. "Thanks for coming," I said.

"I'll walk you both back to the B&B. That's one good thing about that place, by the way. It's easy walking distance from downtown."

So he liked where I was living. But surely he knew people didn't live permanently in a B&B. Did he want me to stay there so I'd leave soon?

That made my heart lurch. I cared about Justin and believed he cared about me — but maybe not in the same way. Or maybe he wanted what I couldn't give, not yet. Not with Warren still in my thoughts, too. Not just caring, but commitment.

On the other hand, we hadn't really talked about it. I'd just been anticipating . . . something.

But not at that moment. "Thanks, Justin," I said brightly. "But Gemma and I will be fine. We'll head right back to the B&B together." *In other words, we don't need you.*

"It's no trouble. I'll go with you. And you need to make a quick stop at the Lucky Dog on the way."

Oh. He needed something for Killer. That was why he was going with us. My heart plummeted again. Maybe I wanted him there for me, wanted him to commit to me even if I was reluctant.

"Well, sure," I said. "What does Killer need?"

"Nothing right now."

We'd started walking west on Destiny Boulevard toward Fate Street, where the B&B was located a couple of blocks north. To get to my pet boutique, we'd have to cross Fate and walk half a block out of the way — no big deal, of course, but I still

41

wasn't sure why we were doing it.

Then it came to me. Of course. "You want to make sure Martha's back in her place and doing well." Martha still lived upstairs from my shop, in an apartment. She didn't walk long distances, hence the wheelchair, but she'd been fine walking up and down the stairway, never tripping — which was a good thing, even though the superstition about falling on your way down and ruining your luck was a lot worse than falling on your way up and causing a marriage in your family.

Justin and Martha were very close. In fact, their closeness was one reason I'd wound up staying in Destiny in the first place, after Justin had practically begged me to help her.

"Yes, we can look in on Martha, too, while we're there," he said.

Too? Then that wasn't his major reason either.

"So why are we stopping there?" Gemma asked bluntly. My good friend the former librarian was nothing if not direct.

"Just want to check on something."

"What?" Gemma demanded.

"Hey, Rory," Justin said. "Maybe you can show me how you're going to display the new pet toys you made. The ones you talked about at your presentation."

We were walking side by side, Pluckie now on the sidewalk ahead of the humans. As usual, she did a lot of sniffing and occasional squatting. I had biodegradable bags with me just in case, but didn't need to use them.

There wasn't a lot of traffic on Destiny Boulevard at this hour, and the light emanating from the streetlamps, which were shaped like Gold Rush–period lanterns, was low but sufficient. Even so, it was hard to see and avoid sidewalk cracks. And although I didn't think anyone had seeded the sidewalks with lucky heads-up pennies at this hour, I still managed to look down a lot.

"So that's why you're joining us?" I asked Justin, deciding to be pushy the way Gemma was.

"Sure," he agreed, but I could tell he was lying.

I wondered then if this had something to do with his work, and he couldn't talk about it. I suspected it had something to do with thefts, since Carolyn had mentioned such things.

But I wouldn't push him . . . now. If he'd wanted to explain, he would have.

We soon reached the Broken Mirror Bookstore, next door to the Lucky Dog. "Let's go in here too," Justin said, making me feel even more certain he was checking for break-ins.

"Really?" Gemma asked, but she did have her key with her and opened the door, flipping the switch to turn on the lights.

The bookstore looked normal, with lots of shelves holding volumes that described and discussed superstitions. The main display at the front was a large table full of *The Destiny of Superstitions,* the book written by the now-deceased Kenneth Tarzal, whose family remained co-owner of the shop Gemma managed.

"Wait here." Justin gestured for Gemma, Pluckie, and me to stay back. What did he expect to find?

Apparently my initial impression had been right. He circled the display area and returned fairly quickly.

"Everything okay?" Gemma looked worried, as well she should when the chief of police insisted on checking out the store she managed.

"Fine," he said.

Our next stop was my Lucky Dog Boutique. Our initial approach was pretty much the same as at the bookstore. Justin walked through the display area, this time filled with myriad pet items, not books, related to superstitions. Justin then called Martha. Yes, she was home, upstairs. She was fine and almost ready for bed. She'd see him soon, but not tonight.

Or at least that was what he reported after going off to one side of the shop and talking to her on his phone.

"Okay," he said. "Lock up well" — he'd told Gemma the same thing as we'd left her shop — "and let's get you back to your B&B."

Since we were here at my store, I decided to drop off the bag of new toys I'd taken to my talk, then locked the door behind us.

I was very conscious of Justin's tall, substantial self as we finished the rest of our walk. Not that I wasn't glad to have him around otherwise, but somehow, after checking the shops as if there'd been a problem there, I felt much happier having his strong police presence along. He'd gotten me worried — and I was irritated, too, since he hadn't explained why.

Pluckie had done a lot more sniffing and squatting by the time we reached the Rainbow B&B. Even so, when we arrived Gemma said, "Why don't you two give Pluckie her last walk of the evening? I'm heading to bed."

She was definitely a good friend — giving

me an opportunity to say good night to Justin.

And quiz him.

"Good idea," I said, then watched her stride up to the ornate, three-story building and walk through the door — beneath a horseshoe for good luck. I knew she'd stroll past the pot of pseudo gold that sat on the lobby floor, a symbol indicative of the origin of this place and of the whole town, founded by Forty-Niners who supposedly found their pot of gold at the end of a rainbow. I really liked this inn.

But now, Pluckie and I were alone with Justin in the parking lot outside. I looked up at him and smiled, sort of. "Okay," I said. "When are you going to tell me what this is all about?"

He bent to pat Pluckie's head, and my little girl wriggled beneath his hand at the attention.

Oh, no. He wasn't going to get me to go away by doing something I really liked. I bent down, too, and put my face almost up to his.

He laughed. The smile on his face — so handsome despite the low level of light — warmed me, but it didn't make me stop.

"Well?" I demanded, although I smiled too.

He rose, and so did I. Pluckie started moving and I allowed her to do her sniff thing. I figured Justin wouldn't let us get too far without following us, and I was right. We were soon on the lawn at the side of the driveway.

"This is Destiny, Rory. You know that." He regarded me with no question in his eyes.

"Yes . . ." I said, hoping to get him to finish his thought.

"I've been told by my superiors — particularly our mayor — that it would be bad luck for me, and for Destiny, if I told people about . . . let's say, an issue that's going on around town."

"You mean that someone's been stealing from some of the shops?" I guessed.

He looked at me. "Who's been talking? I thought everyone was under the same warning."

"Nobody's been talking," I fibbed. Or maybe it wasn't really a fib, since I hadn't had an opportunity to speak with Carolyn. Not exactly. "I just guessed."

"I can't say any more about it, but you guessed right somehow. And please don't talk about it with anyone else."

"You're really buying into that?" I asked. "You, who I thought was as much of a

47

superstition agnostic as I am."

His laugh was wry. "I am. But I suspect that the more word gets around about the thefts, the more there'll be, which wouldn't be good luck for anyone except the thief. I've got patrols out observing, and hopefully deterring anything else. The good thing is that no one has been hurt, which might change if anyone who could potentially be affected hangs out at night in their —" He stopped.

"Shops?" I ventured.

"I've said too much already." He took a few steps toward me and looked down, worry written all over his expression. "Rory, I especially don't want you hurt. I . . ." He stopped.

I wished he'd continue. Was he going to say he cared?

That he loved me?

Or was I just reading too much into the possibilities?

And if he did say he loved me, how would I respond? I couldn't say for certain, but —

His mouth was suddenly on mine, so I couldn't ask him. Didn't want to. Didn't need to then. Our kiss took my breath away. It continued for — how long? I wasn't sure. Forever?

Not long enough.

My arms were around him, pulling him even closer. Good thing we were outside or this might not have been all we did.

But eventually our kiss ended. I didn't pull away at first, even as our mouths drew apart. But Pluckie began tugging on her leash, which was still hooked to my arm, pulling away from Justin's body and mine.

I laughed. "I think Pluckie's telling me it's bedtime."

Justin moved back and patted my dog once more. "She's right." He bent down and gave me a brief kiss this time, again on the lips. Then he accompanied me to the B&B's door, where he waited while I searched in my purse for my key.

"Good night, Justin," I said, standing on my toes to give him one final kiss.

"Good night, Rory." He knocked on the wooden frame around the door. "Stay safe. I'll be in touch."

FOUR

We were finally in our room, Pluckie and I. I was winding down from an initially tense yet always enjoyable evening and was ready to head to bed.

I put my purse down on a chair near the door, its usual place in the chintz-and-lace decorated room, then extracted my cell phone from it.

I remembered then that I hadn't turned the sound back on after my talk. Having any phone go off during a presentation wasn't good luck, and I'd always figured it would be particularly bad luck if it was my own phone.

Assuming there was such a thing as bad luck.

When I unzipped my bag and pulled the phone out, I checked for messages. There'd been none left, but I'd gotten a text from Carolyn commanding me to call her when I got back to my room, no matter what time it was.

Which sent a creep of unease up my spine, even though I thought I knew what she wanted to talk about.

Since I needed to chill out, I quickly changed from my new black dress into a yellow cotton robe, then crawled beneath the bed's canopy and sat on top of the beige coverlet, my legs crossed. Pluckie jumped up to join me.

I couldn't procrastinate anymore. I'd become close enough friends with Carolyn to have her programmed into one of the numbers on my phone, which I pushed.

She answered immediately. "About time you called," she huffed. "Do you know how late it is?"

It was around eleven o'clock, but shop-keepers in Destiny tended to get to their stores early to prepare for the day, so I doubted I was the only one who preferred going to bed reasonably early — earlier than this. Even so . . . "You texted me to call you no matter what time it was."

"I still hoped it wouldn't be this late. I don't want to talk long. But I've been letting all store owners and managers know the little bit that I've learned about what's going on in town."

I sat up straighter, no longer feeling defensive but concerned. "You said something about thefts." I wondered if she could tell me more than Justin had.

"That's right. Our dear mayor issued an edict that no one, not the victims or the cops or anyone else, is to talk about it because it'll rain bad luck down on Destiny — mostly on our tourist industry — but the bad luck is already here, and it consists of these thefts. And vandalism, too."

I didn't bother reminding Carolyn what had happened to the Vardoxes when they'd violated similar commands not to talk about another bad situation in Destiny: their newspaper office had all but burned down. Carolyn already knew, and she'd apparently decided it was best to let people know the information that was forbidden to discuss, even if there were unlucky repercussions.

"And yet you're talking about it," I pointed out. "Which shops have been broken into? Yours?"

"Fortunately, not mine. And I doubt I can tell you all of them. I suspect most victims are heeding the mayor and not talking about what's been going on. But those I know about are the Heads-Up Penny and Wish-on-a-Star. Good luck symbols were taken and bad luck ones were left in their place.

Not only that, but some restaurants, too, were broken into: Beware-of-Bubbles Coffee Shop, Shamrock Steakhouse, and Wishbones-to-Go. I'm not sure whether food was stolen or not, but some of their good luck symbols inside were compromised enough to make it clear someone had been there in off hours. And you know how I found out about all this?"

"No," I said. "I don't."

"From your friend and hostess, Serina. Not much was done at the Rainbow B&B, I gather, but one night the horseshoe over the front door was turned upside down. Serina found out about it right away, called in her handyman to fix it, and did a whole bunch of knocking on wood and crossing fingers, all to ward off any bad luck that might come about."

"Did it work?" My mind raced. Had I heard any guests mention such a thing? Or any hint of bad luck overtaking them, especially if they'd walked through the door with the horseshoe facing the wrong way? I was fairly sure I hadn't.

"As far as I know, it did," Carolyn said. "Anyway, I wanted to warn you so you can take whatever steps you want to protect the Lucky Dog. I've ordered a new security system for Buttons of Fortune, but right

53

now I'm just making sure I lock all doors and windows securely when I leave."

"I just did that at Lucky Dog," I told her. "Gemma and I walked back here with Justin, and he made sure we locked up our shops." I appreciated Justin's concern for my shop and my safety — but was even more irritated that he hadn't explained it until I'd pushed him on it.

The last thing I asked Carolyn, because I always wanted to know, was, "Are Helga and Liebling all right?" They were her long-haired dachshunds.

"They're fine, and they're trying to soothe my frazzled nerves."

I laughed. "They must be exchanging information with Pluckie." My sweet little dog now had her head on my lap.

Carolyn and I said good night a minute later, after wishing each other the best of luck and describing how we were knocking on wood as we spoke.

Although knocking on wood a lot hadn't saved Destiny's public affairs director Lou Landorf, who'd been murdered two months ago despite his habit of knocking on every piece of wood around him . . .

I finished getting ready for bed as quickly as I could, since I felt exhausted. But my mind kept me awake far into the night.

Burglaries and more, in the stores that helped make Destiny the wonderful superstition tourist town that it was . . .

Who would do such a thing?

And how soon would Justin and his police department find the culprit and stop the crimes?

That sleep didn't come easily that night wasn't a big surprise. There were often times I wished I could purposely turn off my mind for a while. But I couldn't, and it kept rehashing the little I knew and worrying about everything I didn't.

Was the Lucky Dog on the target list, assuming there was a target list and it wasn't just random stealing and vandalism? If so, when and how would we be hit?

Bad luck or not, I'd warn Gemma in the morning so she could do what she thought necessary to protect the Broken Mirror Bookstore. That place, in some ways the core of Destiny and its retail businesses, had already had too much bad luck rain down on it. Its original owners were dead as a result — but it had been proven to be bad luck to talk about that.

Maybe as a result, that store would be safe from whatever was going on now.

Or not.

Even if it was, the Lucky Dog Boutique was my responsibility.

I slept a little, but when I woke around six in the morning, I decided not to try to rest any longer. Pluckie seemed happy when I got up and started to get ready.

Before heading to the B&B's breakfast, I leashed Pluckie and walked her outside through the front door. We headed for a grassy area to the side of the parking lot, and I turned to regard the horseshoe hung above the entry.

Serina must have seen us go by, since she came out the door, looked around till she spotted us, and hurried in our direction. "Good morning," she said, waving as she approached.

Serina Frye had been one of the first people I'd met here in Destiny, since I'd moved into in the Rainbow B&B right away. She kind of represented Destiny, for me and for the tourists who were her guests. She emphasized this by nearly always wearing blouses and long skirts in the style of women back in Gold Rush days, when Destiny was founded. Today was no different. She was pretty, around ten years older than me, and a nice and welcoming presence in this town of superstitions.

"Hi, Serina," I said as she reached us and

bent to give Pluckie a pat. "Everything okay with you?"

"You mean, did having the horseshoe over my door turned upside down send some bad luck my way?" At my surprised look, she said, "I saw you staring at it when I came outside. How did you hear about it?"

"I understand it's bad luck to talk about any of the stuff going on around here right now," I responded.

"But you've always said you don't necessarily believe in such things." We were close enough buddies that I'd admitted this to Serina.

"You tell me. Is it bad luck to have the ends of a horseshoe hanging downward rather than up?"

"Depends on who's describing the superstition," she said. "That's generally true. People say that having the ends up turns it into a receptacle that holds good luck in, but ends down means the luck pours out. Although I've heard the opposite, kind of. If the ends are down, luck is released to the people around it. That means whoever turned my horseshoe over might have intended to ramp up my good luck."

"And did it?"

"Who knows?" Serina shrugged her narrow shoulders. Her blouse and skirt rippled in the morning breeze. As often happened, she made me feel underdressed, since I was clad as I usually was to go to the store — in a Lucky Dog knit shirt and nice slacks. At least I had my lucky black dog hematite amulet on, as usual.

"I guess a lot of superstitions can have opposing interpretations," I agreed. "*The Destiny of Superstitions* even says so."

"Right." She paused. "So everything's all right with you and with the Lucky Dog?"

While Serina wasn't exactly talking with me about the thefts, like she had with Carolyn, she certainly wasn't staying silent, either.

"Just fine," I said brightly. "In fact, I stopped by there briefly with Justin and Gemma last night." I hesitated. "I didn't see you . . ."

"I'm sorry I didn't make your talk and the get-together. I had things to take care of. I'll really try to come next time."

I wasn't sure what was on her mind, but, like me, Serina was still trying to get over the loss of an important man in her life. In her case it was Tarzal, author of *The Destiny of Superstitions* as well as a recent local murder victim. The fact that the two of them had all but broken up before his death seemed to have only made it harder for her.

"It's okay," I told her. "Anyway, Pluckie and I want our breakfast."

Gemma joined us in the dining area, where she and I ate a light breakfast — although with everything Serina made available, we could have loaded up on enough to fill us for the entire day.

I didn't tell her about my conversation with Carolyn till we started toward our shops. She took the news grimly but well, all things considered. I didn't mention what Serina had said about the horseshoe, since there was nothing much to report on that anyway, except the controversy about the direction in which a horseshoe should be hung.

The walk to the Lucky Dog Boutique didn't take long. It was early, but there were already tourists on the streets — avoiding the cracks on the sidewalk. I'd have to seed the area in front of my shop with some heads-up pennies later, since that kind of good luck often brought customers into my shop.

My shop. It remained Martha's, of course. But I had pretty well taken over the management. And I had the goal of buying it someday — maybe. If it made sense to Martha, too.

As we reached the Broken Mirror Bookstore, Gemma and I started to say goodbye. She patted Pluckie goodbye, too — or tried to. Pluckie seemed energized. She jumped at the end of her leash, pulling me toward the Lucky Dog.

She'd done this before — on our first day in Destiny. That was when she'd found an ill Martha in the back room and helped to save her.

Was Martha okay?

"Let's go, Pluckie," I told her, exchanging glances with Gemma. "I'm not sure what's going on."

"I'm coming with you," Gemma said.

We hurried to the front door of the shop, where I used my key to enter, Gemma right behind me.

I immediately stopped.

Things — leashes and food, toys and more — were off the shelves, tossed onto the floor. I didn't see the bag I'd left up against the counter, the bag filled with my new dog toys.

Pieces of broken mirror were everywhere, and so was salt.

Whatever was going on in Destiny had invaded my shop.

FIVE

"Call 911!" I yelled to Gemma. "I'm going upstairs to check on Martha."

I closed and locked the door behind us so I could let go of Pluckie's leash. My little dog nevertheless stayed right with me as I crossed the shop to fling aside mesh drapery decorated with dog bones, open the door to the storeroom, and hurry through it to the door to the stairway that led upstairs.

To Martha's apartment.

Was she okay, after the disaster that had happened downstairs in her shop? I crossed my fingers.

Flicking on the light, I began running up the steps, at the same time pressing Justin's number on my phone. He needed to know what was going on for many reasons — because of his warning, because he was so close to Martha, and maybe most of all because I needed his presence for some modicum of reassurance that all, eventually, would be well again.

"Good morning, Rory," I heard in my ear, just as I tripped over Pluckie and fell onto my knees on the stairs.

"Ow!" I gasped.

"Rory, are you okay?"

I'd pulled the phone away from my ear as I caught myself and prevented any further falling, but I still heard him. "Yes," I lied. One of my knees was killing me. "Sort of." I spoke in gasps through gritted teeth as I started back up the stairs, walking much more slowly this time. Pluckie was a few steps ahead of me, sitting now and watching as if trying to apologize. I hoped our collision hadn't injured her, too. Fortunately, she looked fine. "But I'm on my way up to check on Martha. The store was robbed and vandalized last night, like you warned."

"I'll get someone there right away."

"Gemma's calling 911," I told him. I didn't imagine he'd want to duplicate efforts — although he might contact his own people and make sure they were moving fast.

"Good. I'll see you in a little while."

I'd reached the top of the steps, standing right beside Pluckie now. I was panting and about to knock on Martha's door when it dawned on me what had happened.

I had fallen while going up the steps. If it had been when I was on my way down, that would bode bad luck. Going up, it supposedly meant a wedding in the family.

Not in my family. I'd lost Warren, and we hadn't gotten the chance to marry. My mom had passed away long ago, and my father, who still lived in Pasadena, had remarried. We had more distant relatives but didn't stay in close touch. Was one of them likely to marry?

But at the time I'd tripped, I'd been talking with Justin, with whom I was developing some kind of relationship that bordered, at least, on romantic.

Were we now destined to marry?

Hah.

I knocked determinedly on the closed door and yelled, "Martha? Are you awake? Are you okay?"

And waited. She didn't come to the door immediately. I usually called her first, or accompanied her home, so for her to take a while to get to the door didn't necessarily mean there was anything wrong.

It also didn't mean she was okay. I knocked again, then pulled my phone back out of my pocket and started to punch in her number, just in case she simply hadn't

63

heard me.

The ornate wooden door opened slowly, and I could see Martha off to the side, peeking out. "Rory," she said immediately, pulling it fully open. "What's wrong?"

"Can we come in?" I asked, although my gesture toward Pluckie was too late. My dog had already entered the apartment.

"Of course," Martha said. She was still in her pajamas, pink ones I'd seen before. Her silvery hair looked uncombed, but her hazel eyes looked fully awake, narrowed out of concern.

Fortunately, the pain from my fall had dulled to almost nothing. I moved gently past her and into her living room. I always considered it charming and quaint, with its fluffy yellow sofa and antique tables and chairs, but I barely glanced at it this morning.

"There's been —" I stopped and started again. "Did you sleep all right last night?"

She motioned for me to sit down on her sofa, and I obliged as she took a seat at the other end. Pluckie sat beside the long, low coffee table, looking from one of us to the other.

The expression on Martha's wrinkled face appeared wry. "I hardly think you came up here like this to ask about my sleeping habits. What's going on, Rory?"

"There was a break-in at the shop last night." I watched to make sure she didn't look like she was going to faint or anything. When I'd met her, she'd had health issues, and she still was a bit fragile.

Not now, though. She stood and said, "Tell me. Or should I get dressed first and come see for myself?"

I waited for just a moment before I spoke again. Should I let her know the forbidden information Carolyn had imparted to me, possibly raining bad luck down on herself and the rest of Destiny? Or should I heed Justin's warning?

Heck, he'd be here soon and could scold me then if he wanted to. But maybe if more information was out there, this kind of thing wouldn't be happening — notwithstanding our dear mayor's edicts.

"I haven't had a chance to really check it out," I told her, waving her back down to her seat. "I'll go back down in a few minutes, since the cops should be arriving soon. Gemma is with me, and she called 911 and I called Justin. You can get dressed now if you want. I have to warn you, I've been told it's bad luck to talk about it — but we're the latest victims of an apparent serial crime spree in Destiny."

■ ■ ■ ■

I was finally downstairs again, in the store. Martha was getting dressed. I'd told her I wasn't sure of the severity of what had been done at the Lucky Dog; I'd only been in the shop long enough to see the way the merchandise had been thrown on the floor, and how those bad luck symbols — broken glass and salt — had been scattered about. Plus, I hadn't seen the bag of my new toys.

"But the Lucky Dog isn't the only place where this has happened?" Martha had demanded.

"Apparently not. Justin's been acting a bit . . . well, concerned, despite admitting he's under orders not to talk about something. Someone else" — I didn't want to mention Carolyn and potentially get her in trouble — "told me about the thefts."

"We'll see about that," Martha said. "I'll talk to Justin." And with that, Pluckie and I were virtually kicked out of her apartment and told to go downstairs to start dealing with whatever had happened.

I'd heard voices on my way downstairs. I'd proceeded slowly nonetheless, Pluckie ahead of me. I even held on to the rail. No pain now, at least, but one stumble on the steps was plenty for the day. And I most certainly didn't want to fall going *down* the stairs. I'd already had some pretty bad luck that day: what was done at the shop, most likely early that morning. I didn't want to add to it.

The door into the back storeroom was still open when I reached the bottom, but the voices were coming from the shop. I headed there, Pluckie at my feet, and opened that door.

Gemma was still there, near the cash register counter covered in tangled leashes and collars, talking to two people in suits. One I recognized as Detective Richard Choye, who'd been the main investigator in the most recent Destiny murder. He was a fairly slim cop beneath his gray suit, although his shoulders were wide. His hair was short and black, and on the whole he was reasonably good-looking.

I wondered how Gemma felt, talking to him now. He'd been sure she was guilty before I'd helped to find the real killer and absolve my good friend. I doubted that Detective Choye was overly fond of me, or of Gemma, either.

The person with him was a woman. If Detective Choye was of moderate height, then she was one basketball-player-sized female — very tall and slender. Her suit was black, with a white shirt beneath. Her short hair was light brown, and the expression on her narrow face was intense as she focused on Gemma.

Gemma soon focused on me. She must have seen me enter the room and most likely had been watching for me. "Hi, Rory." Although her voice was calm, I sensed relief in it.

"Thanks for staying here," I said to her. "Martha's okay. She's getting dressed and will be down in a few minutes." That was as much for the cops as for Gemma. "Don't you need to get to the Broken Mirror now?" That was solely for her.

"Yes. I need to open in a short while."

I was sure her thoughts were similar to mine. Surely the shop she managed hadn't been trashed, too — had it?

Apparently the detectives were on the same wavelength. "Rory, Gemma, this is Detective Lura Fidelio," Choye said. "She'll be working with me while we figure out what happened here. Detective Fidelio, why don't you accompany Gemma next door to the Broken Mirror to make sure everything is all right there."

"Certainly." The other detective lowered her head so she could look more directly into Gemma's face. "Let's go," she said, and it sounded like a command.

I hadn't been wild about Detective Choye, but he was better than the counterparts of his I'd met previously. And I already had a feeling I'd like him better than his new associate.

But given the current circumstances, maybe it would be a good thing for Lura to be a take-charge personality — especially if there were problems at the bookstore, too. My fingers crossed behind my back in the hopes that everything there would be fine. Unlike at my shop.

Gemma and Detective Fidelio headed out the front door. I pulled Pluckie's leash out of my pocket where I'd stuffed it and attached it to her collar, to make sure she didn't attempt to follow them.

I almost wanted to do that myself rather then deal with the chaos here. Fortunately, since I'd been in retail for a long time, I kept a pretty accurate inventory of all the items we sold, so once I got things back on their appropriate shelves I'd be able to tell what was missing.

I still didn't see my tote-on-wheels. Nor did I see any of the other items I'd designed. Had they been the target of the theft for some reason? If so, that would suggest that whoever had done this had been at my talk the day before. Otherwise, how would they know what to take?

Unless, of course, they'd opened the bag and removed from the shelves everything that matched what the duffle contained.

Yes, I was already attempting to think of ways to solve this crime. Was the detective with me doing the same thing? He was no longer standing beside me but had moved a few steps away, surveying the store with his dark eyes beneath thin, worried brows.

"So, Detective Choye," I began, "how have you been investigating similar break-ins?"

I realized I was goading him, in a way. I wasn't supposed to know about those other break-ins, and presumably he wasn't supposed to talk about them.

"The Destiny Police Department has a standard procedure for investigating thefts of various kinds," he began pompously. At the same time, I heard a noise at the front door and turned.

Justin was outside.

I hurried toward him as he opened the door, stepping over and around the thick piles of items cast over the floor. I was glad I hadn't locked up after Gemma and Detective Fidelio left. That made me remember that I *had* locked the door behind us earlier, when Gemma, Pluckie, and I first entered, and I recognized in retrospect that this might have been a bad move. What if the thief had been here and we'd needed to escape?

Fortunately, that hadn't been the case. Or, if the person had still been here, he or she apparently went out the back door before I'd checked the storeroom. Unless that person was still hiding under a counter somewhere.

But even if Detectives Choye and Fidelio hadn't made sure the room was clear, I felt fairly confident the thief wasn't there. If anyone was still around, Pluckie would have let me know, and she'd been fairly calm since we'd come back downstairs.

Right now, though, she was pulling on her leash in her attempt to greet Justin.

He, in turn, was working his way through the piles of stuffed animals and blankets and other mixed-up items toward me. Well, toward us, since Detective Choye remained at my side.

Which was a shame. I'd have liked to have thrown myself into Justin's arms to extract whatever comfort I could from him. Never mind that I couldn't define our relationship. We were more than friends, certainly, but was there more to come?

Did I want more?

In any case, a hug from him right now would go a long way toward helping me deal with this situation . . .

Hey, he must have read my mind, I thought a moment later as he reached where I was standing and threw his arms around me. I snuggled against him, aware that Detective Choye was there and watching us. Well, so what?

"Damn that bad luck edict," Justin growled. "We shouldn't have kept any of what happened quiet. This shouldn't be happening anywhere in Destiny, and most especially not here. And I intend to make sure it doesn't happen again."

Six

"Justin. You're here." Martha's voice shrilled out from the doorway to the storeroom.

"Yes, I am." He released me and pulled back a little.

Martha was dressed in a beige Lucky Dog Boutique T-shirt over a calf-length brown skirt and yellow athletic shoes. Pluckie immediately navigated over the piles of things on the floor to reach her.

I refused to allow myself to feel anything but glad that Justin had given me that reassuring little hug, the way friends did with one another. We weren't touching now, and I reminded myself that the embrace hadn't meant anything more than that he was one nice cop.

Even though it was far from the first time we'd been in each other's arms . . . but that hadn't happened often with other people around. And whatever Martha might suspect about us — well, no sense giving

Justin's subordinate, Choye, reason to gossip about the chief back at the station.

This time Justin headed over the tossed merchandise toward Martha, who was like a mother to him. It was no surprise that she got a hug, too. And maybe if Detective Choye had reason to be upset about what had happened here, he might get an embrace as well — or at least a masculine handshake.

Okay, my emotions were overwrought. But under the circumstances, that was allowed.

"I've got a crime scene team coming here, due to arrive anytime," Justin said. "They'll look for prints and other evidence we can use to determine who did this."

Too bad he was across the room. I'd have whispered a question about whether they'd found anything at the other break-ins.

Surprisingly, I didn't have to. "Now, I've already warned you, Rory — and I'm telling you not to talk about what I'm going to say, Martha, because it could be bad luck for you and for Destiny — but this is part of a crime wave. Problem is, we haven't gotten much in the way of evidence yet to go after whoever's doing it and prevent it from happening again."

"Er . . . sir," Choye began. He was still standing not far from me.

"Yes, I know, Detective." Justin stepped away from Martha but remained near the door to the storeroom. "We're under orders, and bad omens appear to be threatening Destiny. But we have a job to do, and if doing it means that we tempt fate against us — well, that's just the way it is."

"But what if it brings bad luck to the entire town, sir? And —"

"We'll warn people. And considering what's been going on, I'd say that bad luck has already arrived. Don't you think?"

Interesting that he was soliciting his subordinate's opinion. Or maybe that was just his way of daring Choye to disagree with him.

"Yes, sir," Choye said.

"Right now, I think you'd better lock the front door, Rory, to prevent any customers from coming in. I can help you come up with a sign that says you're taking inventory or something, so the store will be closed for a couple of hours."

A couple of hours. That would never be a good thing, but on the day after I gave a presentation introducing all sorts of new good luck pet toys, it would be terrible.

On the other hand, I really needed to do that inventory and see if I still had even one of those new toys left.

"Okay," I said sadly. I looked at Martha. She was nearer to me now, since Justin had assisted her through the debris. She nodded and looked as miserable as I felt.

I had an idea. "Martha? Justin? You go ahead and close us down for now. Everything in the back looked okay, so I'm going to get on the computer and print out a bunch of coupons that we can leave in the front — lucky coupons saying that everyone who picks one up will get fifteen percent off whatever they buy here within the next two days, after we reopen."

"Let us check out the back room first," Choye said, "and even if it's okay, you still won't be able to touch anything besides the computer."

It was nearing noon now. Justin had dispatched a crime scene investigation team fairly quickly, three of them, and they'd managed to get through the storeroom, then the shop, reasonably fast. I'd already called our assistants, Millie and Jeri, and told them not to come in till the afternoon, saying that I'd explain later.

Which I would, as much as I could without making them worry that I was raining bad luck down on them.

Detective Fidelio had come back after accompanying Gemma to the Broken Mirror, and told us that all was fine there. No one had broken into the bookstore.

The two detectives had hung around for most of the morning, assisting the crime lab techs and asking me questions. As the investigation wound down, I was surprised that the detectives actually assisted me in doing a cursory inventory, primarily for their own crime scene analysis, but it also helped me.

And now all of them were finally leaving.

That included Justin, who'd also remained here, ostensibly helping to pore through everything at the crime scene. Maybe that was, in fact, all he'd intended. But his presence certainly helped me — and Martha — get through a very difficult time.

He even helped clean up the pieces of broken mirror and spilled salt. I removed five dollar bills from our cash register and handed them out, to counter the former bit of bad luck as that superstition dictated, and we each tossed some salt over our shoulder, to offset the bad luck associated with the latter.

I carried the tablet computer I used with me as I jotted down each piece of merchandise. I'd compare it against what was supposed to be here later. Finally, I got a brief opportunity to speak to Martha — with Justin present.

We stood near the shelves where the stuffed dog toys were displayed. Shelves that did not currently contain any of the new toys I'd designed. We'd found none of them in the shop. Although we still had a few of the new products in boxes in the back, not many had been in the front of the store yet. At the moment, none were.

Which again led me to believe that the thief had been at my talk, and, perhaps, had some kind of grudge against me. But who? And why?

Martha hadn't heard any noise from the shop during the night, which she reiterated again, also pointing out that she didn't sleep too deeply these days. But she'd had some bad dreams. "I don't remember them all, but one stood out," she said, a sad expression on her face. "There was a raccoon in it and it was chasing me, so I was running away."

"That does sound pretty scary," I agreed, although it didn't seem terribly bad to me.

Not until Martha said, "You know what that means, Justin, don't you? We've talked about it before. I had one like it when I was in the hospital, around the time Pluckie saved me." She bent slightly and motioned to my dog, who moved from her place beside me to accept a pat on the head.

Justin nodded. "You told me that dreaming about a raccoon means to stay on guard, and if someone you know is chasing you in the dream, it means they're going to turn on you. And to run in your dream means there'll be some kind of change in your life. Right?"

"That's right," Martha said sadly. "I'm going to have to stay even more alert now."

She looked at me as if for my affirmation. Or was she sizing me up as potentially being the person who'd turn on her?

It hurt to think she might believe so. "We'll all stay alert and keep an eye on you, Martha," I told her.

"We sure will," Justin said.

Martha moved her smile between the two of us. "Thank you," she said. "Both of you. For being here for me."

And then she turned and went back to work organizing things.

Finally, with the police departed, we were ready to open the shop. But not to share what had happened, at least not much. Whether or not it would be bad luck for Destiny, I didn't know, but I wanted people to talk about our wonderful, lucky pet items and buy them, not feel sorry for us or gossip about how awful things were here.

I didn't need any reminders of the nasty situation anyway — unless someone came up to me and confessed and returned what was missing. And then let me call Justin to come and pick them up.

I almost laughed at the thought as I leashed Pluckie to the counter, to make sure she stayed inside as she should. Martha, who was finishing the organization of the good luck pet-related amulets in the nearby case, must have looked up and seen me smile.

"What's so funny?" she asked, not sounding at all amused.

I needed to cheer her up, too, so I told her the nonsense I'd been thinking. "What if the thief were to come in here and apologize and return everything? Wouldn't that be the good luck of Destiny?" I knocked on the wood along the counter's frame to underscore what I'd said.

Her aging face looked more youthful than I'd seen it that day. The stress had only added to her wrinkles — even now as she smiled, too.

"What an imagination you have, Rory my dear."

"Not any more of one than anyone else in Destiny."

She held up her hand and we high-fived one another, both still smiling. Maybe things would improve that day.

I certainly hoped so, and so I crossed my fingers as I double checked that Pluckie's leash was securely attached to the counter before opening up the shop. Pluckie was always a good dog, and she was free to roam the store when we were closed, but not when we were open; even good dogs could get distracted by food or other animals, or something else of interest to them, and walk out the door.

There was the usual horde of people outside on the sidewalk. Destiny Boulevard in particular seemed to attract crowds, even at this hour of the day. I glanced at the envelope I'd taped to the door under the sign instructing passersby to collect coupons to use later.

All the coupons were gone, more than a couple dozen of them.

A few people entered right away.

"I'll call Jeri now," Martha said. "I think we'll need some help pretty soon."

I nodded as I started showing the first customers to enter, a young couple with a golden retriever on a leash, some of the leashes and collars with shamrocks and other lucky symbols on them. Maybe our good luck was returning, since they bought a couple of each, one in yellow and the other in green. "We can dress her up more with these," the man said.

As they left, I went to help some people examining chew toys for the pups they'd left at home and saw that Martha was showing off some doggy clothing.

I was surprised, as I was ringing up the first of these sales, to see Brad Nereida of the Wish-on-a-Star children's shop across the street come in. He waved, and as he moved away from the door I was glad to see Jeri come in. She immediately came up to the counter.

"Everything okay?" she asked. Dark-complected and lovely, Jeri had been one of Martha's assistants when I'd first come to Destiny. I'd seen her at my presentation yesterday, as well as at the Clinking Glass Saloon last night. The beige shirt she wore was one from her family's Heads-Up Penny Gift Shop just down the street.

"It is now. Thanks for coming in to help out."

"Sure," she said. "We need to talk later, though. It's supposed to be bad luck, but I need to discuss something with you."

The way she looked at me, her deep brown eyes solemn and concerned, caused me to blurt, but quietly, "You know what happened here last night?"

Those eyes widened. "No, unless . . ." She bent toward me. "We had a break-in at Heads-Up a few nights ago. Did that happen here, too?"

Brad Nereida was suddenly right beside us near the counter. He was medium height, medium weight, and average looking, and he always appeared tired to me — a symptom, I assumed, of being both a store owner and a father of three youngsters. I figured that they were in school now, as this was Thursday, and that Lorraine must be watching the store.

"I couldn't hear you," he said, "but the way you two looked while you were talking, and the fact it took you so long to open your store today, Rory, despite giving a presentation last night . . . did someone break in here? We're not supposed to talk about it, but Wish-on-a-Star . . ." His voice trailed off, and I looked into his pale brown eyes.

Another break-in, another theft. How many shops had Justin been referring to when he'd mentioned the break-ins?

This was terrible. It had to stop.

And I was going to do whatever it took to make sure no one else in Destiny went through this again.

SEVEN

There were too many people in the shop for me to talk. Customers who needed help. Ears that could overhear what we were talking about — and perhaps up the potential of bad luck resulting from a discussion of what definitely needed to be discussed, no matter what the reputed outcome.

I drew Jeri and Brad into the corner near where Pluckie was tied to the counter. My dog stood up on her hind legs and planted her front paws on me, and I absently stroked her head as I told the other humans, "We really need to talk. I think Millie's now supposed to come in around three o'clock, and she can cover the shop."

I looked at Jeri, who nodded. The two part-timers kept good track of each other's schedules, just like they enjoyed taking breaks together to go get coffee.

"Can we three meet somewhere?" I continued. "At — how about Beware-of-

Bubbles?" The coffee shop's superstitious name reflected how bubbles traveling in a cup of coffee are supposed to affect whoever drinks it, and Beware-of-Bubbles was a fairly good place to sit off to the side and talk, especially on its patio. I'd be sure to bring Pluckie if they agreed.

Which they did. I crossed my fingers as I watched Brad leave and Jeri walk up to a youthful group of customers who'd brought in both a little Yorkie and a big standard poodle.

I'd have to curb my curiosity till later. But I really wanted to know what had happened at their stores — and if they had any idea who'd robbed them.

It was a good thing that we had our brief prelude to our later talk when we did. I was suddenly approached by Flora Curtival, who inserted herself into the Lucky Dog as if she had business there — even though she'd brought no pets and, as far as I knew, had none.

Apparently, though, she thought she had the most important business in the world to transact. "Hi, Rory," she said, motioning me to join her as she sauntered among the display shelves and customers. I took a few steps in her direction but stopped. "So glad you're open now," she continued. "I wanted to talk to you before. When I saw you were busy inside I left you alone, but I've got some ideas about properties that I want to run by you."

I wondered how Gemma had avoided speaking with her — or if she had. "Thank you," I said, to be polite, "but I really don't have time to deal with that now. And as I've told you, I'm really not in that much of a hurry."

"That's what Gemma said, too." Flora's glossy mouth turned down into a pout. As before, she was all dressed up, almost like a model rather than a real estate agent, but I figured that was her style. "She had some help in the bookstore, like you do here, but she wouldn't tear herself away to talk to me." Flora glanced around. "Is everything okay here?"

"Of course." But I saw her studying some of the shelves we'd had to restock. She surely hadn't been here enough to notice any difference, had she? Just in case, I said, "We were conducting a quick inventory earlier, so things might be organized a little differently, if that's what you're wondering about."

"Oh. I thought I saw — is that salt on the floor?" She turned and pointed down.

Had we missed some? Apparently so, since

there were tiny grains on the polished wooden floor, right behind where Flora stood.

"Just to be safe, feel free to toss some of it over your shoulder," I said. I'd dare fate this time and not do it. I'd joined everyone in the ritual before, even though none of us were responsible for spilling the salt in the first place.

"Of course." She knelt down, picked up a few granules, and stood again, tossing the grains over her shoulder.

I was glad Pluckie's leash wouldn't let her come this far, since I didn't want her licking up salt. Was that unlucky for dogs? I doubted it was healthy.

"Excuse me." I went to the sales counter, where I pulled a roll of paper towels from beneath it, moistened one from the bottle of water I kept there, and hurried back to wipe up the rest of the salt.

I heard murmurs from customers around the area, including questions to one another about whether they'd seen who'd spilled the salt and whether it was okay to stay in the shop even if they hadn't spilled it themselves.

When I stood again, I smiled and turned around. "Hey, everyone, it's a game. I'm not sure how the salt got there either, but it's good to hear that most of you know about the superstition surrounding spilled salt. Just in case, I'm going to knock on the wooden floor it was spilled on and invoke good luck on each of you, and on the Lucky Dog Boutique." Which I did. When I was done, I slipped through the crowd, which still contained Flora, and returned to the counter.

Martha was there now, appearing concerned. "I like how you handled that," she said softly, "but do we know how that salt got there? I thought we got rid of all of it before."

I shook my head. "So did I, but we must have missed some. Anyway, I think we're all good now."

"Me too." Flora had followed me to the counter. "In fact, this afternoon would be a good and lucky time for me to show you, and Gemma too, some of the houses and condos I've been checking out on your behalf. I can examine them for spilled salt before we enter."

"Thanks," I said, "but it'll have to wait." Not that I hadn't told her that before.

"But —" Flora didn't finish her objection, since she saw me staring toward the front door and turned to see what I was looking at. No, not what, but whom.

Mayor Bevin Dermot had just entered the Lucky Dog.

As far as I was aware, our illustrious mayor wasn't owned by a dog or any other pet, so he most likely wasn't here to buy something for a loved one. I hardly ever saw him here.

Had he heard what had happened, perhaps from Justin?

Did he come to admonish Martha and me and whoever else was aware of last night's episode, reminding us to keep it quiet? Especially now, with tourists visiting the shop in throngs, which could dissipate if they knew what was going on in Destiny stores: waves of bad luck.

I didn't know Bevin well, but I anticipated more of that from him than sympathy for what we'd been going through. Maybe he'd be kinder, though, to Martha.

He glanced around, peering at and beyond the display shelves as if surveying whether all was well. Or perhaps preparing to do his welcome thing for our customers. His glance seemed to stop on Jeri, though, and then returned to me, then swung to Martha. "Good to see you, ladies," his voice boomed. "There are a couple of things I want to talk to you about, so can we go into your back room? You can convey anything

89

appropriate to Ms. Mardeer later." That meant Jeri, whose family store had of course gone through something as well.

I decided I wouldn't necessarily mention to the mayor that she and Brad Nereida and I planned to meet later, and that we'd probably violate his command to keep the thefts quiet, at least as it applied to our own small group. Still, I'd learned that it didn't usually make sense to deny Mayor Bevin anything — or at the least, I tried to make him believe that I was as much of an obedient townsperson as anyone else.

"That's fine." I nodded at Martha, whose return smile looked pasted on her senior face, but I knew she understood and agreed. She rubbed her hands along the hips of her baggy jeans beneath her Lucky Dog Boutique T-shirt, then motioned for us to follow her.

I glanced at Pluckie, who looked just fine lying at the end of her leash attached to the counter, and Jeri stood nearby with several customers. Flora was still there, but she appeared to be studying the glass case filled with lucky amulets, mostly hematite.

I headed in Jeri's direction, briefly mentioned what Martha and I were up to, then followed Martha and the mayor through the door into the storeroom.

Once we were there, near the card table and among the metal shelves and boxes, Mayor Bevin herded us together. He may have been dressed in his usual leprechaun-like suit of green jacket and dark trousers, but his expression was anything but cute or scheming or anything else I imagined a leprechaun to look like.

"Thank you, ladies," he said solemnly, his hands clasped in front of his chubby middle, his back barely touching one of the depleted metal shelves. He looked again from Martha to me, enough of a quiver in his chin to cause his white beard to tremble. "The police told me what happened here last night."

Justin, I wondered? Or someone else?

"Now, to keep Destiny's luck moving in the most positive direction, you must not talk about it to anyone. It's best to not even discuss it among yourselves."

"But if no one knows about it," I said, "what's to prevent the perpetrator from doing it again?" I didn't mention my awareness that our invasion hadn't been the first. Would he mention it?

"I understand," he said evasively, "but what's to prevent tourists from staying away from your shop if they hear about it?"

"They might be curious enough to come

see us anyway," Martha said. She appeared to be playing along, too. Her expression was bland, at least, as she regarded Bevin. "Maybe it would be a good thing."

"Not if they want to derive good luck from Destiny," Bevin argued. "Why patronize a store that's suffered bad luck?"

"And if they enter stores that have suffered bad luck and don't know about it, maybe their luck will remain good." I hesitated, then blurted intentionally, "Hasn't that been the case with other Destiny shops that have been looted?" And restaurants that have been vandalized, I mentally added, but I didn't mention that.

"You've heard?" Bevin's tone sounded scandalized. "How did you find out? Which stores do you think . . ." His voice tapered off, then he demanded, "Are you just guessing the Lucky Dog isn't the first, Ms. Chasen?"

"If I were, your response would have answered my question," I said. "We're not the first. And to keep us the last, we really need to let everyone know — at least all the business owners in town." That, at least, hinted that I knew shops weren't the only victims.

"No." Bevin crossed his arms over his hefty round chest. "You know what happened when the edict not to discuss what happened . . . next door . . . was nearly made public by the *Destiny Star*." He was hinting about the newspaper's initial investigation into the superstition-related deaths of the owners of the Broken Mirror Bookstore — and the resulting fire in the *Star*'s offices.

"I'm not sure of the origin of that command to keep silent, or of this one," I said. "But this situation is different, in any case, since we've got a crime wave going on that might not end until the perpetrator is caught, or at least outed enough for the store owners to protect their premises better." I hesitated for only an instant, then said, "If only I'd known, we might not have suffered last night's break-in." I glared at Bevin, as if he were part of the problem. And maybe he was, with his insistence on people keeping quiet.

"Now don't you start blaming everyone trying to protect you for —"

"We understand," Martha interrupted calmly. "We know you have our best interests at heart." Nice of her to say so, although what I figured was that Bevin had *his own* best interests at heart. "We'll not spread the word around town about what happened, Mayor. You can count on that." She shot me a look that warned me not to contradict her.

I didn't. Not now. And besides, I sort of understood what she was doing. She wasn't promising we wouldn't talk about it, even if we agreed not to make a public pronouncement about it.

Not yet, at least.

"All right, then. Thank you, Martha." With his arms still crossed and resting on his middle, the mayor turned to glare me into submission, too.

"That's fine with me," I said. "At least for now, during the investigation." I didn't mean to dump all the responsibility on Justin and his department, but they were involved. And if they quickly figured out who'd been committing these acts, then the whole thing could go away.

On the other hand, since we weren't the first victims and the situation had begun days, if not weeks, earlier, then relying on an official investigation wasn't particularly wise — not for us, and not for our town.

For, yes, I considered Destiny my town, at least for now — even if I didn't want to jump right in and check out available residences that Flora found for Gemma and me.

"Very well, then," Bevin said formally. "We

will stay in touch."

And talk about what, I wondered as Martha and I followed him back to the door and into the shop.

Jeri was just ringing up a sale at the register — a good luck doggy shirt with a four-leaf clover on it. A line had formed behind the customer, so I hurried over to help. The mayor started schmoozing with some of the other customers. Flora was still there, but she must have noticed how busy I was, since she began working her way toward the other side of the shop.

As she walked in that direction, Martha's nephew, Arlen Jallopia, entered the store. He was a guide for Destiny's Luckiest Tours, and I had in fact taken one of his tours and enjoyed it immensely. He seemed to notice Flora, viewed her up and down. Was he flirting with her? She aimed a smile at him, then walked farther into the shop.

Martha had stayed near me and was helping to pack customers' purchases into bags as they paid. Arlen soon joined us.

It would be no surprise to me if Flora had flirted back. Arlen was a nice-looking guy who resembled a sitcom star. As usual, he wore a red knit shirt with the Destiny's Luckiest Tours logo on the pocket, and his dark hair was combed into spikes.

But I was used to seeing him wearing a smile. Today his face was curved into a worried frown. "Hi, Auntie," he belted out in a surprisingly cheerful tone. "Rory. Good to see you both. I see you're busy now, but can we get together for dinner tonight?"

Now that was unusual. Or at least it was unusual to include me. I supposed that aunt and nephew got together for dinner now and then.

"Sure," I said, then added, "Is everything all right?"

He looked me straight in the face with his dark, concerned eyes. "That's exactly what I intend to ask you."

EIGHT

As Arlen went to talk to his aunt, I saw the mayor leave — a good thing. Some of my tension faded.

Right after he'd left, Millie came in. That was good, too, since it was nearly the time Jeri and I had agreed to meet with Brad for coffee — and a discussion of stuff we theoretically weren't supposed to mention, let alone talk about.

Theoretically? No, if our mayor had anything to say about it — which he thought he did — it was fact, not theory. We weren't to let word get around about the thefts and vandalism, or probably anything else that might give Destiny a bad name, or give its inhabitants or visitors bad luck.

But things happen. And as I'd learned, especially since coming here, even well-known superstitions weren't always consistent with one another in predicting outcomes. So how could superstitions made up by people in power absolutely come true?

That was our mayor, though, and it wasn't the first time he'd done something like this — superstition by edict. And although I fretted a bit about our somewhat confrontational conversation, I found myself puzzling even more over Arlen's comment as I unhooked Pluckie from the counter and, motioning for Jeri to join us, started making my way through the customers surrounding the shelves to get to the door.

Arlen wanted to talk to us. Why? What had he meant by his comment that he wanted to find out from us if everything was all right?

He was still talking with Martha, like the good nephew he was, or at least tried to be sometimes. Maybe that conversation would be enough to reassure him that all was well.

But I suspected that my boss, though she might whitewash how she presented it, would be honest with her nephew. Besides, even if she wanted to reveal to him everything that had happened, she would be reluctant to do so in the shop where they could be overheard.

As a result, I figured, I could count on dinner with aunt and nephew as he'd suggested. Later.

But now, we were headed to Beware-of-

Bubbles, which was right next door. As we walked, Jeri said, "I hope you don't mind, but I invited my mother. She knows a lot more than I do about . . . about what went on at the Heads-Up Penny." Apparently Jeri didn't feel entirely comfortable talking about the situation. *Thanks, Mr. Mayor.*

"I'm fine with having your mother join us," I said to my clearly concerned companion. I didn't know Kiara Mardeer well, but I hoped she'd be unsuperstitious enough to provide some details about the break-in at their gift shop.

On the other hand, heads-up pennies had lots of superstitious connotations, and the Mardeers did live in Destiny. Maybe Kiara wouldn't want to tempt bad luck by talking about what had somehow become forbidden.

On the sidewalk near the coffee shop, I passed the usual vending machine that contained the *Destiny Star.* I generally picked up a copy, but I hadn't seen anything about nasty goings-on in Destiny in the last one. Then again, I knew the Vardoxes had apparently suffered consequences after not complying with the superstition edicts around here, so they might not mention any vandalism or theft they'd heard about, just assuming it was forbidden.

Kiara was standing near the door as we got there, not far from the tables along the sidewalk. She was shorter and rounder than her daughter and pretty, too. Her black hair was decorated with white-streaked highlights, and her deep complexion glowed as she shot us a quick smile. Although Jeri wore a T-shirt that said Heads-Up Penny Gift Shop, Kiara sported a white button-down shirt that was decorated with copper pennies — all heads up, of course.

"Hi," she said. "This'll be an interesting cup of coffee, I'll bet."

"Interesting," I agreed, nodding. "And it'll hopefully lead to some good luck, which I think we all need. Have you seen Brad Nereida?"

"He just got here and said he figured you'd bring your dog. He picked up his coffee and now is saving a table on the patio for us."

"Good guy," I said. The three of us plus Pluckie entered the coffee shop and got in line, which fortunately wasn't very long.

"Everything okay at your store now?" Kiara asked. I heard what she wasn't saying — that she knew it hadn't been okay earlier.

"It's fine now," I responded. When we sat down, I hoped we'd all tell the truth about what each store had experienced.

Or not.

In any event, I noticed that Celia Vardox was here. I'd run into her and her brother, Derek, at the coffee shop before. Apparently the owners of the *Destiny Star* liked to buy their coffee out a lot rather than just keep a pot going at the newspaper office. Or maybe customers here tended to blab gossip that they could write up in articles. Or perhaps they were keeping an eye on how their newspaper was selling at the nearby vending machine.

Celia was sitting at one of the round indoor tables, facing someone with his back toward me. I wasn't sure, but it could have been Padraic Hassler, one of the owners of the Shamrock Steakhouse, judging by the sparseness of his gray hair.

Was he allowing her to interview him? Carolyn had said that his restaurant had been hit by vandalism.

Or maybe they were just friends. Or she was pressuring him to talk but he knew better.

I wasn't about to ask. I'd had my own run-ins with the Vardoxes, especially when they'd done an op-ed piece on me and how I was looking into one of the murders to help a friend. I would have just as soon stayed off their radar — unless they wanted to talk about my new additions to the Lucky Dog inventory, or if I decided to place another ad to promote the pet boutique or my "Black Dog and Black Cat" presentations, as I'd done before the talks had become popular enough to always attract a crowd.

The Vardoxes weren't the only ones I recognized. Beware-of-Bubbles wasn't very big and nearly all its tables were filled, some by people I didn't know, of course — most likely tourists. But I did see Brie Timons, Flora's boss. She was facing toward the coffee line, with someone sitting across from her whose face I couldn't see. Even so, I thought I recognized the person's model-like style of dressing. It was most likely Flora.

I was glad she couldn't see me, but I figured Brie would let her know I was here.

Darn it.

We fortunately reached the front of the line quickly, and I ordered a small mocha plus some water for Pluckie. I stayed by the counter while my mocha was prepared, then slid outside with my pup as soon as I could, the Mardeers close behind me.

I saw Brad Nereida right away. He sat at a table for four, unsurprisingly, in a corner of the crowded concrete patio.

He rose as I got there, then pulled out a chair for me. Ah. A gentleman. Lorraine must have taught him well.

Speaking of whom . . . when he was sitting down again, after also pulling out chairs for Jeri and Kiara, I asked, "How's Lorraine, Brad? Is she watching the store today?"

"No, she and the kids are visiting relatives in San Diego right now. Some of our staff are in charge at Wish-on-a-Star."

I'd become fairly friendly with Lorraine, partly because their store was right across the street from the Lucky Dog. She and Brad had twin boys who were in preschool, plus a daughter a couple of years older. I wondered how the parents had dealt with the difficult situation of the break-in at the store, especially with the kids. Or maybe that was really why Lorraine had taken them traveling.

Now Brad leaned over the table, regarding us one at a time as he held his large coffee cup in one hand. "Speaking of Wish-on-a-Star, I understand you've all had some trouble lately too."

"You know we've been told it's bad luck to talk about that trouble," Kiara said.

"Well, I'm crossing my fingers that the worst is over," Brad replied. We all solemnly held up our hands with fingers crossed. And then we softly began talking about what had happened at our respective stores.

Pluckie must have sensed my disquiet, since she sat right against my leg as I described what I'd found this morning when I got to the Lucky Dog. The others had each experienced something very similar with their stores.

"What do you think?" Jeri asked. "Is someone out to bring bad luck down on us by stealing lucky things and leaving ill omens — broken mirrors and salt and things?"

"Maybe," Brad said. "I want to know more, though. Around here, someone could be doing that part as a joke while they steal things — and money. I know some was gone from my cash drawer."

We'd also had some money taken, but not a huge amount. Even so, he was right. That could have been the real motive for what had been done to our stores.

We talked a little more, speculating mostly about motive rather than who might have done it.

But I couldn't talk long. From where I sat, I could see the door to the coffee shop, and so I could also see when Flora came through it and approached us, wending her way among the patio tables.

"I'm afraid I'm going to have to leave," I told the others. "You can go ahead and continue brainstorming. Jeri can catch me up later if there's anything I need to know." Then, with a sigh, I stood, and so did Pluckie. "Hi, Flora," I said resignedly. I didn't want her to bother the others, so I picked up my mocha. "I was just about to leave."

"Great," she said. "Hi, Brad. Hi to all of you." She smiled at the Mardeers even as Brad glanced at her, gave an unconvincing smile, and mumbled his own hello. Had they met before? Were the Nereidas looking for a new home?

Or was Flora hoping they were, as she was with me?

I tried to use the opportunity to slip away, but Flora remained at my side.

"I was just talking to Brie about some ideas for residences for Gemma and you," she said. "I'll walk you back to the Lucky Dog and we can talk about them."

She didn't give up. Nor did she listen to my repeated admonishments that we weren't in a hurry.

She was, however, in a hurry to scoop us in and try to make a sale, or at least a rental.

Lucky me.

The walk to my shop was quick, and I

105

turned to face her at the door. Pluckie took the opportunity to squat on the sidewalk, waiting for me.

"I'll be in touch when things slow down enough for me to start really thinking about finding a place," I told Flora.

Or not. I'd actually been okay with the idea last night, but I didn't like being nagged about it. And now, given a choice, I wouldn't want this pushy woman to get some kind of commission based on her unwanted aggressiveness.

"I'd like to come in now and look around your shop some more," she said.

"Do you have a pet?" I asked. Maybe I could sell her something, then make her go away.

A strange look came over her too-made-up face, almost causing it to pale beneath the blusher on her cheeks. "I used to," she said softly. "Not now."

"Oh. Sorry." I assumed whoever her pet had been, he or she had crossed the Rainbow Bridge — a euphemism for a beloved pet dying and going to pet heaven.

"Me too. Anyway, maybe another time. I like your store, but I just remembered I need to check with Brie about another client."

She pivoted, which was probably difficult

to do considering the height of her stiletto heels, and walked off.

Which made me glad, yet sorry I'd brought on pain. I hated to do that to anyone.

Even to someone who was starting to drive me nuts.

NINE

Martha's kitchen table was small, but it was large enough for four of us.

It wouldn't have fit five easily, so I'd allowed that to be the sort-of excuse I gave to Justin about why I couldn't see him that evening. As I often did, I requested a rain check. He'd granted it immediately, and I'd almost regretted not inviting him along.

Almost. If he'd been here, I suspected that whatever Arlen wanted to talk about would have turned into a benign superstition discussion — and I'd be driven crazy wondering what he really believed to be so important that he thought we needed to get together in private to discuss it.

Not quite private. He and Martha considered me part of their family now, and I appreciated it. I also appreciated that they'd brought Gemma into the fold as well.

Right now, we were just starting dinner. I'd offered to bring in pizza or even something more formal, but Martha had insisted on cooking. Which was a good sign. Even though she hadn't been well when I'd first met her, now, despite her age, she was going strong. But she hadn't yet booted me out as manager of her store, and I was glad about that. I hoped she never would. Sure, I'd considered trying to buy it from her, and I still had that plan, but I probably wouldn't act on it, not as long as she was able to participate in the shop's management.

Tonight, Martha had made mac and cheese — delicious! I wasn't sure which cheeses she had used, but there were several, and she'd also added bacon, with a slightly crispy coating of bread crumbs on the top.

Apparently Arlen had helped her with the side salad, at least. Everything was great.

Even the company. Especially the company.

But we hadn't yet started discussing the main reason for getting together this evening.

Martha was wearing a pretty lavender housedress. She seemed alert as she finally joined us at the table, looking first at Arlen, her hazel eyes intensely peering from her wizened face. "So spill it, nephew. Why did you want us to get together tonight?"

As always, Arlen looked good, even as he raised his brows at his aunt, his mouth puckering into an expression of wryness. "You aren't going to like it." But he said this not to Martha, but to me as he turned his head. "You neither." This time, his gaze was on Gemma.

My dear friend shrugged her shoulders as she took another bite of mac and cheese, then looked at Martha. "Even if I don't like what Arlen has to say, this makes it worth my coming here." She smiled.

Gemma was still dressed in some of the librarian-like garb she wore while managing the Broken Mirror Bookstore, making her the most formal-looking person at the table. Arlen wore a red Destiny's Luckiest Tours shirt, and I still had on a gray Lucky Dog Boutique T-shirt.

"Why aren't we going to like it?" I demanded lightly.

"It's about superstitions." He looked at me from beneath furrowed brows, as if he anticipated I'd berate him for that.

How could I, here in Destiny?

"Why am I not surprised?" Gemma asked, covering her mouth as if she was yawning.

"And . . . well, it's speculation. But first I want you two to know that I'm aware of what happened in the shop last night."

I looked toward Martha, whose gaze was now pointed innocently toward the ceiling.

"I won't guess about how you learned," I said dryly, "but let's all knock on wood that the discussion, and this one, will not bring any of us bad luck."

We all knocked. Did I really believe it provided any protection?

Heck if I knew.

"Okay, then," Arlen said. "I've heard rumors in town and on tours today that the break-in at the Lucky Dog wasn't the only one recently. And the other reason I think you two aren't going to like what I have to say is that I know you're looking for a place to live other than the Rainbow B&B. Am I right?"

"Possibly," Gemma said. She took a bite of salad without removing her gaze from Arlen. "Why does that matter?"

"Because Flora Curtival is your real estate agent, right?"

"She wants to be," I acknowledged. "Why does that make a difference?"

"Because . . . well, I know it sounds odd, but I think she's the one responsible for all the break-ins."

Dinner was over now. Martha, Gemma, and I sat on Martha's fluffy yellow sofa facing

111

Arlen, who occupied the chair across from us. Pluckie sat beside me on the floor.

"So, are you going to tell our estimable police chief about my suspicions?" Arlen asked me.

"Of course," I said. "Even if it doesn't make a whole lot of sense, that doesn't mean it isn't true. Plus, I suspect the police force can use all the possible angles they can find."

"Particularly in a town like Destiny," Gemma broke in, "where what you've suggested might actually be true."

I took a sip of the after-dinner drink Martha had poured for us, a little bit of sweet wine with a dab of whipped cream on top. I resisted chugging it. It tasted good — and my mind needed a bit of cleansing.

What Arlen had related was that he had met Flora maybe a year ago. She'd come to town with her husband, and they had gone on several tours with Arlen.

"I know I'm not the only one around here who talked to them on that visit," Arlen had said while gazing over Gemma's head and munching on mac and cheese. "They were around for maybe a week. Flora seemed to be all over her man, hanging on to him on the tour bus, clutching at his arm at each place we stopped. I might not have noticed, since we get all kinds of people on the tour, but there was one night when she came back alone to the tour office when everyone else was gone. I'd taken a late tour out and was just taking care of the administrative stuff afterward, and she burst in the front door."

I'd been to the Destiny's Luckiest Tours office shortly after I'd come to town, before heading off on a bus tour with Arlen. It wasn't one of the area's most exotic buildings, being low and concrete and outside the middle of town where everything looked like it was built during the old Gold Rush days.

But someone coming in after hours didn't seem especially memorable to me — until Arlen continued.

"She threw herself into my arms and started sobbing. She said she'd dragged her husband here to Destiny since they were destined to stay together. They had to be. He'd talked about leaving her before they came, and now they were going home tomorrow — and she still thought their marriage was doomed. But what could Destiny do about it overnight? What could *I* do about it right then?" Arlen had shaken his head. "I smelled alcohol on her breath, so I figured she'd been out drinking to try

113

to ease her pain. And I kind of half expected it when she started tearing at my clothes."

"You're kidding!" I interjected.

"Nope," he said. He related how he'd gently pushed her away — which apparently had only added to how upset she was. "She promised revenge on Destiny for not changing her luck. That was the last time I saw her — until she showed up at a Destiny Welcome a few weeks ago. I stayed away from her, but she probably saw me anyway." Looking around the table, from me to Martha to Gemma, Arlen continued, "I know it's pretty weird for me to think this, but is she getting her revenge on Destiny by robbing its shops and planting bad luck stuff in the places she hits?"

I'd pondered his revelation and speculation throughout the rest of dinner — not surprising, since we kept talking about it. And now that I was drinking, too — albeit not the quantity I surmised Flora must have imbibed back then — I let my mind wander about superstitions and why Flora might have thought they could help her in her relationship, and whether there were any superstitions connected with how to exact revenge.

Or she could have made up her own superstitions about revenge, which was more likely. Or maybe she was simply removing or ruining good luck stuff and replacing it with bad luck stuff as the best way to get back at Destiny's inhabitants, even those who'd had nothing to do with her prior trip here and its apparent failure to ensure the result she wanted.

So now I said, "The possibility of Flora being responsible for all this makes more sense than a lot of other potential reasons for what's been going on here, Arlen. I'll definitely let Justin know about it."

I'd also ponder what other ways there might be to determine the truth of what Arlen had said.

Maybe even asking Flora about it.

It was nearly nine o'clock by the time Gemma, Pluckie, and I departed from Martha's and the Lucky Dog downstairs.

Arlen remained in his aunt's apartment after we left, as a good nephew should — assuming he was just keeping her company and taking care of her and not asking for money or something like that. But I'd never gotten that impression about Arlen. He'd moved here to Destiny after his aunt did. He had a job that he seemed to enjoy: taking tourists all around the area and showing them the fun stuff about our town and its

115

superstitions.

Our town? Again I recognized that I'd begun thinking of Destiny as my town. Which was why, whether Arlen was right or not, I really wanted to figure out who was trashing our stores — including mine — and trying to change our good luck to bad.

If it was Flora? Well, she certainly wasn't going to get my real estate business, but she would get something from me. Revenge of the arrest kind, at least — if I could do anything at all to help collect the evidence that Justin and his crew would need.

"Why are you so quiet?" Gemma asked as we turned the corner onto Fate Street.

The November night was cool but dry, and we'd both donned jackets before setting out onto Destiny's sidewalks, now nearly tourist-free in the downtown retail area.

"I'll bet you can guess," I answered wryly. For one thing, Gemma knew me well. We'd been friends for a long time in LA before moving here. For another thing, after the discussion we'd had with Arlen, she could have undoubtedly figured out my thoughts even if we'd been strangers.

In short, we now had a potential suspect for all the nasty stuff that had been happening in town — including at the Lucky Dog.

And that suspect wanted something from us. Something that she believed would result in a commission.

"I'm going to play Justin here," Gemma said. She stopped walking, drew herself up a little taller, and appeared to attempt to broaden her shoulders — a not-very-good imitation of Justin, if that was what she was doing. I laughed as she said in a deeper voice, "Don't do anything foolish, Rory. Tell me what you know, then let me do the investigation. Got it?"

"I hear you, Justin," I said, batting my eyelashes so Gemma could see them under the nearest Destiny streetlight. Then Pluckie and I continued walking.

"You hear him a lot," Gemma huffed, catching up to us. "But do you obey him?"

"What do you think? And do you think I'd have been able to figure out the murder you were all but accused of committing if I'd gone all girly and done everything the police chief said?"

A few cars passed by, and one pulled into the B&B's parking lot just as we arrived there. I didn't recognize the two couples who started to pile out — tourists, I supposed.

"You're right, Rory." Gemma stopped outside the B&B's door, letting the newcomers file in ahead of us. "Let me know what he has to say about your new suspicions."

"Sure," I said. "I think I'll go ahead and call him tonight."

After our walk, Pluckie didn't need another outing, so we went upstairs with Gemma. I didn't see the tourists, so they must have hurried up to their rooms.

"Good night," I called to my friend, whose room was farther down the second floor hallway than mine was.

"Good night. Will you be joining me for breakfast?" she asked.

That was our usual arrangement, so I said, "Sure."

"Good. Oh, and by the way, Stuart is supposed to arrive in town tomorrow for a short stay." Gemma's smile looked casual, but I knew better. She had gone through a breakup with her former boyfriend a few months ago, and a couple of other men had stepped in, vying for her attention. Stuart Chanick had seemed like the winner — even though, when Gemma had followed a superstition by eating an apple and looking into a mirror to see the face of her true love, she hadn't seen Stuart. She didn't recognize who she'd seen, actually. Still, she and Stuart remained in touch. Close touch, I'd gathered.

Plus, Stuart had made an offer to buy the Broken Mirror Bookstore. As far as I knew, that was still pending.

As the editor of *The Destiny of Superstitions,* Stuart had been the one who'd helped Gemma get started as the new manager of the Broken Mirror. His publishing house was located in New York, but he did manage to come to town every few weeks, ostensibly to ensure that the company's bestselling book remained that way. But I knew he also came to see Gemma.

"Great," I said. "Will you be talking to him tonight, too?"

"Yes, to make some plans." She paused. "We can compare notes tomorrow if you'd like."

Our conversations with Justin and Stuart, respectively, were likely to be very different. "We'll see," I equivocated. Then I found my old-fashioned key, appropriate at this place that imitated Gold Rush days, and Pluckie and I entered our room.

TEN

I decided to call Justin right away rather than get ready for bed first — which is what I often did when we spoke late at night, especially when we hadn't spent the evening together.

Not that it replaced a real evening or night with Justin. And, yes, we were now engaging in close-up fun on some of those occasions.

But sex with the good-looking guy I was seeing wasn't on my mind that night. Well, it took second place to what else I was thinking about.

I sat down on the edge of my bed, beneath the canopy and on top of the coverlet, and pulled my phone from my pocket. Pluckie must have understood phones to some extent, since she lay down on the floor, cradling her muzzle in her paws. I pressed in Justin's number, not trying to suppress the smile I felt at the thought of talking to him.

"Hi, Rory," he said almost immediately. "I was just thinking about you."

"Are you in bed?" I asked spontaneously, then basked in his deep laughter.

"Not yet, but I can still think of getting you there again one of these days."

I laughed, too. Then I grew serious. "I know full well that it's supposed to be bad luck to talk about —"

"About the stuff we've been sort of talking about," he finished. "And I know it hasn't stopped you from discussing it before. So — what do you want to say about it?"

Taking a deep breath, I related what Arlen had told us.

When I was done, there was silence at the other end of the phone.

"I know it might be a stretch, Justin, but —"

"But it's a possible lead. I've been taking notes. I'll get someone started on checking it out tomorrow. And before you ask, yes, we have extra patrols on the streets tonight. We'd had extra before, but apparently not enough. Even if this doesn't result in shutting down the problem, we'll get it done somehow."

I certainly hoped so.

"Keep me informed," I told him.

"Without talking about it." I could tell by his tone that he was smiling. "Hey, with this and some other matters, my day tomorrow is going to be pretty full. But will I see you at the Welcome show tomorrow night?"

"Count on it."

Gemma and I didn't say anything at our B&B breakfast about our discussion with Arlen and Martha the previous night. As always, the place was crowded. Our hostess, Serina, flitted between tables, ensuring enough food was prepared and saying hi. No need to let anyone learn what was on our minds.

We left for our shops soon afterward, and broke away from them briefly around eleven to get coffee together at Beware-of-Bubbles. We ordered separately inside and headed out to the patio to drink them, since I'd brought Pluckie.

I'd ordered plain black coffee and was shocked when the cup the barista handed to me had — what else? — bubbles in it. Never mind the name of the shop; I almost never got bubbles in my coffee here. And these were large ones, two of them right in the middle. Without saying a word, I showed

Gemma.

She looked straight into my eyes with her soft brown ones and also appeared shaken, but she sloughed it off immediately and grew all businesslike. No, all librarian-like, as if she knew everything — and probably did. "You're probably as aware of this as I am, but drink that coffee quickly, since you may come into money if you're done before the bubbles disappear."

Yes, I'd heard that one. I'd also heard others. "But . . . large bubbles," I said. "Doesn't that mean I'll get bad news?"

"It can also mean a friend will arrive soon."

"I should give this to you, since Stuart is due here soon."

"Right, but it's your coffee cup. He's a friend of yours, too, so maybe that's what it means."

"Sure," I said, but I doubted it. I wondered what the latest was between the two of them, but that wasn't why we were here. I'd wait to ask that — maybe until after he'd arrived.

We sat at a table. Since it was a cool day, the patio wasn't as crowded as it sometimes was, so we could talk privately. Gemma had ordered a steaming mocha, so we both had warm drinks. Pluckie's was her usual bowl of water.

"So . . . any other thoughts about what Arlen said last night?" Gemma kept her voice low.

"Lots of thoughts, no conclusions." I'd already let her know I'd spoken with Justin, although I hadn't mentioned his reaction. I did now — but all I could say was that he'd been interested and promised to look into the situation.

"Have you heard anything from him yet?"

I shook my head.

"Well, then?" She put an imaginary phone up to her ear.

I shrugged and pulled my real one from my pocket, pressed in his number, and held it up to my own ear.

He answered immediately, a surprise at this time of day when he was usually so busy with chief-of-police kinds of things. But I wasn't surprised that he essentially said hi and bye. The real reason he'd taken the time to answer, though, I figured, was that he added, "That matter I said I'd look into? So far, no one has located the person we discussed."

I heard what he wasn't saying. He wanted to know if I had any idea where to find Flora.

I didn't. "Sorry," I said, "but if I get any

information I'll tell you right away." After hanging up, I related that bit of conversation to Gemma.

"Interesting," she said. "I'd imagine they checked her apartment and the real estate company she's working for here."

"Probably."

Just then Pluckie rose and gave a little woof from beside me. I half expected that my lucky dog had understood what I was saying, and I looked up quickly to see if Flora had joined us here.

Instead, it was a couple of tourists with an inquisitive Malamute who'd just come onto the patio. The other dog had also spotted Pluckie, and they were having a canine communication session of sorts, both standing their ground and wagging their tails.

I handed Gemma Pluckie's leash, dug into my purse for one of the promotional brochures I always carried, and approached the couple. I donned my tourist-welcoming demeanor, handed them the flyer, and told them to come visit the Lucky Dog Boutique with their beautiful companion, whom I patted softly on the head between his erect ears.

It dawned on me then. Tourists? Welcoming? "And by the way, in case you haven't heard, there's a wonderful Destiny Welcome program planned this evening at the Break-a-Leg Theater. Hope to see you there."

I had attended a lot of Welcomes, although not every one of them. My happiest times at the theater occurred whenever I gave a "Black Dogs and Black Cats" program about pets and superstitions.

And at my last talk, when I'd been able to show off samples of the new dog toys I'd designed.

The ones that had been stolen.

But I wouldn't think about that now. Or at least, I wouldn't focus on it. And I certainly wouldn't discuss it here, just in case it really would be bad luck.

Townsfolk were encouraged to attend the Welcomes, along with our visitors, to show how committed we all were to Destiny — and to its superstitions. Even those of us who remained skeptical about the real effects of superstitions were willing to encourage more tourists to visit by showing how much we liked our town and its quirkiness.

Besides, rumor had it that it was good luck to attend a Welcome. And given what I'd been told in the last couple of days, I could have used some good luck.

Gemma and I, and Stuart Chanick, who'd arrived in Destiny that afternoon, were just entering through the wide doors at the front of the charming, old-style theater, admiring the building's golden Art Deco façade and rounded arches. We weren't the only ones. A large crowd containing some familiar faces, and some that belonged to tourists, was lined up and starting to move inside. The noise of many conversations filled the air around us.

Millie arrived, pushing Martha in her wheelchair, as was their usual routine. I really liked Millie and her attention to her boss and friend. Like Justin, Millie had helped to convince me to stay in Destiny to help Martha.

I didn't know if Arlen would come to the show tonight. He sometimes did.

Not Pluckie, though. I'd shut my sweet girl in my room at the B&B after giving her a nice healthy dinner and taking her for a short walk.

I guessed that a lot of us townsfolk, who knew about the things-that-must-not-be-mentioned, would be here tonight in case hints were given about what had happened and what was being done about it.

"Let's find seats toward the rear," I suggested to Gemma and Stuart.

Stuart was a good-looking, tall, slim guy. Professional that he was, he wore a suit.

Gemma and I had both changed clothes from the promotional garb we wore at our respective shops. She had on a long-sleeved black and white shirt dress, and I wore a slightly frilly apricot-colored blouse and brown skirt. As always, my hematite, dog-faced good luck pendant hung around my neck.

"Why? Do you want to try to sneak out?" Gemma's voice was droll and so was her expression. "That could be bad luck."

"Do you want to enumerate all the other things around here that could bring us bad luck?"

"How about nearly everything. Maybe you should have brought a copy of *The Destiny of Superstitions,* Stuart." Gemma glanced up at the guy beside her, who smiled.

"I don't think you'll find the superstitions in play right now listed in that book," I began.

I stopped talking as I saw Justin enter the theater from a door at the other side. He wore a suit and had several other cops with him, detectives who were also dressed up as if this were a special occasion, including Detectives Richard Choye and Lura Fidelio.

In some ways, the Welcome was always special. But I suspected this group was not here just to promote the welfare of Destiny.

"How about these?" Gemma gestured toward some empty seats at the end of the third row from the back.

"Fine." I slid in after Stuart and her. I looked around. Justin and his associates had also found seats, scattered throughout the descending rows of red plush chairs. That was probably good. Even if the tourists recognized them as cops, they could easily think they were here to enjoy the show with the rest of the townspeople, not necessarily here on official duty.

I figured, though, that the latter was the case.

At precisely eight o'clock, Mayor Bevin Dermot scaled the steps at the side of the stage, a microphone in his hand. Of course he wore his green leprechaun-like suit coat. "Welcome, everyone," he shouted into the mic, immediately gaining the crowd's attention and silence. "Thank you for coming to the Destiny Welcome!"

He didn't work off a script, but with the exception of the Welcomes where he had townsfolk take charge and talk about their own stores or businesses, Bevin would deliver a standard spiel about Destiny and how it was established by those Forty-Niners who found gold after following a rainbow here, and how everyone who visits here can have the best of luck — assuming they comply with all superstitions.

Then he proceeded to describe some of the most basic, well-known ones, like crossing fingers, knocking on wood, and picking up heads-up pennies, and also how wishbones, rabbits' feet, horseshoes, and more can deliver good luck.

When he was through, he invited anyone so inclined to come up to the stage: residents who wanted to talk about their shops, or tourists who had questions. A few of the latter happened and visitors asked the standard kinds of things, like whether everyone in town knew enough to make sure their luck stayed good.

"We try," was Bevin's standard reply to this question. "And we help each other, even as we try to teach all of our visitors what they can do, both here and when they get home, to ensure good luck. But as we all know, fate sometimes intervenes."

Fate — in the guise of people who did nasty things such as invade local businesses to steal good luck items and leave bad luck items. But, hey, it would be bad luck even to talk about that. Wasn't that what Bevin had decreed?

Okay, I realized I was letting my mood go

sour again. I needed to stay calm and let Justin and his guys do their thing — mainly, finding Flora and determining if what Arlen said had any validity.

Since so many of the town's policemen were here, I assumed they hadn't found Flora to question her. And I didn't see her at the theater, either.

Soon the Welcome ended, and Bevin thanked everyone for coming. We all started filing out to the lobby.

Sometimes, after the Welcomes and events like my talk, a bunch of us went out drinking, as we had the other night. But I thought I'd just go back to the B&B, although first I'd check to see what people I liked, such as Gemma — and Justin — were doing.

When Gemma and I reached the lobby, I could tell that something was going on. The usual crowd noises were superseded by shouts. People were rattling the doors, apparently trying, without success, to open them and get out. Some were yelling and cursing, too.

Martha, in her wheelchair, sat in a corner with Millie right beside her. Near them was Serina, along with Carolyn Innes, Jeri and Kiara Mardeer, Brian Nereida, Padraic Hassler, and other store and eatery owners, all of whom I'd seen seated inside. Arlen's bosses at the tour company were there, too — Evonne Albing and Mike Eberhart — although I hadn't seen Arlen at the show.

Theater employees, including Phil, wearing garb reminiscent of Art Deco days, were attempting to use keys to unlock the doors, with no success.

What was going on?

Then I heard a voice emanating from the public address system, which was usually used to tell people when it was time to enter the theater. This loud voice sounded familiar.

It was a voice that had suggested, over and over, that its owner intended to find me a new home.

Flora.

But what was she up to? Why was she on the PA system?

All I knew was that what she was saying was — unsurprisingly — superstition-oriented. And it sounded scary.

ELEVEN

"All you storeowners and restaurant owners and everyone in Destiny," said the voice, "you all lie. That's why your good luck has turned bad. Thanks to me. I came here before, trying to turn my own bad luck around, and you failed me. I was working to save my marriage, and it didn't happen thanks to all of you. I followed what you said, that stupid stuff about pulling a hair from my husband's head to make him love me and burning salt at midnight and throwing it into a fire to bring my unfaithful husband back to me. I even got a sweet, supposedly lucky dog when we got home. Well, my husband is now my ex and he's the one with luck who kept the dog. So now I'm getting my revenge."

At the far side of the thick and obviously frightened crowd, I saw Justin and his gang trying to break open the doors into the ticket booth, presumably the area where

Flora was speaking from. Or maybe they just wanted to find a way to let everyone out of here.

"And don't think this is the end." The voice had gone up an octave. "Ms. Rory Chasen, I know you weren't around back then, but I'm singling you out now because you've been singling me out. Before you started pushing, everyone knew it was bad luck to talk about what was happening at the stores. But now you've talked to the cops about me and claimed I'm the one who's done it all, that I've broken into places, removed good luck and left bad luck in its place. Well, you're right. I did it! And you can be sure I'm not done — and I have no intention of being arrested. Thanks to you, though, I had to run and hide today. I heard I was being hunted when I listened to the police scanners." Now how had she done that? "So watch out for your own luck, Rory Chasen. It's crap now. And that goes for anyone else who attempts to stop me."

A huge noise like a thunderclap reverberated throughout the lobby.

Then there was silence.

Some cops arrived outside the theater soon after that, and the authorities finally managed to get all the doors open. I figured they'd conduct an investigation to learn how the doors had gotten locked in the first place.

Flora surely wasn't some kind of technical genius, was she?

Rumor had it she'd used some really strong super glue, which set immediately, although that wouldn't have kept everyone inside for long. Yet it had kept us all there long enough to hear her tirade, and somehow she had found a way to use the theater's audio system.

And her mention of listening to police scanners? Rumors escalated about that, too, and one was that an empty cop car had been broken into outside a restaurant. Undoubtedly Justin and his department would also be investigating that.

They'd have a lot of questions for Flora when they caught her. But that didn't happen after the Welcome. She'd somehow disappeared.

Anyway, I had no opportunity to talk to Justin about those issues or anything else. Not then. He was clearly busy. But I'd have liked to get his sympathy and more after Flora's rant, especially at me.

We walked back to the B&B quickly — Gemma, Stuart, and I, as well as Serina. Some tourists, too, walked the same direction we did.

At one point, I stopped quickly. Why wasn't I surprised to see a black cat crossing the street in front of us as we turned onto Fate Street?

Also unsurprising was the presence of Catrice, the mysterious woman who seemed to care for the black cat or cats of Destiny — we were never sure how many there were. Catrice wasn't seen often, and she always hid in the shadows next to buildings. Residents of Destiny weren't supposed to talk about her, but this night I could see her eyes shining in the faint light from the street lamps. She was protecting the black cats from people, but who was protecting people from the possible bad luck brought by the black cats?

We arrived at our B&B. I needed to take Pluckie for her last walk of the night, and Gemma and Stuart kindly offered to go along. But we soon returned and separated, heading for our own rooms.

I did try to sleep. I should have been able to, since the authorities were on it. Justin was on it. I had no doubts but that his subordinates were patrolling the streets of Destiny, looking for Flora, making sure she caused no more mischief.

Even so, I was a bit scared, because she

had mentioned me in particular. I was angry, too. Since I was highest on her list of people to hate, would she go back to the Lucky Dog tonight to cause more mischief? If so, what kind of mischief?

My mind kept going over all the nasty things she could do beyond what she'd already done. She'd stolen good luck stuff, left bad. But what if she decided to destroy the shop?

Set it on fire? Set off explosives?

With Martha asleep upstairs?

Justin would have considered that, too, and he thought of Martha as a mother. Surely he'd concentrate his patrols there.

Or here? Flora knew I was staying at the B&B.

I suddenly realized I wouldn't sleep at all unless I made sure everything was okay around the B&B and at the shop. I wasn't going to act stupid and try to find Flora. I was simply going to check things out, re-assure myself that the cops were actually on it — and that everything appeared okay.

I couldn't leave Pluckie, so after I got dressed again, I fastened her leash on her.

Serina always left a dim light on to il-luminate the stairs in case a guest used them at night. I stood in the hallway first, listen-ing for anything unusual, watching to see if

137

my dog, with her much better hearing, reacted as if she'd heard anything. She didn't.

I crept downstairs carefully, Pluckie ahead of me.

I glanced out the lobby windows, again seeing nothing unusual. We went outside and I closed the door behind us, checking to ensure that it locked. We hurried to my car in the front parking lot. I turned on the engine quickly and got it in gear, so the doors locked automatically.

I pulled slowly out of the nearly full B&B parking lot, looking around. I didn't see any cop cars at the moment, but that didn't mean they weren't patrolling. I'd keep watch for them as I continued. And hoped I'd see many. The whole town needed protection this night from the woman who'd already vandalized a bunch of businesses.

I needed protection, too. Maybe this outing was foolish, but I couldn't just lie there in bed and hope that nothing was happening.

And if it was? If I saw something?

Well, I'd at least be able to say something. I checked my cell phone, made sure it was hooked up to my car's Bluetooth, then drove down the street.

I drove around for maybe half an hour, mostly in the downtown business area but also in the vicinity of where I thought the apartment was that Flora had rented. Not that I really knew, but she'd referred to the area during one of our conversations about her plans for relocating Gemma and me.

I wasn't alone on the streets. I wasn't sure whether tourists were checking out the sights at this hour, but I didn't recognize any of the other cars.

One could have been Flora's and I wouldn't have recognized it.

Did I see Flora? No. Did I see any official police vehicles? Yes, maybe half a dozen, which was a lot in this small town at this late hour. Most had lights flashing, and they made themselves obvious on Destiny Boulevard and other important retail streets in town. They might not capture Flora that way, but hopefully they'd deter her from any further vandalism, at least for that night.

I drove slowly by the Lucky Dog Boutique, as well as the Broken Mirror Bookstore next door. I saw no lights inside either one, not official ones or anything resembling a flashlight glow. Those were the two shops I cared most about. Plus, I cocked my head so I could look up toward the upper floors of my shop to see if there was any light on there, any indication that Martha was awake . . . or that some mischief was going on.

I saw nothing, fortunately.

I also took in the Wish-on-a-Star children's shop across the street, as well as Carolyn's Buttons of Fortune, the Mardeers' Heads-Up Penny Gift Shop, and more.

Nothing seemed unusual, although I admit I almost never came by this area so late at night.

I also realized that my being out here wasn't helping anyone except myself and my own fragile state of mind. Fortunately, none of the cops decided to stop and question me.

Finally I decided it was time. "Let's go back to our room," I told Pluckie, who lay sleeping on the rear passenger seat, a safety harness holding her there. She woke up at my voice and wagged her tail, which made me smile.

We soon pulled back into our parking spot in front of the B&B. I sat still for a while before turning off the engine, once more scanning my environment for anything amiss, any danger.

Any indication that Flora was nearby.

I didn't see her, or anything else.

"Let's go in, Pluckie," I said.

Of course I let my dog do some sniffing and squatting before using my key to enter the lobby. Once inside, I shut the door behind us and again checked to ensure that it had locked.

I also checked around but didn't see or hear anyone in the B&B. Probably everyone was already, wisely, in bed.

It was, after all, nearly two o'clock in the morning.

"Let's go to bed," I whispered, and Pluckie and I walked up the stairs together.

I ushered us quickly into our room and again made sure the door locked behind us.

Only then did I start getting ready for bed again, feeling particularly glad that this B&B had individual bathrooms for each room. They were small, it was true — but at least I didn't have to go back into the hallway.

Yes, I was that nervous. That upset after Flora's tirade and the apparent inability of Justin's police force to find and apprehend her — let alone after my own fruitless search for her and thinking she might be out there doing something horrible.

I felt exhausted, but I couldn't imagine I'd fall asleep easily, even though it was late — and I didn't. But when I finally dropped off, Pluckie awoke me.

I soon realized why, because I heard it, too.

A dog was howling somewhere.

And previously, the dogs I'd heard howling in Destiny had been harbingers of murder.

TWELVE

I sat up in bed, looking Pluckie straight in her highly concerned, fuzzy black face. Did my dog know what those howls were supposed to mean? What they *did* mean?

"What do you think, Pluckie?" I asked, and she nosed against me in a snuggle I knew was meant to comfort me and probably herself, too.

I figured Justin was either out on patrol with his subordinates or sleeping — probably not very deeply, with an important search going on. I didn't want to bother him . . . and yet, though neither of us admitted to believing in superstitions much, this particular one had seemed to have some merit in the past.

Of course, at least once when I'd heard a howl and a death had ensued quickly thereafter, someone involved had piped the sound in. But people had still heard it, and there had indeed been a death, so maybe the actual source of the howls didn't matter.

This time, I needed whatever knowledge I could get, and some extra comforting wouldn't hurt, either. Trembling, I took my phone off its charger on the bedside table and pushed the button for Justin. He didn't have to answer, after all.

He did answer, though — immediately. "Rory. Are you okay? I was about to call you but received some other communications first that I had to deal with. Did you hear —" He hesitated.

"A howling dog?" I finished. "Yes. So I gather I wasn't the only one who heard it." If it was just some ordinary dog who'd gotten upset about something normal, like getting lost or being hungry, how could Justin have heard it, apparently at the same time I did, and apparently from his home? My B&B was north of Destiny Boulevard. His house was on Quail Street, several blocks south of downtown.

Recognizing this made me shiver all the more. Maybe there really were such things as omens, at least in Destiny.

But if so, that meant . . .

"You're right," Justin was saying. "Maybe everyone in town heard it."

I looked toward the closed window not

far from the left side of my bed. Some light shone outside, the usual amount from the dim lanterns at the front of the B&B. Did I dare go look out the window?

Why not? If the sound had projected everywhere, it was unlikely that a dead body would be lying outside in the parking lot.

But did a dead body lie somewhere else in town?

"Are you home, or did you hear it somewhere near the B&B?" I asked.

"I'm home," he said, "but not for long. I'm just glad that you —"

He stopped. Had I heard a quiver in his voice? Then I realized he might have been concerned about me, especially after Flora's nastiness at the Welcome.

"You're glad I'm not the person who died, if anyone did?" I spoke as lightly as I could, considering all the emotions that were passing through me — including that, if I was right, Justin apparently gave a damn whether I lived or died.

Well, heck, I did, too. And I definitely was glad to talk to him, to confirm that he also had survived whatever had happened, if anything.

"Justin," I said softly, "I know you'll be busy tomorrow sorting out whatever is going on, but could we possibly get together for dinner?"

"Count on it," he said.

I'm sure I dozed off now and then as the rest of the night passed, but I never slept deeply. Eventually, when Pluckie started nuzzling me, I figured I'd tried long enough. Time to take her out and get ready to go to the shop.

I got dressed quickly so I could accomplish the first of my goals fairly fast. As Pluckie and I walked downstairs, I wasn't surprised to see a lot of people hanging out in the lobby of the B&B, as well as inside the breakfast room, talking.

Among them were Gemma and Stuart. I figured he was staying in her room, although he could have been renting a room by himself. If they were together, as long as he treated Gemma well and made her happy, that was fine with me.

Even if his face hadn't been the face she'd seen in the mirror . . .

"Hi, Rory," Gemma called up the stairs as soon as she saw me. She had a cup of coffee in one hand and backed away from the group of people she'd been talking to, although Stuart stayed with them. "Did you hear — ?"

"The howling dog?" I'd reached the bottom of the stairs, thankfully, so I didn't have to shout about it. "Yes. Did you and everyone else?"

She nodded. Her brown eyes looked huge but excited. "Not everyone knows what that omen means, so, since this is Destiny . . ."

"You and Stuart remedied that," I finished. "I assume Stuart knew, at least, having edited *The Destiny of Superstitions.*"

"Exactly. So . . . well, no one has figured out if anybody died last night. The local news hasn't said anything, and I checked the *Destiny Star*'s website. Have you heard anything? Like, from Justin?"

"No." I mentioned talking to him right after I'd heard the howl, and that he hadn't had any information at that point. "Even if something happened, I doubt he'd call to let me know, but if I hear from him, I'll fill you in on it."

"Great. Come join us for breakfast when you and Pluckie are ready."

I took my dog outside then, or rather she led me out the B&B's front door, under the horseshoe — which faced the correct way now, ends up. I hesitated there, scanning the parking lot and Fate Street beyond it, listening for . . . well, anything unusual.

Everything seemed normal, at least around here.

When we went back in, I kept Pluckie with me even though we were heading for the dining room. She was family, and Serina never told me to keep her outside. On the way, Pluckie sniffed at the pot of pseudo gold in the lobby. Would that ensure that she — we — had good luck today? I hoped so.

In the breakfast room, a long counter was filled, as usual, with the special food Serina prepared daily for this meal — omelets, toast, pancakes, biscuits, home fries, you name it. I most often stuck to toast and jam, with an occasional half-omelet, and that's what I grabbed now, along with coffee, before sitting down at the table with Gemma and Stuart.

It was a long table, and some of its occupants looked only a little familiar to me — tourists.

For the next twenty minutes, we talked about Destiny and superstitions and what that howling dog last night meant. Yes, nearly all of the guests at the B&B had been awakened by the sound. Since I was now an almost-official Destiny resident, they regarded me as an expert who could explain what the sound meant.

I kept my tone as light as I could, as did Gemma and even Stuart, as we discussed

148

what the traditional interpretation was. "It doesn't mean anyone's even been injured, you realize," Gemma said as she finished her explanation. "That's the superstition, the possible omen, but we can keep our fingers crossed that all's well with everyone."

Which I was already doing — under the table.

Because Gemma hadn't been around for some of those previous howls, she could believe, or pretend to believe, what she wanted.

Yet I was also hoping that this time, the howl was benign.

Breakfast was over. Gemma, Stuart, Pluckie, and I were walking down Fate Street toward Destiny Avenue and our shops.

That's when I started hearing sirens in the distance.

No howls accompanied them, but Pluckie's ears moved forward and so did she, pulling her leash.

"What's going on?" Stuart asked.

"I don't even want to guess," I told them. But I was guessing internally.

Sure, it could be a car crash or small house fire or something not great but relatively normal.

Or it could be because someone had found a body.

Sadly, my bet was on the latter. After all, this was Destiny, and we'd all heard that cursed howl.

It was eight thirty by the time I got to the Lucky Dog. Gemma and Stuart came inside to help me check things out, which I really appreciated. All was fine. No nervous reactions from Pluckie. No further thefts or vandalism.

No dead bodies.

But when my friends entered the Broken Mirror Bookstore, would they find a dead body there?

It wouldn't be the first time.

Before they left, I walked through the curtained door into the storeroom, faced the door to Martha's apartment upstairs, and called her, putting my phone on speaker since Gemma had come in with me. Was Martha okay?

She answered right away. "I'm fine," she reassured us. "But yes, I heard that howling dog, too. If you happen to learn of anyone who's . . . who didn't make it through the night, will you let me know?"

"Of course."

"I'll be down in an hour to help you open the shop," she said, "but if I get any calls or hear anything on the news before then I'll call you back."

I thanked her, and Gemma and I returned to the shop. Stuart was looking out the front window, Pluckie standing beside him. "Destiny Boulevard's already full of people," he said. "I'd imagine they'd really like to find some reassurance that all's well in town, since rumors are undoubtedly flying around today, even among the tourists."

"I'll seed the sidewalk with some heads-up pennies in a little while," I said.

"I have a few, and if you've got a lot, we can guarantee the presence of pennies on the ground between our two shops," Gemma said.

I'd left my purse in the back room but went to the cash register, where I kept some shiny new pennies in a plastic bag in the drawer. I gave Gemma a dozen, plenty for the small expanse of sidewalk. "Here," I said. "And let's all wish for some really good luck today." I crossed my fingers and bent to touch my lucky black and white dog.

Pluckie licked my fingers, which made me smile.

Surely all would be well today — wouldn't it?

Gemma and Stuart left then, and I started fussing around to make sure we had enough

151

dog toys and lucky food, collars, leashes, and more on display.

Gemma soon called to say that all was well in the Broken Mirror. "Fingers crossed things stay that way," she said before hanging up.

Like me, she was becoming accustomed to at least acting as if superstitions meant something real. But I didn't know for sure whether she believed in them any more than I did.

After we hung up, I realized I could use some more hematite amulets in the glass-fronted display case near the checkout counter, so I went into the storeroom in the back. It was probably a good thing I wasn't involved in doing any financial tasks for the store that morning, like balancing our bank account or calculating profits so far for the month. My mind was still obsessing over that dog howl.

At about nine forty-five, Martha came downstairs, as promised. When she entered the store, I was revising the display of stuffed dog toys, wishing I had some of the new ones I'd designed to place there. I'd already ordered a new supply, but they'd take some time to get here.

"Everything okay, Rory?" Martha asked as Pluckie dashed over to greet her.

"Sure," I said with no hesitation. The only thing that wasn't okay was the way my thoughts had been going, particularly about last night's howl.

"Excellent." My senior friend started doing pretty much as I had, checking out our great product displays. She puttered a bit but apparently I'd done well enough, since she didn't move things around much.

At ten o'clock, it was time to open the doors. Immediately, several groups of customers entered, including a family with three kids and two dogs, and an older couple who seemed to feel guilty that they'd left their pets, a dog and a cat, back home in Phoenix.

Both kinds of groups were often good for ringing up substantial sales, which proved true once again.

Martha took care of one of the groups and I helped the other. I was glad Jeri was due in fairly soon. If this continued, we'd definitely need more help.

I went behind one set of shelves to grab some dog kibble for one of the customers, and when I came out, Celia Vardox had arrived. She had a notebook and pen in her hands, so I had a sinking feeling she was here as a reporter and not as a pet owner.

I nevertheless said, "Hi, Celia. What do

you need for Charlotte today?" Charlotte was her black Labrador retriever. Her name had come from the name Charlottetown, a town in Labrador, Canada.

"Nothing right now," Celia said. Her short hair was about the same shade as her dog's, and today she wore brown slacks and a lacy beige blouse. "I just wanted to get your re-action to the latest murder."

My heart plummeted even as my head started to throb. "Murder?" My voice came out as a soft croak.

And why was she specifically looking for my reaction?

Though the possibility of it had crossed my mind earlier, I had a sudden insight into who'd been killed.

Someone who'd singled me out from the crowd of people she disliked in Destiny, who'd distinguished me from the rest.

Celia had simply confirmed it.

She maneuvered a recorder's microphone toward me, but I shook my head. I didn't need to have this conversation, however it progressed, preserved for posterity.

Celia frowned then, even as Martha, who must have seen my expression, turned toward us. With her pen poised over a clean sheet of paper in her notebook, Celia re-garded me expectantly with her gleaming, inquisitive brown eyes.

"Rory Chasen," she said, in a tone that made me wonder if she had some kind of backup recorder hidden in her tote bag or elsewhere on her person, "as you most likely know, Flora Curtival, your real estate agent, was found murdered last night. What is your opinion about that?"

THIRTEEN

Unable to catch my breath for a few seconds, I just stared at Celia.

"Ah, then you didn't know about it?" She smiled at me calculatingly, as if trying to read my mind.

I shook my head. "What happened to her?" My voice shook.

This explained the howl, at least. This was the fourth time a death had occurred after I'd heard a howl in the middle of the night. If I didn't watch out, I'd start really believing in Destiny's superstitions, or at least those that were supposed to be omens.

"Right now I'm just gathering information, not giving any out. But actually, I haven't heard any details," Celia said.

"What's going on?" Martha came over to us, followed by Jeri, who'd just arrived. Martha's face was scrunched in a frown of concern as she looked at me.

I figured my angst was visible in my

expression. "That howl —" I began slowly.

"I heard it, too," Jeri broke in. She looked horrified. "Are you two just discussing the superstition, or did someone die?"

"The latter," I managed.

"Who?" Martha croaked.

"That real estate agent, Flora." Not only a real estate agent, I thought. The vandal. The woman who'd mocked Destiny and said she'd continue to exact revenge on the town and its inhabitants for not being lucky enough to save her marriage.

The woman who'd mentioned me in particular.

Oh, no. I wouldn't become a major suspect, would I? Heck, there were a lot of shop and bar owners and managers in town who had just as much motive as I had.

Almost.

"Tell us what happened," Martha said. But even if Celia had decided to change her mind and reveal she knew more, some new groups of customers came through our door.

"I'm still checking things out," Celia said. "You'll be able to read about whatever I learn in the next *Star* and on our website. I imagine you'll see something on the local TV stations about it too, even though I won't be their source." And then she left.

157

Trying not to sigh — or panic — I asked a couple of teenagers, who'd come in with their mother and a Yorkie, what I could show them. I was glad to focus on something else for a while — or at least stay as focused as I was able.

Had Celia wanted me to just nod my head and smile and admit to knowing Flora was dead? Or maybe even confess to having murdered her?

We weren't the best buddies, Celia and I, but she surely knew me well enough to realize I'd never do that. Any of it. I wouldn't kill anyone, even someone goading me. And confess to a murder? No way, even if I had done it. Which I hadn't.

While I helped the customers, I managed to walk near Pluckie a couple of times. She seemed to sense my awful mood and stood up, pulling at the end of her leash that was tied to the counter. I patted her and said some soothing words, even though what I wanted to do was pick her up, unfasten her, and hug her tightly to me as consolation for all the torment in my mind.

This latest group bought a substantial amount of merchandise, all apparently to give their little dog the best of luck via her toys, which included four-leaf clover and horseshoe chews. My stolen toys might have worked out well for them, but the few we'd had left had been sold, and this family was only in town for another day.

As I packed up the things they'd bought, I stroked each of the toys. I had a feeling I might need all the good luck I could get.

But maybe I was wrong. Maybe, despite Celia's insinuations, there was no mystery about how Flora had died. Did the police have her killer in custody?

Or maybe, even if she was dead, Celia had gotten it wrong and Flora had died of natural causes.

Or . . .

I was driving myself even more nuts. Since Martha and Jeri seemed to have our current cache of customers in hand, I slipped into the storeroom by myself. I wished I'd brought Pluckie for company, but I didn't want it to look too obvious that I planned to be out of the store more than momentarily.

Mostly, I just wanted to talk to Justin. But if there had been a suspicious death last night, he would be unlikely to answer my call.

I could leave him a message, though. And we'd already talked about getting together for dinner that night. Hopefully he'd still be available.

I pushed his number and was delighted that he answered on the second ring.

"Hello, Rory."

Uh-oh. He sounded almost formal. But he could be with some of his subordinates or others at the station, discussing what had happened.

"Hi," I said. "Justin, I just heard —"

"Are you at the Lucky Dog?" His tone hadn't changed.

"Yes," I said tentatively, suddenly wondering if I should admit even that. What was on his mind?

"Good. I'll be there in a short while. Detective Choye will be with me. He has a few questions for you."

He has a few questions for you. Not: *I* have a few questions for you. Or, much better: gee, Rory, I'm still so glad you're okay, especially since there really was a homicide here last night.

That brief phone call with Justin really hurt. And worried me.

I helped a few more customers as I waited, rejecting the urge to flee the store, flee Destiny. Flee Justin. After all, I had nothing to feel guilty about.

But Detective Choye was coming, and he had a few questions for me.

I was ringing up another sale behind the counter when Justin and Richard Choye came in. I hadn't told Martha or Jeri that I was expecting visitors, but now I motioned for the cops to join me as I unhooked Pluckie from the counter. At least my dog should be able to get a walk out of this.

I didn't want anyone from the store eavesdropping on my upcoming interrogation. Nor did I really want to talk as we walked. Tourists probably wouldn't hang out in the vicinity and listen in, but just in case . . .

"Is it okay with you if we just take Pluckie for a short walk, then go into the storeroom through the back door and talk there?" That way, Martha and Jeri were less likely to know when we were there, so we'd have some privacy. I hoped.

"Fine," Justin said, looking at Choye as if giving him an order. The detective nodded.

The walk outside was, indeed, short, and all we did then was exchange pleasantries about the November weather here in Destiny. I glanced toward the Broken Mirror and was glad not to see Gemma. I didn't want to have to explain what was going on. I wasn't even sure myself what was happening — although I had a sinking feeling that I could figure it out.

We walked through the parking lot at the

rear of the Lucky Dog and I used a key to open the back door. I went inside first, scanning the stockroom from the perspective of conducting a conversation there, not grabbing products. It still looked much as it had months ago, when Pluckie had discovered an ailing Martha on the floor — lots of shelves and boxes, plus a card table in the center where Martha, and now I, often sat to conduct financial calculations and plans. There were now two chairs pushed under it, and another folding chair against the wall.

Soon we were all seated around the table, with Pluckie sitting alertly at my feet on the concrete floor. My poor, sensitive pup undoubtedly felt the tension among the humans.

Justin was clad in a button-down blue shirt and dark slacks, his usual while on duty. Although he didn't always wear it, today his chief's badge was pinned to the pocket on his chest. He had his acorn-shaped hematite amulet around his neck.

His subordinate Choye wore a dark suit and a snide smile.

And both of them stared at me across the table.

"Let me begin, Rory," Justin said, "by telling you that Flora Curtival is an apparent homicide victim." His blue eyes stared intensely into mine, as if attempting to read my internal reaction.

I nodded. "Celia Vardox was here before. She told me." Was she supposed to know? Was she allowed to talk about it? Heck, she was a journalist, so yes on both counts. "Can you — I mean, what happened? Do you know?"

"The matter is under investigation. And since you and I are . . . friends, Detective Choye will be the one to question you, as is being done with the principals at all the businesses that were apparently vandalized by Ms. Curtival, according to her confession at the theater last night."

Good. The way he phrased it indicated I wasn't being singled out as the main suspect.

Or was I? What he'd said might be the truth, but it might not be the whole truth.

"I will be here only to listen. Do you understand that? And would you like to have an attorney present?" Justin's expression had turned blank, as if he wanted no emotion to show up on his face.

I swallowed hard. Maybe I *was* being singled out. "Are you reading me my Miranda rights?"

"No," Choye said. "Not now, at least. You're not under arrest." I heard what he'd left unsaid: *yet*.

I thought about offering to brew a pot of coffee. But I wasn't sure getting caffeine in me would be helpful. And what if the bubbles in the cup I served myself suggested bad luck? Besides, I'd have preferred a glass of wine or something even harder. But we didn't keep any of that here.

Choye kept his head bent slightly in my direction, his dark eyes regarding me with an intensity so sharp that I had a sense he wanted to slice me open and insert a confession that would blare out of my mouth. He'd asked first if talking to me was okay, as if I had a choice, and was both recording and taking notes on our conversation.

He started by asking me what I'd done after the Destiny Welcome last night. I told him I'd gone back to the B&B with Gemma and Stuart.

"Okay. Then what did you do?"

"I went to bed." Oh, heavens. That was true, but of course I hadn't stayed there. I'd driven my car around town. And I couldn't keep that to myself in case someone had seen me. "But —" I began.

At the same time, Choye asked, "And did you go to sleep immediately?"

"No," I replied. "I was just about to say that I couldn't fall asleep right away after the — after Ms. Curtival's tirade at the theater. I was concerned about the Lucky Dog and other shops, so I got up again, and Pluckie and I drove around town checking to see if there were any lights on in shops where there shouldn't be any."

I risked a glance toward Justin, expecting him to aim a chastising expression at me for daring to put myself in harm's way, but his face remained blank.

Which made my heart sink. Did he think me guilty? Was that why he didn't seem to care if I'd done something foolish?

"Right. And did you see anything . . . suspicious?"

"No."

"And did you go anywhere else?"

I'd folded my hands on the table, and now I looked down at them. In retrospect, under the circumstances, what I'd done was definitely stupid. "I . . . I drove through a residential area, including California Street, around where I thought Flora had rented an apartment."

"I see. And did you notice anything wrong there?"

"No," I said, realizing I sounded a little curt. "No," I repeated more softly. "Sorry. I didn't see anything anywhere that would give the impression that Flora was doing as

165

she'd promised and causing more harm to people of Destiny. And so Pluckie and I drove back to the B&B, and I went back to bed."

"And that was all?"

"Not quite," I said, looking from Choye's suddenly interested expression to Justin's frown, then back again. "I heard that dog howl in the middle of the night, which suggested someone had died in Destiny. But I only learned this morning that was true." I drew my lips into a grimace of sorrow and closed my eyes, but only for a second. "Look, Detective Choye — and Chief Halbertson. I'd been a little irritated with Flora prior to last night, for being such a pushy real estate agent. But I had no idea until then that she'd been stealing from our shopkeepers and vandalizing our shops — shops that included the Lucky Dog. Even when she pulled that stunt at the theater and confessed and threatened — well, I worried about what else she'd be up to. But, heck. I think I have a relatively good relationship with the Destiny PD."

I looked again at Justin, whose dark eyebrows lifted. Was that amusement or irritation on his face? In either case, he still said nothing.

I continued talking. "If I'd seen anything,

166

I'd have said something — to the cops. Isn't that what concerned citizens are supposed to do? 'If you see something, say something.' But I wouldn't have endangered myself if I'd noticed a problem. And I certainly wouldn't have endangered Pluckie, who was with me." Then I drew myself up, shoulders back, as determined and truthful an expression on my face as I could produce. "And I definitely would not have killed Flora Curtival."

"Well, I think we're done here," Choye said, without acknowledging whether he believed me or thought I was a bald-faced liar. "I'll be in touch if we have any further questions."

He didn't bother to thank me. Justin did, though, as they both stood and headed toward the back storeroom door.

Pluckie got up, too, and began following them. So did I, half with the intent of making sure they left and half just to lock the rear door behind them.

I was relieved they were leaving without arresting me.

I was also furious with Justin for letting me be interrogated that way.

Okay, that was his job, but —

I was about to shut the door behind him when he stuck his head back inside.

"Are we still on for dinner tonight?" he asked.

Shocked, I just looked at him for a second before saying, "I . . . I guess so."

"Good." And then he was gone.

FOURTEEN

I closed the shop, as always, at seven. Martha, a bit tired, had headed up to her apartment an hour before that. I'd let Jeri leave early, too, since she wanted to go to the Heads-Up Penny to make sure her family had heard of the apparent murder of the person who'd ransacked their shop.

I didn't think Jeri was the killer, and although I didn't know her mother very well, I doubted Kiara would have murdered Flora, either.

But like everyone else in town who now had reason to dislike Flora, the Mardeers could become suspects.

Pluckie stood beside me on the wooden floor, looking up expectantly. "Do you need to go out right away?" I asked. I'd taken her for a brief outing just before Martha had left, so she was probably okay. "We'll be going for a walk any minute now." When Justin arrived, I meant. I wasn't sure what we were doing for dinner, but even if we were driving there, I could walk Pluckie for a few minutes beforehand. He'd called me only long enough to let me know he'd come by the shop at closing time to get me.

My dog and I didn't have to wait, though. Only about a minute after I'd locked the door to customers, I heard a knock. I looked outside and saw Justin standing there. I opened the door immediately.

And saw he wasn't alone. That new detective with the DPD, Lura Fidelio, stood near him, off to one side — maybe so I wouldn't see her the instant I pulled the door open.

Why was she there?

Was I about to be arrested? Was Justin the one to knock to soften the situation a little — or to make sure I didn't just keep the door locked?

"Hello, Justin," I said coolly, looking up at his blue eyes instead of over his shoulder at the tall, grinning woman behind him. Heck, I didn't really need to be polite. I took a step to one side, without inviting either of them in, and glared at the detective. I talked to Justin, not her, though. "What's she doing here?"

In the meantime, Pluckie had made her way through the door and was standing on her hind legs pawing at Justin for attention, which he provided in the form of several pats on the head. I was holding the end of her leash, so I wasn't concerned about whether my dog would try to say hi to the other person standing there.

"Let's walk toward the Shamrock Steakhouse, Rory," Justin said, "and I'll explain a little more about what's going on."

That caused my curiosity to rise at least a degree or two above my irritation. "Okay."

As was often the case in Destiny, the sidewalk was still crowded with tourists. Justin walked on my left side, and I wasn't pleased when Lura took her place on my right. Today her suit was charcoal and her blouse a lighter gray. Even though my height was average, I felt awfully small between these two tall people. My uneasiness caused me to stroke my hematite necklace, although I tried to hide it a bit by fluffing my straight hair, which was much longer than Lura's — and if she took it as a criticism of her very short light brown hair, then too bad.

"Here's the thing, Rory." Justin's voice was as serious as it was loud. Apparently he wanted Lura to hear and didn't care if the strangers around us did, too. "People I work with know that you and I have been seeing each other."

No surprise there. We hadn't been keeping it secret, even though we weren't sure how serious it was. At least I wasn't, although sometimes I hoped . . .

"And now, well —" As he hesitated, I looked up into his blue eyes. They looked both serious and sad. "You're a suspect in the murder of Flora Curtival."

"What!" My voice was even louder than his.

"That doesn't mean you're in imminent danger of being arrested, Rory. Although if you want to call off this dinner, I'll understand."

"Or get my lawyer to join us."

He stopped short, then caught up immediately. His tone now was ominous. "So you did lawyer up?"

If I had, would he take that as a sign of my guilt? "No," I responded curtly. "But maybe I should."

We continued onward. We must have looked somewhat grim — or at least business-like — since people moved aside to make room for us as we walked. We took our time, though, since Pluckie was checking out the ground.

I wished Killer was with us, since Justin seemed to act softer with his dog around, but he'd most likely hired one of his neighbor's kids to drop in on Killer.

172

"Have you looked at the *Destiny Star* website today, Rory?" That was Lura.

"No, although Celia Vardox came to the shop early to try to interview me. I didn't tell her much. I didn't have much to say, anyway."

"I was going to show you the article when we got to the restaurant, Rory, before we started talking," Justin said. "What's there is public, whether or not it's true. And that means I can mention it — but I can't talk about the official investigation or give any opinion about the accuracy of what's in the article or otherwise, or . . ." His voice tapered off, and I looked up into his face again. He looked sad now. "The thing is, Rory, I have to be very careful here, as I indicated when Detective Choye interviewed you. Because of our relationship, I'm staying away from pretty much everything official to do with the case, and I also want to make sure no one thinks a conflict of interest is leading me to do anything to compromise the investigation."

A conflict of interest. I assumed that meant that the world — or at least his associates — recognized that there was some sort of relationship between us.

Under other circumstances, I'd like hearing this. But I nevertheless couldn't help making one of my regular silent apologies to my deceased fiancé, Warren.

"That's why I'm joining you this evening," Lura broke in. "I'm your chaperone. I'll be able to report back to the mayor and city council and everyone that your friendship didn't lead to any inappropriate revelations."

I slowed my walk, and, looking down at the sidewalk, shook my head. "I. Don't. Know. Anything. To. Reveal." I looked up again, from Lura to Justin and back again.

"I'm sure that's what Chief Halbertson hopes," Lura said with a smile.

I didn't say much more till we arrived at the Shamrock Steakhouse. It was only a couple of blocks down Destiny Boulevard, on the other side of the street from the Lucky Dog. It was another Gold Rush–looking building, a couple of stories high and pseudo-Victorian. Thanks to Pluckie, we were shown to the back patio, where heat lamps were already fired up even though it was a relatively warm evening.

Servers in green suits that made them resemble leprechauns — even more than Mayor Bevin did — hovered around us, showing us to one of the round tables and bringing menus. I ordered a glass of wine. I needed it. And of course a bowl of water for my dog. Both Justin and Lura ordered beers. "We're officially off duty," Lura explained, "even though I'm fulfilling an assignment."

By then I was ready. I retrieved my cell phone from my pocket and pulled up the *Destiny Star* website. There, on the front page, was an article about Destiny's latest bad luck: another murder.

It included a photo — and I gasped when I saw it.

I assumed it had been edited, at least somewhat, since although it depicted the back of a woman apparently lying on the floor, the angle was such that not much was visible — not her outfit or her face, or blood if she'd been killed violently. Just a relatively benign photo of a body.

But it wasn't benign to me.

For one of the things that kept the details of her body from being visible was the array of items on the floor surrounding her.

They looked much too familiar.

They were all stuffed toys, lucky characters such as a rabbit with large feet, smiling black dogs and black cats, ladybugs, and woodpeckers.

The toys that I had designed and manufactured, that Flora had stolen from the Lucky Dog.

They had turned up again.

With Flora's dead body.

I waited until after our drinks had been served to make any comments. Until then, I continued reading the *Destiny Star* story on the apparent murder.

Some of the article was clearly conjecture, but either Celia or her brother Derek had apparently spoken with Flora's boss, Brie Timons.

Brie had found Flora's body.

She'd gone to a condo she'd listed for leasing to meet with Flora, who was supposed to have inspected it after a cleaning. Flora was slated to show the unit to some people who were seeking a new place to live in Destiny.

Could that have been Gemma and me?

If so, that might give the authorities additional reason to consider me a suspect. Theoretically, Flora could have told me about it, including its address. What if I'd happened to show up unannounced when just Flora was there and wanted some kind of retribution for what she'd admitted to doing at the Lucky Dog — and for singling me out in her tirade?

That was what circulated through my mind, but I didn't mention it.

"I'm not sure what you can and can't talk about," I said, first to Justin, then to Lura.

Our drinks finally arrived, and I waited until the green-clad server, complete with leprechaun-like hat, had left again before continuing.

Justin beat me to it. "We can talk about the existence of that article. Since it's public, we can also confirm that Ms. Curtival is deceased and her body was found by her employer, Ms. Timons, at a condo unit she had listed for rental. But don't ask anything about how she died or anything else that could become evidence."

"I get it," I said, mostly meaning it.

"And by the way, Ms. Chasen," Lura said, "Detective Choye said you admitted driving around last night."

"Well, yes, but that doesn't mean I —"

"I'm only mentioning it because it was a good thing you brought it up. You see, there were a number of police vehicles out cruising then. Your car was photographed on several dashcams and its license number was jotted down by some officers, too."

"If you'd attempted to hide it, you would have appeared guilty," Justin explained unnecessarily.

The article didn't give the address of the condo, but I had little doubt, especially after this part of the conversation, that it was located on or near one of the streets where I'd driven last night.

Our server came back. I ordered only a salad. I wasn't especially hungry, not with all that was going on.

For the rest of the meal, we mostly talked about other things, not Flora Curtival or what had happened to her. It actually was quite pleasant. Maybe that was because I crossed my fingers often beneath the table in hopes that we could continue to be civil toward one another — and that I would be allowed to return to the B&B later rather than get arrested.

And that, maybe, I'd get an opportunity to talk to Justin alone, even briefly.

That moment came when Lura excused herself to head for the restroom. "Feel free to give your little dog a few pieces of the steak still on my plate," she said as she stood and began finagling her way through the crowded patio.

I obediently picked up a couple small pieces of sirloin. As if she'd understood, Pluckie had sat up and was now regarding me with expectant dark eyes.

After I'd given her the steak, I looked at Justin.

"I didn't do it," I told him.

"Of course you didn't. I didn't need to be there at your questioning by Detective Choye, or to see your reaction to that *Star* article, to be certain of that."

I felt a huge wave of relief. "But . . . well, to protect yourself and the integrity of your job, does that mean we won't be able to see one another till the real killer is caught?"

"No," he said. "Having Lura along tonight was just a precaution, since I wanted to go on record as having been seen with you, having a pleasant get-together, where someone neutral could testify that yes, we discussed what happened, but it was all aboveboard and I clearly know better than to discuss any part of the ongoing investigation, even with you."

"Even with —"

"Heck, Rory. As I've said, people know we're seeing each other. I'm really happy we are. But at the moment, we — especially I — need to be particularly careful. Know what, though?"

"What?" I asked hesitantly, even as my eyes were captivated by a look from his that looked downright lusty.

"I'd love for Pluckie and you to join Killer and me for dinner again tomorrow. At our house."

FIFTEEN

Surprisingly, I did get some sleep that night.

For one thing, I didn't hear any howls, and apparently neither did Pluckie, since she didn't wake me up.

I supposed I was feeling at least somewhat optimistic after getting confirmation that Justin didn't really believe I was guilty. On top of that, he was figuring out ways he could see me, and talk to me, notwithstanding the fact that some of his superiors or associates seemed to believe he had a conflict of interest.

Maybe the fact that he himself felt he had a conflict of interest helped as well. The chief of police wasn't staying away from me, despite the way things appeared. He was acting supportive, and as if he truly wanted to be in my presence.

I woke up, as usual, to the sound of music emanating from the clock radio on the small table beside the bed. "Good morning,

Pluckie," I said to the pup, who stood on the coverlet beside me wagging her tail.

Still lying there, I considered how to approach this day. I'd certainly look forward to getting together with Justin later, but I had things to do in the meantime.

Managing the Lucky Dog came first, but until the police figured out who'd really killed Flora, I was likely to remain a suspect.

Though not if I could help it.

Not if I could determine who was more likely to have murdered her. Better yet, I might be able to not just point to a group of possible suspects, but prove who'd actually done it. That would get me off the hook, plus Justin would again feel comfortable talking to me.

Okay, how could I be lucky enough to achieve all that? I couldn't be certain, but even so, I made sure to get out of bed on the same side I'd crawled into it — the requirement of a superstition. Nothing unusual about that. I also knocked on the wooden table that held the clock radio and crossed my fingers.

Too bad I'd kept all the lucky dog toys I'd designed at the store. I might never get back the ones that had become evidence, and in fact, that was fine with me. They might now be unlucky, or at least people who believed in superstitions would think so. We'd sold the few that Flora had missed, and the new ones I'd ordered on a rush basis still weren't due to arrive for another few days.

I would just have to rely on the luckiest thing — no, luckiest being — of all. "Come here, Pluckie," I called. She came running from where she'd lain down on the floor near the door and, as I knelt, she threw herself into my arms. "Give me some luck, you wonderful black and white dog."

I imagined I felt some good karma radiating out of her, *imagined* being the key word. But, heck, this was Destiny and I needed some good fortune right about now. Why not talk myself into believing, at least for the moment?

I gave Pluckie an extra hug, then stood, showered, and dressed.

When Pluckie and I got downstairs, I peeked into the breakfast room before taking her for a walk. Gemma was there, sitting alone among the crowd, and I didn't see Stuart.

Was he still sleeping? Or had he left town . . . or Gemma?

If she had figured out who she'd seen in that mirror, I felt certain she'd tell me about it. Even so, that wouldn't necessarily mean she'd have no further relationship with Stuart.

I took Pluckie outside before trying to find out, and then, when we returned, I directed my dog to Gemma's table so my friend could watch her while I got food.

"How's Stuart?" I asked.

The calm expression on Gemma's always-pretty face didn't change, which was a good sign. "We thought of something to check at the store, so he headed there early." She didn't move her gaze before asking, "And how's Justin?"

"We'll talk later," I said, knowing she would understand my cryptic response to mean I didn't want anyone to overhear what I said.

Serina came over to say hi, and Gemma and I talked with her and others over the usual amazing B&B breakfast. When we were done, it was time to walk to our shops together, with Pluckie sniffing the sidewalk, and the air, and the noses of other strolling dogs as we talked.

That's when I really told Gemma what was going on: my dinner with Justin and Detective Lura Fidelio last night, and why Lura had been along.

"Interesting dilemma," Gemma noted as we moseyed down Fate Street. "I feel for the guy — and like him, too, for working around it in clever ways."

I then told Gemma what was really on my mind. "Your prior situation as a murder suspect? It gives me some extra smarts in that area, which I now intend to use to help myself."

We paused at the end of the block to cross the street, and Gemma asked, "You're up to more amateur sleuthing?"

I nodded. "Sounds as if I don't have much choice."

"Don't ask Justin about it," Gemma observed wisely. "But go for it, girl."

"And if you don't mind," I said, "I'd like a little help, at least with my cover. Do you have an hour or so today when you can break away from your shop?"

"Absolutely," she said, "especially with Stuart in town. So tell me what we're going to do."

I did, and as I finished, we reached the Broken Mirror. I smiled as Stuart came out the front door to greet us — or, at least, Gemma.

"See you later," she called to me as she entered the shop with him.

Rising Moon Realty was on Luck Street, not far from the offices of Destiny's Luckiest Tours, where Martha's nephew Arlen worked.

I'd left Pluckie at the shop with Millie and Jeri, who were both working there today. I wasn't sure what Brie thought of pets since I'd never seen her with one, at the Lucky Dog or otherwise. I wanted there to be nothing but friendliness and empathy — and information — between us today. Would she be at the office? It was Sunday, after all. But surely real estate brokers, like retailers, never rested.

Rising Moon Realty was located in yet another building that looked as if it had materialized from the Gold Rush days, but it was so well maintained on the outside, I figured it was a lot newer than that. Gemma and I walked up the six steps of the wide stairway onto the porch and I pushed open the wood-trimmed glass door.

The inside was all modern: a nest of four wooden desks, two occupied by smartly dressed and apparently busy people — one man and one woman, neither of whom appeared familiar. The white walls around them were decorated with a plethora of photos of lovely homes.

Yep, they were open and busy this Sunday.

The man was the first to look up, a huge smile on his young and professional-looking face. "Hi, may we help you?"

"Is Brie here?" I asked. "Er . . . I'm Rory Chasen and this is Gemma Grayfield. We heard about what happened to poor Flora last night. Our deepest sympathy to all of you."

He and the woman both nodded and appeared stricken. But then the woman took charge. "Wasn't Flora trying to find you a place to rent here in Destiny?"

So much for grieving, if a deal could be made . . .

"Yes, and that's why we'd like to talk to Brie," I said firmly, causing the woman's expression to freeze.

"Hello, Rory. Gemma." Brie had just walked through a door in the wall behind her apparent flunkies' desks. I wondered which of the two empty desks had been Flora's.

"Hi, Brie," Gemma said in a low voice that was overflowing with emotion. "Rory and I just came here to express our sympathy. We'd seen quite a bit of Flora. She seemed determined to find just the right living situation for us — before she . . ."

Appeared to totally unwind and go bonkers, was the ending to that sentence, which went through my mind.

"I — I just don't understand." Brie shook

her head. "And then —"

I saw how her employees were staring at her, as if encouraging her to describe exactly how and where she'd found Flora.

"May we go into your office and talk?" I asked Brie sweetly, glancing briefly from the man to the woman and back again.

"Yes. Yes, of course."

In a minute, we were sitting in a room as large as the other one but containing one desk instead of four. These walls, too, were covered by photos of properties, from houses to apartment buildings to town-houses. Were they all in or around Destiny? I didn't think so, but I wasn't totally familiar with the residential areas.

Brie had already asked her underlings to bring us coffee, and both seemed eager to comply — whether to gather brownie points or eavesdrop on what she had to say wasn't clear. She'd asked the guy — Pratt, I think she called him — to fill her order. He'd smiled at the woman as he rose to start the process.

Now Gemma and I sat in comfortably upholstered chairs across a desk filled with neatly organized files. Brie was dressed for business, in a pantsuit once more, but her attractive middle-aged features were sagging and sad now.

"This whole situation must be particularly difficult for you, Brie," I began. "I know that Flora was your employee for a few months, but she only recently approached me with the possibility of finding a place for Gemma and me to live. I'd been talking about it with some of my friends in town, so I wasn't surprised." What had surprised me was Flora's pushiness, but I wasn't about to mention that here — especially since I figured it had probably been encouraged by the chief broker here, her boss Brie. Nor did I mention that I'd tried putting Flora off for at least a while — or maybe forever.

"We're still interested," Gemma added.

We'd talked about this before coming. The more Brie figured she could make a commission off of us, the more likely she was to talk to us. I therefore nodded eagerly.

We stopped talking when Pratt and the woman brought in our coffee. The three of us thanked them and they left, although neither looked especially happy about it.

Then I said to Brie, "Did you — I mean, had anyone complained about Flora, or had you heard about the vandalism and thefts downtown? That could be something a real estate broker would want to know about, even if you didn't know who was doing it."

I sipped my coffee. Not bad.

"I hadn't heard anything." Brie sighed and took a sip of her drink, too. "Not till the Welcome, just like everyone else. Flora always seemed so happy, so eager to complete our transactions, and so glad to be around people here in Destiny . . . I had no idea." She shook her head.

"Interesting that she hid it so well, and not just from you," I said. "And I heard — we heard — that you were the one unlucky enough to find her . . ."

"How awful, Brie," Gemma added, leaning forward with sympathy written all over her face. "What horrible luck. Tell us what happened."

Brie closed her eyes. "Bad luck? Absolutely. And I try so hard, here in Destiny, to ensure my employees, our clients, and myself the best luck possible. I don't take listings of places that have the number thirteen in their addresses or unit numbers, and I never close deals on Friday the thirteenth. But I'm always happy to take on listings that have the lucky number seven in them. I look around for black cats each time I inspect the places. I tell clients some of the superstitions I know, like not moving in on Friday the thirteenth, and leaving the brooms behind in the home you're moving out of, so you don't bring dirt and other negative aspects of your old life with you. You should enter the new place with a new broom, too."

I kept nodding even though I didn't know about all of these superstitions — mainly the ones about brooms. "You were really diligent," I said to Brie.

"But not diligent enough." I saw tears in her light brown eyes.

"Where — how — did you find poor Flora?" Gemma asked gently.

I'd already heard, read, or speculated about what I knew Brie was going to describe.

"There was a place I'd just gotten a listing on, a condo unit for rent, but it needed some cleaning." She spoke so quietly, it was hard to hear her. "The owner said he'd take care of it, but I told Flora to go check it out before she started showing it — and I was hoping she'd show it . . . yesterday." Tears rolled down Brie's cheeks. "To you." She sobbed slightly.

"Oh, I'm so sorry," I said, not wanting to mention to her that I hadn't agreed with Flora to look at that place or anywhere else.

"Me too," Brie continued. She lifted her chin as if bracing herself to go on. "I told Flora I'd meet with her first thing the next

morning, and so I went there, and . . . And
—"

This time she really did start crying, and I
felt sorry that we'd been pushing her to talk,
even gently.

But then she continued. "I'm not sure the
police want me to discuss this at all, but I
thought you, at least, should know, Rory.
They were saying it appeared she'd been
struck on the head first, then smothered.
There were some toys on the floor near her,
and though I wasn't sure, I saw some labels
and things and they were apparently toys
for dogs, not kids, even though some looked
like stuffed animals."

"Yes, we have that kind of dog toy at the
Lucky Dog," I said, not mentioning that the
ones she'd seen had been the ones I'd
designed, and then were stolen by Flora —
and then showed up in the photo around
Flora's dead body.

"The thing is . . ." Brie hesitated, then
looked me straight in the face as she sucked
at her wizened lips. "And I really don't think
I'm supposed to mention this, in case . . .
Well, I'm going to anyway. One of the toys
was pushed right into Flora's mouth, almost
as if taunting good luck. You see, the toy
was a stuffed rabbit, and the part shoved

into Flora's mouth was its oversized rabbit's foot."

Sixteen

I didn't say anything for a long moment.

I saw the immediate shock cross Gemma's face, then disappear, replaced by a sympathetic look toward me.

No wonder I was a top suspect. My special Richy the Rabbit's foot stuffed into the murder victim's mouth? That sounded a whole lot worse than just having the new Lucky Dog products on the floor around her.

After all, if I was angry about Flora's thievery, what better way to show it than ramming my own creation down her throat?

Knowledge of that part of the murder scene might just cause all the fingers in town to point toward me as the killer. Flora had stolen my dog toys. Logically, who besides me would lash out at her by shoving one of my stolen toys into her mouth?

On the other hand, if someone had wanted to frame me and protect themselves, doing that might have been a really smart move, right?

Not really — not to any cop with brains. Unless they figured I'd done it to point suspicion away from myself.

Oh, great. I wasn't aware of superstitions involving circular arguments, but if there were any, they'd surely apply now.

I didn't bother revealing my absurd thoughts to those in the room with me.

Brie knew the toy had come from my store, but she might not have known its origin and I didn't want to discuss it with her — or I'd find myself admitting it was my creation and crying out that I didn't kill the woman, even if my denial made it sound like an admission.

Instead, I said to Brie, "That's terrible. Your finding her dead had to be an indescribably awful experience, and having symbols of good luck appear all around her . . . well, I know she'd admitted to trying to mess up some of our local stores' luck with her actions, but killing her and using symbols around her that way just seems to make the whole situation so much worse for everyone in Destiny, especially you."

Not to mention me, I thought, but again kept quiet about it.

"Yes." Brie looked down at her desk. "I

194

feel responsible in some ways — not for her death, mind you, but for letting her, as my employee, run rampant all over town conducting all that terrible mischief without my even knowing about it, without being able to protect our citizens, those who really understand Destiny."

That wouldn't necessarily include me, I thought, but I knew what she meant: people who were here because they believed in superstitions or wanted to believe or wanted to know more. Not those — if there were any others, besides Flora — who felt cheated or hurt by what Destiny was and wanted to pay the town and everyone in it back.

"What she did isn't your fault," Gemma said soothingly to Brie. "And she certainly seemed good at hiding what she was feeling inside, when she wanted to."

Except for a certain rabbit's foot dog toy, I thought but didn't mention.

"I guess you're right." Brie had kept her gaze downward but now looked back up, first toward Gemma and then toward me. "Well, I can't do anything about Flora, what she did to others, or what happened to her. I know that. But what I can do something about is helping you two ladies to find your next home here in Destiny."

Ah, the bright and effervescent real estate

195

broker was back.

"Well, we'll think about it," I told her.

"And so will I. I'm sure you won't want the place we were going to show you before, even after the police are done with it. But I'll find some other apartments and condos that you'll like even better." Brie's smile was huge, and she gestured toward the computer at the side of her desk. "Just give me a day or so and I'll get back to you."

I wanted to tell her not to bother. But what she said presented us a good opportunity to flee her presence. I doubted we'd learn more from her anyway.

"Fine," I said, and looked at Gemma, who nodded.

And then we got out of there.

On the way back to our shops, we discussed what we'd heard.

"In some ways, it's even worse than I imagined," I said with a sigh, watching the cracks in the sidewalk both to avoid them and to keep myself from looking up.

"It certainly isn't good," Gemma agreed. "But you know Justin is smart. He may not be able to discuss the case with you, but he surely knows that whoever killed Flora and left her that way must somehow want to hurt you, too — just not by murdering you."

She stopped in her tracks. "Oh, Rory, I hope that's all it is. But maybe whoever it is *doesn't* want to just frame you. You've got to be particularly careful."

"While finding the truth," I said. My mind was swirling again. "What if whoever it was knew that I've already helped find a couple of killers and did this to point suspicion at me — not just to warn me off, but also to get me arrested so I can't figure out who really did it?"

We were walking again now. "Maybe so," Gemma said. She looked at me. "I know Justin didn't want you to get involved investigating the other murders, Rory. I was grateful that you helped me. And I know that this time, since you're a suspect, you have even more reason to figure out who did it. But I'm going to be really worried about you till that person's caught."

So am I, I thought.

It was evening now. I'd closed the store on time and made sure Martha got upstairs all right.

Pluckie and I had headed back to the B&B for my car so we could drive to Justin's. On the way, I pondered what to say — or not say — to him.

I'd reached no conclusions by the time we

arrived. I looked around his neighborhood, though. Was he jeopardizing his reputation as a fair cop, an excellent chief, by having me visit, rendering his appearance of neutrality a farce?

Maybe he'd invited one of his detectives over to join us tonight.

Or maybe no one would even notice I was there. I didn't see anyone out and about, after all.

Besides, knowing Justin, he wouldn't talk about anything he shouldn't, which would probably drive me nuts. Maybe, despite his expressions of concern and having his subordinate detectives question me and listen in on our conversations, everyone who knew him was as aware of his integrity as I was, so he would come out of this situation just fine.

Would I, though? Or would he be so straight, so careful, that he'd allow me to be arrested because of the planted evidence that pointed to me?

What superstitions were involved here? What could I point to that would get me off the hook by making it clear that my bad luck was caused by something outside my control?

I decided to call Justin to make sure he didn't want me to sneak my car down his driveway so Pluckie and I could enter the house from the rear patio.

"No, come on in," he said. He sounded amused.

Well, heck, he was the one whose reputation could be jeopardized here.

Mine already was.

"Okay, Pluckie," I said. I parked my car, a medium-sized blue sedan, at the curb. I checked to ensure that my dog's leash was fastened onto her collar, looked to make sure there were no cars coming down the street, and got out, almost strutting in case anyone was watching.

Hey, I was visiting the police chief, with whom I had at least some kind of relationship. And despite possibly being a murder suspect, I was innocent.

Justin's house was a single-story home on a nice wide lot. It was built of white stucco with a red Spanish tile roof, and extended farther back on its lot than it appeared from the street.

As Pluckie and I approached the front door, it opened and Justin came out. No neat blue shirt and dark slacks on him now. No, he wore a snug gray T-shirt and jeans. He always looked good, but tonight he appeared especially handsome. And sexy. And — well, I guess part of my attraction toward him was that he apparently wasn't throwing me to the wolves but supporting my innocence, at least until I was proven guilty.

Which should never happen — *should* being the operative word.

"Hi, Rory," he said as we reached him. Good thing he bent to give Pluckie a pat. Otherwise I might have thrown myself into his arms and given him a great big kiss out here just for acting so normal — for now at least.

I needn't have worried, though. Once we were inside and he'd shut the door behind us, Justin was the one to take me into his arms and share that kind of kiss with me.

I smiled up at him, then couldn't help asking, "Is that the way you treat all murder suspects?"

He laughed, but his smile got a little grim. "Only those I care about. And believe me, this is the first time."

Yes, I believed him. He was too astute, too smart, to fall for someone who truly was a murderer. But if we hadn't had a kind of relationship before now . . . ?

No use worrying about that.

Killer had joined us, and Justin's Dobie was now trading sniffs and tail wags with Pluckie.

"I hope you don't mind," Justin said, "but

I just brought home a roast chicken dinner with side dishes from the supermarket outside town."

"That's fine with me." I followed him into his kitchen as I wondered silently whether what he'd brought would include chicken feet or gizzards. I'd read in *The Destiny of Superstitions* that eating either would make you beautiful, and it had sounded so odd, even for a superstition, that I'd remembered it. I needed something encouraging like imagining myself turning beautiful that night.

On the other hand, would I really eat chicken feet or gizzards even if they were available?

He led me down his wide hallway, past the living room and into his kitchen. As always when he invited me here to eat, his butcher block table was already set with red pottery plates and simple flatware.

I helped him place the chicken and side dishes on the table as well as some wine glasses and a bottle of Chianti, and then we were ready.

I took a chicken breast as well as some salad and rice. I saw no feet or gizzards, but that was fine.

After pouring some wine, I started sipping it, then sipped some more when Justin asked, "Okay, Rory, let's poke that elephant in the room. Tell me what you've learned so far about Flora's death and the evidence against you . . . and others."

"But I thought you weren't supposed to talk about any of that." I stared at him.

"We're alone here now, and anyone who knows we're together will figure that's what we're talking about. Or that we'll talk on the phone or at the station or whatever. It's no big secret that we've been seeing each other." His blue eyes looked so serious that I almost melted into the thick wooden chair I sat on.

"But you seemed so careful before. Justin, I don't want to do anything, even through appearances, that may hurt you."

"I appreciate that." He smiled. "I did tell people I might continue to see you socially, and if I happened to learn anything from you, I would simply turn the information over to detectives to follow up on."

"But I don't have any information to —"

He interrupted me. "First thing — Choye, who questioned you, has already filed his report about what he asked, what your answers were, and how I responded. Fidelio filed a report, too. I thanked them and told them to keep going with their investigation, to keep an open mind as much as possible and to review anything that smacked of real evidence, whether against you or against someone else. They trust me. I've also talked to the city attorney, with them along. Anything I say about your innocence, or submit as evidence to prove it, is to be further investigated and treated with suspicion until the real murderer is caught. Any evidence I provide indicating your guilt is also to be investigated, but is less likely to be ignored."

I knew my eyes were huge. I felt like crying. No, screaming at him. Maybe both.

But I did understand what he was doing, and why. Or I thought so, anyway.

"Then maybe I should leave and not talk to you again, Justin," I said softly.

"That's up to you." His tone was gentle. "But the thing is, Rory, this case has to be solved. I know you didn't do it. But not everyone will be so certain. And since you helped to solve those other murders, I know you're checking out this one, too, and you'll do it even if I tell you to leave it alone and let my department handle it. That's who you are, and this time it makes even more sense for you to get involved, no matter how much I hate it. Just be cautious and keep me informed, and don't put yourself in danger." He stopped and rolled those blue eyes of his toward the ceiling. "Right. Maybe I should stay at your side all the time, both to protect you and to help you solve this."

My short bark of laughter was rueful. "Sounds like a good idea to me."

After that, the ice was broken a little. I did tell Justin about the conversation Gemma and I had had with Brie Timons, so he was aware that I had more information about how Flora had been found . . . including the fact that the rabbit I'd designed had had its foot in her mouth.

He still didn't reveal anything about the official investigation to me, though, despite my asking. Yes, his discretion was unquestionable.

"Next to me, who's your lead suspect?" I inquired, taking a chicken wing to eat next so I could pretend to look hungry.

"You know I can't talk about that."

"But we've been talking about the situation."

"Mostly I've been telling you how I'm playing this — and listening to you about how you're conducting your own investigation." He smiled, darn him. I took a quick and deep sip of wine, and as I did so he asked, "So who's your favorite suspect so far?"

I couldn't help it. As bizarre as I found it, I laughed aloud. "You know," I said, "I really don't like this unfairness in our discussion. I'm supposed to tell all and you're supposed to tell nothing."

"Yep."

As a result, I didn't bring up anything more about Flora's murder. And in fact, I really didn't want to talk about it with Justin. It divided us too much.

We soon finished eating, and so did our dogs. With Justin's okay, I'd given Pluckie some of Killer's food, since it was good and lucky stuff he had bought at the Lucky Dog.

We took the dogs for a walk and once again I looked around, but no neighbor was obviously watching us. Subtly watching? I didn't know, and neither did I ask.

The more I thought about it, the more I admired Justin and how he was handling this. Realistically, he could remain with me, even question me about any evidence I found, or whether I'd taken more of a role in this case than I would admit to. Which of course wasn't the situation, but he could keep his associates informed about what he was learning from me — to a point, of course; nothing personal.

Back in the house, we kissed again. Then Justin led me to his bedroom — not the first time I'd joined him here.

And I hoped it wouldn't be the last, especially if what wound up keeping me away was that one of his underlings would decide there was enough evidence and arrest me.

Whether it was fear, frustration, or simply the lust that had continued to build between us, we had a wonderful time. At least I did. And I'd every reason to believe that Justin enjoyed himself, too.

"So is this supposed to be when I confess all," I said as we lay in his bed afterward.

He grinned at me. "Sure, if you've anything to confess."

"I do," I said. "Even though you don't like it, I really am trying to solve your damned case — to protect myself."

"Surprise, surprise," he said and kissed me again.

Later, he walked Pluckie and me to my car. Neighbors or not, I couldn't stay here all night. One way or another it would be bad luck, mostly for Justin, I feared.

But I knew I'd have to hatch a plot tomorrow to get this situation resolved as fast as possible — and catch the murderer to clear myself.

I let my mind wander on our drive back home.

What was I going to do next? Continue to investigate the murder?

Absolutely, but how?

I came up with an idea.

SEVENTEEN

I recognized what a bad idea it might actually be, even as I started putting it into effect the next day.

Since I didn't have any idea who the killer was, talking to people at random to conduct research could wind up being dangerous, especially if I happened to interrogate the right person in the wrong way.

Which meant I needed to be extra cautious.

I'd told Martha, who was in charge at the Lucky Dog that morning, where I was going, but I'd lied about why.

After all, it had been a while since we'd run an ad in the *Destiny Star*. So why not do so now, to let townsfolk and tourists know we were going strong . . . notwithstanding the fact that locals might be aware that the shop's manager — me — might have some terrible things happening to her, like being a murder suspect?

Even worse, they might think I could actually be the killer.

But running a cheerful, come-see-our-shop kind of ad wasn't the whole reason Pluckie and I were heading for the local paper's offices several blocks east on Destiny Boulevard.

I continued to ponder the pros and cons. For one thing, maybe I should attempt to enlist Arlen as an ally. He surely wasn't the killer, and he heard things as a tour guide, rumors and more. Maybe he could make suggestions as well as relay anything interesting he heard to me.

It didn't take Pluckie and me long to get to the newspaper office. I glanced through the glass windows facing the street but couldn't tell who was inside. I opened the door and entered.

A long counter ran the length of the room, and beyond it was the large, open office area, which contained several desks where computer screens dominated everything else.

Celia Vardox sat at one. Her brother Derek sat at another. There were no other people present. I didn't recall seeing additional employees at the *Star* the few times I'd visited previously — assuming there even were any.

Did I want to talk to both Vardoxes? I'd

originally thought of only Celia, but she'd certainly tell her brother what I suggested, whether or not she agreed to do it.

Maybe, by speaking with them both, I'd get a better sense about whether my bad idea might, in fact, work, or whether I should retract it immediately.

"Hi, Rory," Celia called. Her metal desk was closest to the entry. Yes, metal. This place was all business and didn't pretend to have the antique, Gold Rush ambiance of the rest of Destiny.

"Hi." I maneuvered my way down the counter so I could look at them without peering over one of the several stacks of the latest edition of the *Destiny Star.* The paper generally came out weekly, and I noticed that this one was a few days old. It therefore wouldn't contain anything about Flora's murder. They updated their website daily, though. Maybe hourly, or minute by minute. So even if one or both of them was still working on the print story about the murder, they had surely, immediately after the event, splashed the basic information about it across their website, sharing it with the whole world.

I knew that. I'd seen it.

"What brings you here?" Surprisingly, Derek was the first to face me across the counter. He had sandy-colored hair on top of his head, and some on his cheeks in a bit of beard stubble. His shirt was checkered blue and white, over jeans. Not a bad-looking guy, yet the combined amusement and curiosity in his brown eyes bothered me.

But he was a reporter, so I should have expected it.

"Well, I want to buy a small ad for the Lucky Dog, for one thing."

"So people in the know will be aware the shop will continue, despite some possible glitches like theft and vandalism that we may still not be allowed to talk about without incurring bad luck," Celia said. She had joined us and didn't make her statement a question. The beige top she wore today was long and belted at the waist, over a brown skirt that touched the bottom of her knees. She resembled her brother, something I noticed a lot more when they were together like this.

"Not to mention that its manager is a possible murder suspect," Derek added, "which could lead to a loss of employees there, depending."

"There is that," I agreed. "You never know when the police may make a mistake and arrest an innocent person. But one thing I intend to do is prevent that — and that's another reason I'm here. I'd like your help, and in exchange I'll keep you informed about what I learn about the case, as long as you promise not to make anything public till I say it's okay. Otherwise it could compromise what I'm doing to save myself."

"Don't try to tie our hands," Derek said, his look as stern as his tone.

I stared back at him. "I thought this could be mutually beneficial, but if it only goes one way, forget it."

"Who says you'd come up with anything new?" he challenged, leaning on his arms toward me over the counter. "And if you come up with something we already have, you could say it's all yours and claim we can't run with it."

I shrugged one shoulder in my Lucky Dog shirt of the day, a deep blue T-shirt. I'd dealt with Derek before, but usually in situations where he was clearly interviewing me or others. Even if his subject was controversial and his manner too pushy, we'd never really argued. Before.

"There'd have to be an element of trust," I agreed. "Both ways. But maybe this is a totally bad idea. I wondered about that when I came up with it."

I started to rearrange the leash in my

hand, to steer Pluckie toward the door, when Celia called, "Wait."

I stopped and looked back at her, doing just that: waiting. But inside, I figured we were through here.

I wasn't even going to buy an ad if we didn't at least talk.

Standing at the counter beside her brother, Celia said, "I want to hear your idea, Rory. If we can work something out that's useful to you and to us, then why not?" She was looking at Derek now, who'd raised his eyebrows and one side of his mouth into a dubious-looking expression.

Well, let him be dubious. In fact, maybe that was a good thing. I could tell them what I was thinking, and if he kept that doubtful, negative attitude, I'd still just tell them to forget it.

"Come over here and sit down with us," Celia continued. "Would you like a cup of coffee?"

"Sure," I said. If nothing else, I could get a little caffeine out of this conversation. Although my adrenaline, considering the atmosphere, was bound to keep my nerves edgy anyway.

I went to the opening at the end of the counter and passed through into the office area, Pluckie with me. There, Celia moved a chair around so I could sit between her desk and Derek's.

"Okay," she said. "What's your idea?" She approached the shelves near the far wall where a coffee maker sat and brought back a paper cup with a sleeve on it for me. I took a sip as I pondered what to say next.

I was a retailer, not a writer, so I hoped I could articulate it in an understandable way, one that both they and I liked. I started by underscoring that I hadn't killed Flora, and added, "I'm still not exactly sure why she singled me out in her rant after the Welcome, but that only matters because it puts me in the authorities' line of fire. So to speak."

Celia and Derek already knew my toys had been found with Flora's body. I wasn't about to tell them the additional bit of knowledge I'd obtained from Brie, about Richy the Rabbit's foot shoved into Flora's mouth, in case they hadn't heard that yet. As far as I was aware, only Brie and the cops, and now me, knew of that detail. But if my idea worked out, I might let the Vardoxes in on it later — despite it pointing to me as the killer. Or maybe because of it, since someone was attempting to frame me. I wouldn't mind that part of all this becoming public.

"You know that I helped figure out who committed the other murders in town recently." I looked from one Vardox to the other, and they both nodded. "I don't really know what I'm doing when I conduct an investigation on my own, but like you, I ask questions and dig in where amateurs aren't really supposed to go."

"We're not amateurs," Derek growled.

I raised my eyebrows as I looked at him. "You're professional journalists. But you're not professional investigators. And . . . well, did you solve those murders?"

He clearly didn't like my challenge. "You're correct. We're professional journalists. It's our job to learn and report the stories, not solve criminal cases. But you —" His glare turned almost scornful. "You're only a retail store manager. We know a lot more about crimes and investigations than you do, thanks to our research and writing."

"This is getting us nowhere," Celia cut in. I wanted to hug her, or at least thank her. Instead, I just smiled at her.

She didn't smile back. "What's your plan, Rory?"

"Coordination," I replied. "In her rant, Flora said she felt harmed by storeowners and restaurant owners and others in Destiny, since the protective superstitions she'd been told about on her prior trip didn't help her. I figure you've probably already interviewed some business owners for your articles." I paused and looked at Celia, who nodded. "I don't suppose any of them confessed to being among the people Flora might have been angry with, right?"

"That's right," Derek said, and I turned my head to look at him.

"You know, it was said to be bad luck to talk about what was going on here," Celia added.

"And you of all people know what happens if you violate that Destiny rule," I replied, looking from one of them to the other. I was sure they'd never forget the fire in their office, the apparent result of one such violation.

"You got it," Derek responded glumly.

"But now the black cat's out of the bag, so to speak," I said, wondering where the nearest black cat, or their caretaker Catrice, might be. Maybe she'd know something useful, considering how she roamed the streets of Destiny at all hours with her dark-furred charges. That would be another avenue to try, but it wasn't where I was headed now.

"The bad luck we were warned about has

216

already occurred — to Flora," I continued. "From her confession, we know who perpetrated the crimes at the shops. Since any damage to Destiny's reputation has already been done, I think it'll be okay now to talk about the whole situation so that the remaining crime — Flora's murder — can be solved and everything put behind us."

"I agree," Celia said, looking at her brother.

"I'll interview Mayor Bevin about it before we get in too deep," Derek said, "but I think you're right, Rory. The murder certainly overshadows any other kind of bad luck that might have resulted from talking about the harm done to Destiny and its businesses."

Good. We were heading somewhere.

"So what if we try this?" I said. "Together, we choose a store owner, or manager, or worker from the shops that we know were looted or vandalized by Flora. Those were the people she was angriest with, right?"

"That's the impression," Derek said. He paused. "Do you actually know which businesses were involved? Besides yours, I mean?

"I've heard some fairly strong rumors," I said, recalling my conversation with Carolyn as well as with the Mardeers and Brad Nereida. "We can start with those shops, at least. As well as any that you two have heard about." I didn't want to mention the names of the stores yet, not till we had a deal, but I figured that people like Celia and Derek, who were nosy for a living, probably had an even better idea than I did about who'd been broken into.

"Then what do we do?"

"My idea is for you to approach the shop folks individually, in an order we agree upon. Push them a bit for descriptions of what Flora did to their place of business, after telling them why you don't think it's bad luck anymore to talk about it. See if you can get quotes from them. But then get really pushy and tell whoever you're talking to that you really think they're a major suspect in the murder. Tell them you've got the ear of one of the police detectives, whatever."

"No one will confess because of that," Derek scoffed.

"And we're certainly not going to do a story that's all speculation without any proof," his sister added.

"Of course not," I agreed, although I wasn't so sure. "But here's what'll happen after your interview. I'll go see each person right after you've talked to them. Tell them I heard you were badgering them, accusing them, in the interest of sensationalistic journalism. Empathize with them."

"Ah, I get it," Derek said.

"Me too," said Celia. "And I like it. If whoever you're talking to knows more about the murder —"

"Their empathy with me will be pretty darn strong, and might lead to more clues . . . or even a confession of guilt," I finished.

"So who's first?" Celia asked with a big smile. "And by the way, were you serious about buying that ad you mentioned before?"

I could hardly say no now.

Eighteen

That conversation occurred in the late morning, and I was back in the Lucky Dog's storeroom soon after, ostensibly checking inventory. No, actually checking it, since it didn't take all my concentration. Many of my thoughts were focused on my recent conversation and what was going to happen next. Could I keep myself patient enough to wait till I heard from one of the Vardoxes?

We had ended our impromptu meeting by discussing which owners and managers of the vandalized and burglarized shops to approach, and in which order. We realized that this list might grow as we got further into our research. But as with everything else we'd talked about, we didn't necessarily agree on the details. The two siblings didn't always see eye to eye, either, and my agenda and needs were quite different from theirs.

In the end, we came to an agreement about the first couple of people they'd approach, not only because each of these business owners apparently had a motive to do Flora in, thanks to what she'd done to their stores, but, equally importantly to the Vardoxes, they might ultimately make the most interesting news stories. The *Star*'s owners didn't want to write articles that were just speculations about murder, but they could certainly report on their interviews with Destiny shopowners.

Hopefully that way, the reporters might learn something that not only would trigger the next step in my investigation, but would help make it more effective.

Cryptic? Yes, even to me. I needed to discuss this with someone else. Someone I could trust.

So, a short while after entering the storeroom, I called Gemma and asked her to join me for coffee that afternoon. She might have heard the emotion in my voice, or maybe she was just curious after our last discussion, which of course ended with her acknowledging her expectation that I would try to investigate Flora's murder.

"Okay," she said immediately, in response to my invitation.

Several hours later, we met outside our shops. I'd wanted to bring Pluckie along, but since we were heading to Beware-of-

Bubbles, it was critical for us to find a spot where we wouldn't be overheard by anyone — especially the owners or wait staff — and I thought it would be better if we could choose a table in whichever area seemed least occupied, whether inside or outside.

As it turned out, inside worked best for avoiding a crowd. It was a temperate day for November, and apparently that drew people to the patio. A small corner table farthest from the door and counter seemed our best bet. Even at that, Gemma and I moved our chairs close together, turning them so we could see if anyone approached.

I'd gotten a latte and Gemma a mocha. I particularly kept watch for the shop's owners. Carolyn had said that Beware-of-Bubbles was one of the victims of Flora's tyrannical attempts at revenge, so Marypat and Dan Dresdan appeared to have as much of a motive as the others. Could one or both of them have acted on it?

They weren't the Vardoxes' first target, but it still wouldn't hurt to talk to them.

"So what's going on?" Gemma finally asked in a low, librarian-style voice. Despite running a bookstore now, she still maintained some of her old mannerisms. And as usual, she wore librarian-like garb — a nice skirt and blouse today.

I hesitated for an instant and nearly kicked myself. This was Gemma, the only person in town I trusted to be innocent.

Well, almost the only one. I didn't suspect Martha, for example. Or Justin.

Enough.

I began to explain my idea to Gemma, acknowledging right up front that it sounded odd and hokey.

"But sometimes odd and hokey ideas work," she said with a small grin.

I told her about my arrangement with the Vardoxes, and my larger plan behind it: how I thought their interviews with the store-owners could help get people I didn't know well to talk to me. "Of course, whoever actually killed Flora could be someone different altogether," I finished. "Someone who followed her from her hometown, for example."

"Like her ex-husband?"

I shrugged. "Justin said the authorities are looking into that angle, so I'm laying off it." That had been among his orders when we did talk about what I — not he — was doing. "Unless, of course, I happen to hear that her ex is visiting Destiny or someplace nearby. But even then, since Justin mentioned it, I'd probably just let him know what I heard."

"You don't know who in town is being officially investigated, though," Gemma said shrewdly, taking a sip of her mocha.

"Except for myself." I attempted to sound more amused than glum but most likely didn't fool my friend.

"Right. Except for you."

Neither one of us said anything for a moment after that, which most likely was a good thing, since a young couple sat down at a table near ours.

"So, who's up first?" Gemma asked somewhat nebulously, raising her eyebrows and nodding slightly to our new neighbors. She was trying to keep the wording of her question discreet, but I knew what she meant.

"I've got a little craving for a steak," I answered. I figured she would stretch out that thought and come up with the Shamrock Steakhouse and therefore its owner — Padraic Hassler.

"Me too. Maybe I'll join you."

That was actually a good idea, since I didn't want to show up there alone to eat a meal and then attempt to start crying on Padraic's shoulder to get him to start crying on mine in return. It would look too odd, for one thing. I'd eaten there before with Justin, among others, but I was definitely not inviting him along this time.

"Good idea," I told Gemma. "I'll have a better idea tomorrow about if and when I'll need to satisfy that craving."

"Well, I'll do the Destiny thing and knock on wood that it's tomorrow," Gemma said, doing just that on the wood-topped table.

"Good idea." I did the same, smirking at myself. I certainly adhered to superstitions when it seemed they could benefit me, even if I still couldn't really bring myself to believe in them.

Too bad I'd neither picked up nor seeded the sidewalk with lucky heads-up pennies on our short walk over here.

But perhaps triggered by that wood-knocking, I happened to see one of the owners of the coffee shop, Marypat Dresdan, come into the room with a tray full of small paper cups. She stopped at the nearest occupied tables and handed a cup to each of the patrons sitting there. I assumed she was giving out samples. Although I knew who Marypat was, that was about the extent of it, since although I'd seen her sometimes at the coffee shop and occasionally at a Destiny Welcome, we'd hardly spoken except to say hi.

Marypat appeared to be forty-something going on twenty-five. She was chubby and her face was beginning to show age lines, yet she dressed in clothes I thought were a bit young for her — too short, flowing, high heeled, and rather risqué for her size. I was maybe ten years younger than she was and perhaps a little jealous, since the clothes that worked best for my pet store were promotional T-shirts. But I tended to be more conservative than she was even when I did get dressed up.

With her tray, Marypat now stopped by our table and greeted both Gemma and me effusively. "How nice to see you here," she said. "Would you like to try our cappuccino drink? We're giving out samples to hopefully step up its popularity."

She handed me one of the cups. I did a double take, since despite the small size, the whipped cream on top had somehow been styled to resemble a cat face — not a black cat, though; a white one.

"Cute," I said. And then, after taking a sip, I added, "Tasty, too. I'll bet you sell a lot of them."

"I hope so." She rested the tray on the table momentarily to cross her fingers, and Gemma picked up a cup, too.

As she walked away, Gemma whispered, "Is she on the list?"

"Yes, and her husband as well." I kept my voice low. "Which is a shame, since she's apparently an animal lover. But that doesn't mean —"

"Exactly," Gemma agreed. "She could still —" She looked around, as if trying to see where the vandalism to Beware-of-Bubbles had occurred. Vandalism that might have made the Dresdans angry enough to do something to the perpetrator.

Or not. In any event, I wasn't going to find that out this afternoon.

We'd been here long enough now. I'd already imparted to Gemma what I wanted to tell her about my murder investigation.

Yes, murder investigation, since that's what it was.

We hadn't stood up to leave yet, even though Marypat had moved on to give out her samples at other tables. I started to get my stuff together — cup and purse — when I glanced toward the coffee shop's door.

And drew in my breath. Justin stood there.

He wasn't alone. Detective Choye was with him, and they both started scanning the room.

Until their gazes both stopped on me.

"Uh-oh," Gemma said softly.

"They're surely not going to interrogate me here, in public," I said with more confidence than I felt.

They both made their way around the

tables toward us.

"Hi, Rory," Justin said. "Martha said she thought you'd come here. Hi, Gemma."

Choye said his hellos, too.

"We were just about to leave," I told them both.

"Let us treat you to another round," Justin said. He looked straight into my eyes.

What was going on?

I was quivering inside and hated feeling this way. Maybe all was well. Maybe they'd found me to let me know they'd arrested someone else for Flora's murder.

Maybe —

They started talking about the weather, of all things. Rain was predicted for tomorrow.

" 'Rain, rain, go away. Come again some other day,' " I chanted. That was a kind of superstition, too: the idea that reciting the short poem would in fact prevent rain from falling.

"So I know Rory didn't kill Flora," Gemma began, changing the subject. I looked at her, eyes wide, hoping she'd just shut up. "You know it, too. Who's your main suspect?"

"Other than Rory?" Choye asked. "That's still privileged information, and the case is under investigation." His wide grin nearly made me stand and flee.

"Why are you really here, then?" I demanded.

"My boss wanted to come and say hi now, while he could. Before we arrest you." Detective Choye's grin grew even wider.

"Oh, cut it out," Justin said. "We stopped in at the Lucky Dog to see you, and Martha directed us here. That's all. We just wanted to say hi to you."

And I just wanted to solve the murder — fast — so this nervousness I felt about everything could finally go away.

Nineteen

That wasn't all there was to it, though. Quietly, and with his characteristically snide manner tuned down just a bit, Choye indicated he was glad that Justin was being up front about things. Yes, he was aware we'd spent some time together last night. He also smiled and shrugged as he said — only somewhat jokingly — that things could go easier on me if I admitted any wrongdoing to the chief of police, and that he would always be around to back his commanding officer.

The good thing was, I figured Justin was handling the situation as well as he could — in a manner that wouldn't keep us totally apart or require us to always have a chaperone along.

The bad thing? Well, there were quite a few, including the fact that Justin's associates wouldn't consider me exonerated based on anything Justin said or did, yet they'd jump on it if he claimed to have wrangled a confession out of me. Or if they found real evidence that they believed pointed conclusively to me, which I certainly hoped wouldn't happen, either.

We all left a short while later, each carrying a paper cup with a sleeve on it as we headed out the door.

I fortunately had no bubbles in my coffee refill, so I didn't have anything I needed to interpret — except for Justin's presence and Choye's sarcastic attitude.

I managed to hang back a little, allowing Gemma to walk near Choye as they headed onto the sidewalk. That gave me a moment to ask, "What are you really up to, Halbertson?"

"That's Chief Halbertson to you," he said solemnly, but with a twinkle in his blue eyes as he looked down at me. We both tried to get through the door at the same time, which led to our bodies touching, though not suggestively. Even so, it made me think about our growing relationship — or at least, I'd kind of hoped it was growing. As recently as last night. But now . . . ?

"Okay, *Chief* Halbertson, what are you really doing here?"

He motioned me over to one side of the front of the coffee shop. "Seriously, Rory,

I'm here because I'm concerned about you. I brought Richard along for appearances and so I could check out his attitude, which seems appropriate, at least for now. But don't be surprised if I hunt you down at any hour of the day or night to make sure that no matter how you're approaching your foolish investigation, you're not in any danger."

"*Foolish* investigation?" My tone was suddenly harsh. "You, or at least your department, consider me a prime murder suspect, and I'm just supposed to go on with my normal life and ignore it till I'm arrested? I can hang out with you and let you keep your staff involved and even make fun of it, all so you can minimize your apparent conflict of interest? And then I'm supposed to suck it all up and smile?"

"Well, somewhat, but you can be sure I'm having other potential suspects checked out, and —"

"By those same minions of yours. I get it. But I also understand that if they think it's all for show — to let the chief create an appearance of giving the benefit of the doubt to a friend who's nevertheless probably guilty — they're not going to really investigate the others as they should."

Scowling, Justin opened his mouth, clearly

to object, but I didn't let him get a word in. "Yes, I know you're in charge and you can tell them what to do," I said. "And you trust them and train them and all that. But they'll do what they think they should, too, and humor you till they decide it's really time to arrest me. Then they'll get you on board . . . or go above your head to the city government." My voice had started to turn shrill, so I took a deep breath. "Anyway, you do what you have to, and I'll do what I have to, too."

I pivoted and started walking through the tourists toward Gemma and Choye, who were waiting for us halfway between the coffee shop and the Lucky Dog.

I looked at Gemma, grimly smiled my thanks that she'd kept Choye away, and headed for my shop.

When Gemma and I got there, we stopped outside the door and I thanked her again. "I'll keep you informed," I told her.

"Keep me informed, too," said a no-nonsense voice behind us.

I turned and looked up again at Justin. "Only if you promise to do the same for me." I waited for an instant, as if I had some hope — which I didn't — that he'd say he would. Then I hurried into my store.

■ ■ ■ ■

I relaxed on my bed at home, Pluckie at my side. We'd returned to the B&B after closing up shop, eating dinner on the way. Under other circumstances, I would have wanted to invite Justin and Killer to go for a walk with us. Even though it was dark outside except for streetlights, I really had an urge for a nice long dog outing. The air was a bit cool, but at least it wasn't raining yet. It was a good time to walk, although not with the person I'd previously preferred.

Sure, apparently Justin and I could continue acting like friends in public, and somewhat in private, as long as he could supervise my murder investigation. Well, I could use him similarly, or at least try to. If he continued telling me nothing, though, it might not work.

Still, maybe I could finagle an answer or two out of him now and then. As long as our interactions remained private. I was mad, but I didn't want to get him in trouble.

I considered calling Celia Vardox to ask if she wanted to walk, bringing along her black Lab, Charlotte, but then it occurred to me I'd be a lot better off not appearing to be friends with the Vardoxes, since we were conspiring and working together, sort of, to find the killer.

For now, I invited Carolyn Innes to join us, along with her two dachshunds, Liebling and Helga. I also invited Gemma, but she and Stuart had other plans for the evening. I didn't ask exactly what and she didn't tell.

I hadn't seen a lot of Stuart since he'd arrived, but that was because Gemma was taking advantage of his presence to leave him in charge of the Broken Mirror when she left, and for longer periods of time than she was comfortable doing with her usual assistants, who were young and somewhat inexperienced. I had seen Stuart at the B&B some mornings and evenings, though. I still considered him to be nice, and potentially a good fit for Gemma, but that was up to her. And to whomever it was she'd seen in that mirror . . . if anyone.

But my own potential relationship, complete with seeing Justin's face in the mirror? That was certainly in jeopardy, if not dying.

Which made me think of my poor Warren yet again. "Let's go," I told Pluckie firmly, and we headed out the door of the B&B. We were supposed to meet Carolyn and her dogs on the corner of Destiny Boulevard.

I couldn't help turning to look toward the horseshoe hung over the B&B's front door.

Its ends remained facing upward now, as they should. Had Flora been the one to turn it over in the first place? Most likely. But if that had caused anyone to suffer bad luck, or if someone walking beneath it had had good luck pour into them, I hadn't heard about it.

Even so, the place had suffered some of Flora's vandalism, so although I didn't truly mistrust Serina, I had to keep her in mind as a possible suspect.

Carolyn, on the other hand, hadn't had any harm done to her button store. If I considered people suspects only because their shops had suffered Flora's wrath, that meant I could remove Carolyn from consideration. But again, I resolved to keep an open mind. At least for now.

The walk with Carolyn and her dogs was fun. And a relief. Her short little dogs scooted along in the low light just as well as Pluckie did. Astute Carolyn let me direct the conversation.

"I figure you're doing something to find out who the real killer is, right, Rory?" she asked as we passed the Broken Mirror and Lucky Dog stores. She wore a Destiny hoodie, which hid all but a few curls of dark hair skimming her cheeks, over jeans and short boots.

I'd thrown on a dark sweatshirt over the regular store outfit I'd worn that day, but added athletic shoes for the walk.

"I'm thinking about it," I hedged.

"Well, think hard. And well. And if there's anything I can do, be sure to let me know."

I told her I would. We started talking about other things, including how cute our respective dogs were. Neither of us had recently heard of any superstitions that were new to us to share with one another.

Maybe that was a good thing. As a sort-of accused murderer, with some townsfolk staring at me suspiciously, I'd had an urge to leave town for good. But people like Carolyn and Gemma made me rethink it. Not to mention all the dogs in town, both living here and visiting.

Then there was Justin. He was a big factor in my staying right now — not because of any relationship between us, but because if I left, he would come after me, or have his subordinates do it, since they'd consider my flight some kind of confession.

So here I'd stay, for now, at least.

And in the meantime, I'd investigate. "Okay, you're right," I eventually admitted to Carolyn.

We'd walked several blocks to the civic center, passing her Buttons of Fortune shop on the way. Then we crossed Destiny Boulevard and headed back toward our starting point. Even at this hour, there were still tourists out and about, apparently window shopping and keeping their eyes open for cracks in the sidewalk and heads-up pennies. And maybe even lucky buttons, although Carolyn only seeded the sidewalks now and then. But there wasn't the kind of crowd these sidewalks attracted during daylight hours.

"I'm trying to figure out who really killed Flora, to get myself off the hook," I continued. I moved slightly to face Carolyn. "Do you have any ideas?"

"I'm sure you're looking into everyone Flora affected with her vandalizing and thefts, right?"

"Yes, but I can't tell you how."

"Well, those people would be my main suspects. If I come up with anyone else, I'll be sure to let you know."

I recalled that in prior conversations, Carolyn had hinted about some strangeness in her own past yet had never responded when I'd tried to get her to talk about it. I decided to stay away from the subject that evening. There was already enough controversy going on around here.

We were nearly back to where we'd part

ways, and Pluckie and I would head down Fate Street.

That's when I saw a black cat cross our path.

Was that a sign I'd suffer bad luck? Never learn the truth? Not be able to save myself from being arrested?

"You saw that?" Carolyn asked, underscoring my sudden pang of fear.

"Yes," I croaked.

"You know," she said, "I have a theory about those of us who live in Destiny. We can turn any superstition around to our favor, don't you think?"

I didn't really think so — assuming I even believed in superstitions, and at this moment, maybe I did. But I loved her attempt to make me feel better.

"Sure," I said. "And thanks for joining us on our walk." I hugged her first, then stooped to hug Liebling and Helga.

"Any time," Carolyn said. "Now go get 'em, detective."

When, startled, I looked into her face, she winked at me, turned, and led her two adorable waddling dogs away.

The next day started out a lot better. After breakfast at the B&B, I walked with Pluckie, Gemma, and Stuart to the stores. Business was great, with noisy crowds ready to spend money from the moment I opened the Lucky Dog.

Even luckier, a delivery person brought several boxes. The new supply of the toys I'd created were starting to arrive!

With Millie and Martha working in the store helping customers, I extracted everything from the crates, including several Richy the Rabbits, and then brought them out to put in their appropriate display spots.

Surely, that was a sign that all was looking up for me — assuming I was superstitious enough now to look for signs and omens and such.

And I didn't see any black cats, nor the Destiny cat person, Catrice.

I didn't see Justin that morning, either. Under other circumstances, I might have considered that bad luck. But I didn't feel like verbally sparring with him or any of his detectives that day. If I chose to try to protect myself by conducting some kind of amateur murder investigation, that was my business, not his. At least sort of. He was in charge of the official investigation, of course.

I received an email from Celia that was bland and didn't really say anything, except that she'd conducted an interview yesterday and was I ready for a more in-depth interview from her?

That was kind of the code we'd decided on, in case anyone breached the security of our emails. It meant that she, or perhaps Derek, had pushed the first person on our list and it was my turn to follow up.

I was therefore happy when the busy day at the store ended and Gemma and I got together to head to the Shamrock Steakhouse for dinner. She'd asked if it was all right if Stuart joined us, and I figured it wouldn't hurt.

As a result, we all went back to the B&B to change clothes. I fed Pluckie, took her for a short walk, and left her in our room. Then all the humans headed back to Destiny Boulevard, where the steakhouse was just across the street from Buttons of Fortune.

We were seated right away by the maître d' at a table right in the middle of the not-quite-full, dimly lit but noisy dining room. I was used to sitting outside with Pluckie when I came here, so not only the food but the ambiance would be a treat. The aromas in the steakhouse stoked my appetite, so I ordered a delicious-sounding small sirloin with a Cobb salad.

All the while, I talked with Gemma and Stuart about my day and theirs, how many copies of *The Destiny of Superstitions* were still being sold daily, and other interesting stuff that was noncontroversial and good dinner conversation.

I kept watching for Padraic but didn't see him, nor did I recognize any other member of the family that owned this restaurant — although he seemed to be the head of it all. As a result, after we ate our salads, I rose. "Excuse me," I said. "I need to find the restroom."

Actually, I needed to find the restaurant offices, which I did, down the hall from the restrooms.

I didn't pretend to be lost. I just kept going till I reached the closed door marked *Private.* I knocked, then opened the door without waiting for a response.

Fortunately, it was Padraic's office. He sat there behind a large desk, working on a computer. The place was small and a bit messy, mostly occupied by that desk.

Padraic, however, was tall and well groomed. In a green suit, sure, but his gray hair was short and nicely styled.

He rose immediately as I came in. "Rory! What are you doing here?"

I continued to approach him. "I really need to talk to you, Padraic," I said. "About Flora Curtival and what happened to her.

The police keep harassing me, and the Var-doxes are pestering me as well. It's terrible!"

"Tell me about it," he said, still glaring at me. "Those damned reporters are now on my case."

"You too, then," I said with a sigh. "I'd wondered about that. I would really like to talk to you about it, so maybe we can figure out a way to make them all back off."

"Good idea," he said. "At least for me." Then he drew closer, until we were close enough for him to touch me. Or punch me. "Why the hell don't you just confess, Rory?" he yelled. "So they'll leave me alone?"

Twenty

I just stood there, blinking at him. I wasn't surprised at his reaction, and all I needed was to get him talking.

I was, however, a bit surprised, and somewhat pleased, when my eyes actually teared up. Yes, he'd hurt my feelings. And being confronted by a regular citizen who thought I might be guilty was painful.

The point, though, was that this could just be an act on his part. I'd play my role, real tears and all, and see his reaction.

"I didn't do it," I said in a throaty whisper. "I assume from your reaction that you didn't, either. What have the police said to you? And did the Vardoxes also ask you questions?"

I'd previously considered Padraic a little young-looking to have such a gray head of hair, but the sad and almost scared expression on his face aged him. His skin was soft-looking and there were lines beside his mouth and eyes. He blinked at me from behind glasses that he must just wear in his office, since I hadn't seen them on him before. Not that we were good buddies, but as with many of the shopowners in Destiny, even those I didn't know well, I'd met him and seen him in various venues in addition to his place of business.

"Okay, maybe it was a bit much for me to accuse you like that." He truly did look regretful. "But I think I convinced the cops it wasn't me. Yes, the b—er, witch — heck, I shouldn't speak ill of the dead, especially in Destiny. The poor deceased woman included my restaurant on her hit list of thievery and vandalism, and I don't understand why, except that maybe this was one of the places she came to with her ex-husband, on that trip she mentioned. I don't know. There are so many tourists who come here, which is a good thing, and I didn't recognize her."

I nodded encouragingly as he spoke, attempting to look empathetic, which I actually was — as long as he truly wasn't the killer.

"Anyway, even though the cops just questioned me and left and that seemed to be it, Celia Vardox barged in yesterday and started demanding answers for an article in her

245

damned *Star.* Unlike the cops, she seemed to think I was really guilty, at least judging by her pushiness."

"She treated me that way, too," I said. I didn't mention that the cops still had me high on their list. He undoubtedly knew it anyway, as did everyone in Destiny. And I certainly didn't mention that I was now colluding with Celia.

"I told her I didn't do it. That, yes, I'd been upset when someone came into my steakhouse in the middle of the night and not only trashed it but left some bad luck symbols, too, like salt on the floor and pieces of broken mirror."

Flora apparently hadn't had much imagination about what bad luck symbols to leave in the places she vandalized — although I couldn't think offhand of something else that was both an ill omen and easily transported.

"She did that at the Lucky Dog, too," I said. "Plus she stole some of our merchandise."

"If she took steaks or any other food or drinks I wasn't aware of it," Padraic said. "But she did overturn tables and chairs and left the place a mess. I'll tell you, I wanted to choke whoever did that . . . but I didn't." His eyes widened as he looked at me.

"Damn. I shouldn't have even said that. Yeah, I was damned angry. But when she made her speech at the end of the Welcome and I finally knew who'd done it, some time had passed. If I could have had her arrested or whatever, sure. And I honestly can't say I'm peeved with whoever offed her. But whether or not you believe me, it wasn't me."

I did believe him. And even though I hadn't found my answer, I'd achieved part of my purpose. Padraic had been "peeved" enough to talk to me after being irritated by the *Destiny Star.* So I thought I had my answer about Padraic Hassler, even if it didn't solve the murder.

"Same goes here," I told him as I stood to leave. "I appreciate your talking to me. I feel a little better speaking with someone in a similar position." I paused at the door. "And whether or not you believe me, too, I didn't kill Flora."

I returned then to my table with Gemma and Stuart. They were finishing their main courses — steak for Stuart and chicken for Gemma. There was no plate at my setting, and Gemma told me she'd requested that our server keep it warming in the kitchen.

"I told the wait staff you had a phone call

you needed to deal with," she said as I sat down again. "I didn't want them to think you'd become ill from the salad."

We soon motioned for the server to bring my steak. When it arrived, I ate a few bites, but I wasn't particularly hungry. Nor did I want Gemma and Stuart to feel obligated to continue to sit there and watch me eat. I decided to take the leftovers home.

In the meantime, I could tell that Gemma was just itching to ask me how things had gone with Padraic. I wanted to let her know, but not here in this semi-crowded room, and most importantly not in front of Stuart. He was a nice enough guy, but what I intended to tell Gemma was likely too much information to share with him.

I realized I might not be able to tell her what happened until the next day. So I just said, "All went well, kind of as I anticipated. We'll talk later."

"When I'm not around," Stuart said, raising his thick, light eyebrows that almost met over his prominent nose. He'd worn a suit that night as he often did, a deep brown one this time. He was astute, as always.

"I'm sure you understand the sensitivity of the situation," I said. I figured that Gemma had filled him in, at least generally, on the reason for this dinner, even though

I'd asked her not to give details about what I was doing.

"I do," he acknowledged, and then started a conversation about whether someone should be researching a sequel to *The Destiny of Superstitions.*

"I thought Tarzal's book was pretty comprehensive on the subject," I said. "Are there many more superstitions that can be described?"

"There are always more superstitions," Stuart said.

I laughed and nodded. "I've been learning that nearly every day in Destiny."

The server soon returned with my steak in a foam container. We paid the bill, split three ways — which kind of surprised me, since I'd figured Gemma and Stuart were on a date. But I wasn't about to ask. They might have such things arranged between them.

We walked briskly back to the B&B. The evening had grown quite nippy, plus I'd left Pluckie alone in my room long enough. She'd need her last walk of the night — and so did I, with just her as company so I could mull over my conversation with Padraic in private, as well as plan my next conversation.

According to our agreement, either Celia

or Derek was to have spoken with — no, pushed and prodded — two more shopowners on our list today, including Kiara Mardeer, Jeri's mother and the key person in charge of the Heads-Up Penny Gift Shop. I hated the idea of being nasty to Kiara. I liked her, and liked her daughter even more. But this procedure was designed as much to knock people off the suspect list as to come up with who'd actually done it — although that, of course, was the ultimate goal.

We soon turned the corner from Destiny Boulevard onto Fate Street and reached the parking lot in front of the B&B.

Noticing one particular car in the lot, I stopped briefly. It was a black sedan and looked a lot like Justin's official means of transportation.

But there were surely other black sedans in the area. I wasn't close enough to check the license plate — or to see if there was a red light mounted inside on the dashboard.

Besides, what would Justin be doing here?

As if I couldn't guess.

I hung back just a fraction of a second as Gemma and Stuart approached the door first. I geared up for a conversation I didn't want to have, but resolved not to let it turn into a confrontation.

Maybe I was wrong, though. Maybe it wasn't Justin's car.

Or if it was, maybe there was a good reason for him to be here — not that I wished any problems on anyone that would require a cop's presence, let alone the chief's.

A few moments later, I passed under the Rainbow B&B's now-perfectly hung horseshoe — a good thing. I just might need a bit of good luck.

"Hi, Gemma, Stuart," said a familiar masculine voice as my friends preceded me into the lobby. "Hi, Rory," he added as I followed them in.

Sure enough, Justin was here. Serina was with him, in an old-fashioned dress as usual.

"Hi and bye, all," Serina said. "Time for me to head to bed so I can get up in time for breakfast tomorrow." She waved as she headed up the stairs.

"Me too," Gemma said, following Serina.

"G'night," Stuart said, following both of them.

Leaving me alone in the lobby with Justin. He was dressed casually in a sweatshirt and jeans, so, official sedan or not, he was off duty.

"I'm tired, too," I told him. I turned my back on him and hurried into the breakfast

251

room, then beyond it so I could put my steak into the kitchen's refrigerator after writing my name on the container.

When I came out, Justin was still there. "I bet you have to walk Pluckie." The expression on his much-too-good-looking face was pleasant, but I nevertheless had an urge to do or say something to annoy him and make it go away.

"Yeah, I do. And I imagine you want to come."

"You got it."

"And later you'll tell all your friends and associates that you were once again just encouraging me to spill more beans about what I know about Flora's death, especially if I killed her." I tried to keep my tone and expression light, but I didn't really feel that way and figured my irritation showed.

"You got that, too," he said. But now he sent me a teasing grin, which made me sigh and, almost unwillingly, grin back — for a few seconds, at least.

He said he'd wait right there. If I hadn't loved my dog and appreciated the B&B as much as I did, I might have just stayed upstairs and allowed Pluckie to do what she had to on the floor, or maybe try to find a newspaper for her to do it on.

But, hey, why allow this man to annoy and

disrupt me like that — and Pluckie, too? I hurried up to our room, opened the door, and knelt to hug my lucky black-and-white pup. "You're more important than he is," I told her. I got her leash and we headed downstairs.

Without turning toward Justin, even when Pluckie hurried over to say hi, I headed for the lobby door and unlocked it to go outside. Justin followed.

I let Pluckie lead me to where she wanted to go, past the cars in the parking lot and into the grassy area beyond. She stopped there, and so I stopped, too.

So did Justin. "I assume you're not wondering why I'm here tonight," he said.

I turned to look up at him. Here, where the light was dim and false, his face appeared even more angular than usual. But I still liked the way he looked. Maybe too much.

"No," I said. "I figure you just want to continue to give me a hard time."

"In a way," he agreed. "Like I told you before, no matter how I have to play this with my staff and the city politicos on my case, I'm concerned about you. Were you off somewhere tonight conducting your murder investigation?"

I could simply lie, or not tell the whole

truth and just say I'd been having dinner with friends.

But in fact, I actually felt a bit warm and gooey inside thanks to his obvious concern. Plus I wanted to goad him a bit more, as he continued to goad me.

"I was having dinner, a strange thing to do during the evening, no?" But I didn't give him time to respond. "But yes, you're right. I was doing more than that — I was investigating. In my way. But have you solved the murder in the meantime so I don't have to?"

"That's still a work in progress," he said.

"Well then, so's my amateur investigation. And unlike you, I'll probably even tell you when I can prove who actually did it."

"I wish I could tell you that now, Rory. That way, maybe you'd give up your chase and stay safe." His tone was serious, and he looked straight into my eyes even as Pluckie started pulling a bit on her leash.

The gooeyness inside me thickened, but I turned away. I had to, thanks to my dog's machinations. She now seemed to be following a scent track along the grass, and I followed her.

"I'm being careful," I told him when Justin reached my side again.

For the next few minutes we both followed

Pluckie. And when she seemed to be done, Justin accompanied us back to the B&B door, which I opened again with my key.

Before I went inside, though, he took me into his arms — and I liked the feeling. "Please, Rory. At least tell me what you're really doing so I can be sure someone's around as your backup."

If I did, he might stop me from doing anything at all.

"Thanks," I said. "I appreciate it. But I'm not putting myself in danger." At least not yet, not by conducting follow-ups to newspaper interviews in public places.

"Okay." But he sounded dubious and frustrated and even sad.

I couldn't help it. I reached up and pulled his head down toward mine.

We shared a long, sexy kiss that gave me the urge to invite him inside and up to my room. But that would be a bad idea for both of us. Especially for him, and his already too-obvious conflict of interest that he was hiding in plain sight, literally.

When I finally pulled away, I tried to catch my breath. "Good night," I said. "I'm sure we'll be seeing each other again soon." I hoped. And I crossed my fingers it wouldn't be because he felt compelled to arrest me.

"Count on it," he said, bending down

once more to kiss me.

I took a few steps into the B&B lobby. "Good night," I repeated more loudly, pulling slightly on Pluckie's leash to get her to leave Justin and come with me. "Be sure to give Killer a good night hug from us, too." And then I hurriedly slipped farther inside and shut the door.

TWENTY-ONE

I couldn't help it. The next morning at breakfast I slipped away from Gemma and Stuart, leaving Pluckie with them, and went into the kitchen where Serina was cooking more food for her guests.

Justin had been here last night, presumably waiting for me. But he'd been waiting with Serina. She'd experienced a bit of Flora's vandalism at the B&B, of course, and therefore, like so many others, she remained on my suspect list.

Had Justin asked her anything about what had happened here?

Should Serina be on the *official* suspect list?

I hoped not. I liked her, liked her attitude about people and dogs and Destiny and superstitions. I hoped to eliminate her from my list eventually.

"Anything I can help with?" I asked, after entering the large, modern kitchen that contrasted with the rest of B&B's decor.

Serina stood behind the stove, her mitted hand holding the handle of a large pan that contained a few omelets. Her upswept brown hair was precisely in place. She looked near perfect, in fact. As if she knew exactly what she was doing.

She'd done this often enough that she probably did.

"No, thanks. I'm nearly done with this batch." She turned to look at me. "But why are you in here? You almost never come in to volunteer to cook." She was smiling, but her look appeared somewhat skeptical, as if she wouldn't believe anything I said. Her light brown eyes glommed onto mine, as if her gaze would somehow evoke real answers from me.

In a way, it did.

"I was just curious," I said. "About Justin being here last night. Was he just waiting for me? Or was he asking questions? Trying to figure out a certain murder — whatever?"

While I hadn't suggested to Celia that she interview Serina, that didn't mean I didn't want to try to push Serina to talk to me about how she was innocent. I truly believed, and hoped, that she hadn't killed Flora, but with the bad luck of an upside-down horseshoe over her entry door, she'd perhaps had a tiny motive to kill, at least for a while.

Maybe I should have told Celia, nosy reporter that she was, to play the bad guy here as well as with the others.

But it was too late now. I'd blown it by asking Serina about Justin's questions. If only I'd just asked why he was here, and acted all gooey about the possibility that he only wanted to see me . . . but I hadn't.

"He did ask a few questions about my upside-down horseshoe," Serina said. "But yes, I think your potential main squeeze was just waiting for you."

I felt my eyes grow huge as we continued to stare at one another. I looked away first.

"He's not my potential main squeeze," I said, both softly and hoarsely. "He certainly can't be now, with me being a major murder suspect and him being police chief."

"Don't be too sure about that." Serina gently put the handle down so the pan again rested on the stove. She then approached me, and I felt the layers of fabric on her Gold Rush era skirt — partly covered now with a full-length bibbed apron — brush against me. "He doesn't think you killed Flora, and he wants to protect you."

I pulled back, realizing my incredulity

probably showed on my face. "Did he say that?"

"Not outright. But he did ask about you right when he arrived — if I knew where you were, that kind of thing. It didn't sound like he was chasing you down to arrest you, but like he gave a damn. And I asked him about the murder case." At my blink, she laughed a little. "Yes, I'm fully aware of the belief around here that asking anything about the vandalism or anything related to it could bring bad luck."

Not that anyone appeared to be paying much attention to that now. I smiled back. "So did Justin tell you anything interesting?"

Serina shrugged her narrow shoulders. "Not really. But I told him a couple of things I overheard here, some of my guests' speculations about who could have killed Flora. Nothing of great note or that he probably hasn't already thought of. But the really important thing?"

"What's that?" I followed the cue she'd given me.

"I told him that in a way, I thanked Flora for turning my horseshoe upside down temporarily. It's a good topic of conversation, and since the superstition it covers can go two ways, I don't think it brought bad luck here. Nor did anyone tell me their luck had changed for the better after they'd walked under it. No harm, no foul, in either case. Even so . . ."

"Even so?" I again heeded her prompt.

"He shouldn't look here for the killer. At least not at me. I didn't do it."

I smiled as she again turned to the stove to work on her omelets.

I believed her, and so I decided not to get Celia here to stress her out.

I thought again about Justin's admonition to stay safe and let him know what I was up to. But it certainly wouldn't be dangerous for me to visit a fellow Destiny retailer after I opened up the Lucky Dog this morning — especially since I would be accompanied to the Heads-Up Penny Gift Shop by one of the owners, who also worked for me.

I didn't speak to Justin that morning, and I had no intention of letting him know what I was up to. I was going to do what I needed to. And yes, I'd try my best to stay safe.

Around ten-thirty, I headed to the Heads-Up with Jeri to visit Kiara and any other member of their family who happened to be working in the gift shop, leaving Martha and Millie in charge of the Lucky Dog. The timing seemed good, since we weren't extremely busy that Wednesday morning.

The reason I gave Jeri for wanting to visit her shop was that I wanted to ask her mother about the suppliers of their products, especially products they'd had specially made. I intended to claim that I'd had some issues with the business that was manufacturing my dog toys, even though the newest items they'd sent seemed to be as good quality as the first batch, and they'd gotten them to me even more quickly than I'd anticipated.

So I was grumbling to Jeri about all this — both the quality and the timing — and she seemed to somewhat defend our supplier.

"I'm not sure any company my mother works with would do any better," she told me as we made our way through the crowd along the sidewalk on Destiny Boulevard, heading toward our destination. As usual, she wore a shirt that said Heads-Up Penny Gift Shop, this time a coral knit one over slender jeans. Pluckie walked with us. Jeri and my dog were buddies, and my assistant had said that her family always enjoyed having dogs visit their shop, too — especially lucky ones.

Jeri and I then talked about generalities, not superstitions — or vandalism — as we walked along, and she continued to stick up for the company I'd commissioned to make my good luck dog toys. Having already given her my ostensible reason for going to her family's shop, I didn't want to bring up anything else, so I listened as she gave her approval of our latest toys' quality and how soon the replacement batch had arrived once ordered.

"You may be right," I acknowledged, "and maybe it's still my angst over the vandalism and everything else that's making me wonder, but it won't hurt to jot down some other possible suppliers to try out in the future."

"You're right," my young assistant said as we walked up to the door of the Heads-Up Penny shop.

As was traditional here in Destiny, the shop was located in a retro, Gold Rush–type building with an ornate facade and wide windows displaying an attractive and inviting array of the shop's merchandise. Jeri preceded me in, then held the door open for me.

I'd been here before, of course, as I had with probably all of the shops in Destiny. Even so, I looked around with curiosity. Since this was one of the other places Flora had rampaged, I tried to see any residual damage.

But the shop looked much as I'd seen it before, with its carved display shelves of antique-looking dark wood, possibly mahogany. As with the Lucky Dog, it was divided into areas for specific kinds of goods. One section held garment racks displaying dressier shirts on hangers, and nearby were shelves of T-shirts and other clothes. I couldn't see them well from the door, but I knew they all had good luck symbols of some sort on them — four leaf clovers and crossed fingers and more.

Another area held a couple of display cases for jewelry, including hematite pieces, like the dog amulet I wore every day. Other areas contained hanging racks of belts and shelves of candles and candle holders — along with brochures about how to burn candles without incurring bad luck and which color candles stood for what, including my favorite, brown, which stood for protecting pets. A metal display held good luck magnets.

I took most of this in quickly, since I saw Kiara come out from behind the counter and approach us. There were five customers at various spots in the store, but they all appeared to merely be looking, at least for now. Kiara smiled at a couple of them as she walked past but didn't stop. Today, her slightly plump body was dressed in a beige button-down shirt covered with green, ends-up horseshoes, over light brown slacks.

"Hi, Rory," she said as she hugged her daughter. "What brings you two here?"

Jeri quickly explained my supposed reason for coming: finding another company to manufacture my dog toys. "Do you know of any to suggest, Mom?"

"A couple. But — Jeri, could you take care of our customers while Rory and I go into the office? Jilli's due here soon, so she'll be able to help out."

Perfect, I thought. Jeri's older sister was on her way. Meantime, I'd get Kiara alone and, hopefully, in a situation where I could appear to cry on her shoulder to get her to talk.

"Sure." While Jeri approached a customer who'd turned toward us with a couple of shirts in her hand, Kiara led Pluckie and me through the store and into her office at the left rear.

This room also maintained the appearance of the Gold Rush era, with antique furniture consisting of a small desk that appeared to be made of redwood — perhaps carved back in the days when cutting down redwoods was no big deal. The couple of chairs around it were lighter in color, and although their backs were carved with designs, they didn't appear to be quite as old as the desk. A narrow wooden set of shelves fit into the corner, and fluffy lace curtains hung around the office's single window.

Appearing a little out of place, though, was Kiara's modern desk chair. And her computer. She gestured for me to sit and lowered herself onto her chair. She then turned to the computer monitor on her desk and started typing on the keyboard.

I did as she directed, and Pluckie obediently followed, lying down on the shining wood floor.

"I'll bring up a few of my suppliers and print them out for you," Kiara said, "including the ones I deal with directly to create some of my stuff that's unique to this shop, like our good luck shirts and all."

"Thanks," I told her. My gratitude was genuine. I had no idea when and if having that kind of information would become imperative. Then I brought up what I'd really come about. "And . . . well, you and I have already talked some about what happened when your store, and mine, were vandalized, so whatever bad luck supposedly can result from discussing the situation has already been triggered — and you haven't seen any, have you?"

She shook her head, her wide mouth pursed. "Fortunately, not. Have you?"

"Well, no — although the police have been talking to me, and . . . well, I've been kind of seeing Justin socially. You might know that. He's taking great care to ensure that he's not compromising the investigation because of what may look like a conflict of interest."

"I've wondered about that." Kiara shot me a look that appeared somewhat sympathetic.

"It's sometimes a little hard to deal with, but even so I can't really consider any of that to be bad luck. Not yet, at least. But what is bad luck? Maybe being confronted by Celia Vardox of the *Destiny Star*. She was doing an article on the murder, which I can understand, but she seemed so accusatory."

Kiara's deep brown eyes widened. "You too?"

"You mean she also *interviewed* you?" I drew out the word "interviewed" so she'd recognize that what I really meant was "interrogated" . . . or worse.

I wasn't completely surprised when Kiara pulled back in her chair a little. I saw her eyes well up with tears.

Which told me something. Either she was as innocent of Flora's murder as I thought she was, or she was one heck of an actress.

"Yes, she did," Kiara replied hoarsely. "But she was so nasty, so accusatory. She acted as if she knew for sure that I killed Flora. Which I didn't." She stopped talking and aimed those moist eyes at me as if demanding that I acknowledge her innocence.

"Of course not," I said, and I meant it — unless things were to change in this conversation or otherwise. "Look, tell me what she asked you and how she asked it. And what you said. I'll tell you the same, and if it ever seems appropriate, we can file a complaint with the police, or even go public and rebuke the *Star* in other media, social or otherwise. That can't be bad luck."

"Well . . . sure. Two of us fighting that nasty paper and the Vardoxes — well, that's bound to be better than just one of us trying it."

Kiara began talking about how Celia had come into the shop yesterday, her tablet in hand for making notes. She'd looked around, demanded that Kiara show her what kinds of things Flora had damaged. When Kiara had balked at the idea of media attention, given the original order that shopkeepers keep quiet about what had happened for fear of getting bad luck rained down on both them and the town, Celia had shrugged it off — even when Kiara reminded her of the fire at the *Destiny Star* offices when the Vardoxes had violated a similar edict.

"Yes, I reminded her of the fire, too," I inserted, just to show I was still with Kiara, on her side.

"The thing is," Kiara said, "Celia isn't a stupid woman. I told her I came in one morning to find that someone had thrown things on the floor, cut up some of the clothing we sell, broken candles and other things, and then left broken mirror pieces and salt all over, as I guess happened at the other shops. She has to know that even if I did kill Flora, I certainly wouldn't admit it to anyone, particularly not a member of the media."

"Of course not. Same thing with me," I said.

But I would still talk to Celia later, get her impression about her interview with Kiara, and her interview with Padraic, too. I needed to find out whether, as she'd verbally attacked them, either of the business owners had shown any indication of lies or hedging.

I didn't imagine they had.

Which meant I had yet another Destiny shopowner who I'd considered a potential murderer to remove from my list. That would be the outcome of today's investigation.

But I wished I knew who to interview to end up with the knowledge that I'd actually found the killer.

TWENTY-TWO

Justin stopped in at the Lucky Dog later that morning. I was not only surprised to see him, but also surprised that he had Killer with him. Wasn't the police chief on duty today? His dog was a pet, not a K-9.

Jeri started to approach him, but, smiling, I nodded to her and she understood. I'd be the one to wait on him — assuming he was here to buy something for his dog. Otherwise, I wanted to talk to him. Maybe. As long as he didn't give me a hard time.

I released Pluckie's leash from the counter and we walked toward Justin and Killer, making our way through a group of tourists looking at doggy toys — including those I'd designed. I'd intended to help them out, but under the circumstances I allowed Jeri to head that way. Both Martha and Millie were talking with other customers. We'd gotten busy not long after Jeri and I had returned from the Heads-Up Penny Gift

Shop, so it looked as if we'd have a good and profitable day.

"Hi," I said as we neared Justin. I didn't have to fake a smile, though my pleasure felt a bit tentative. Why was he really here?

"Hi," he said back, but instead of addressing me further, he bent to pat Pluckie's head, setting her long black-and-white tail wagging.

I, in turn, bent slightly to stroke his Dobie's back. "So what would you like today, Killer?" We stood near the store entrance where the displays held special leashes and collars, some with rhinestones and all with symbols of superstitions, including the ever-popular four-leaf clovers and rabbits' feet. A couple toy displays were near here, too, some of the old style stuffed animals and a few of my new ones. But all the food and treats were near the back of the store, and I figured that if Killer could voice his preferences, they'd be at the top of his list.

"I decided to take an extra-long lunch hour today to come here and buy him some lucky food. Plus check out your new toys, since I see you've just gotten them in," Justin said, looking around.

I wondered right away if he intended to buy a Richy the Rabbit for Killer. I'd briefly considered not ordering any more after hearing from Brie about the enlarged rabbit's foot stuck in Flora's mouth by her killer. But I loved that design. And it wasn't Richy's fault, or mine, that he'd been used in such a terrible way.

Besides, most people didn't know about that — at least not yet, while the crime was still being investigated.

But Justin knew . . . I was curious as to whether he'd buy a Richy and, if so, whether he wanted to look more closely at this toy that had appeared to be some kind of symbol in the murder.

As it turned out, though, the toys he bought Killer were ones with holes in the center into which treats could be inserted and removed as a dog played. The ones we carried resembled large rubberized acorns.

After he paid for them, he asked, "Would you and Pluckie like to go for a short walk with us?"

Ah ha. That must be the reason he was here. Was he going to ask me more questions? Give me a hard time again?

And in fact it was a little of both. "So how's your investigation been going today?" he began as we started walking east on Destiny Boulevard. He carried a plastic bag with the items he'd bought.

I couldn't help glancing toward the Broken Mirror Bookstore as we passed it, in case Gemma happened to be looking this way. If so, what would her comment be next time we saw each other?

"Me? Investigate?" I tried to make my voice sound completely shocked, and we stopped because Pluckie did. "I'm just living my normal life. How about you? How's your official investigation been going?"

"Me? Investigate?" he mimicked. But then he added, "Same as last night — still ongoing. I don't suppose you happen to have picked up any . . . ideas you'd want to pass along to me?"

"No," I said. "And before you ask, you can see I'm doing just fine." I started walking again, and so did Pluckie.

We'd crossed Fate Street, and, in the middle of a crowd of tourists, were facing the 7-Eleven. Continuing down Fate Street would bring us to the Wishbones-to-Go eatery. It was nearing lunchtime, so I decided to pick up some sandwiches — and wishbones — for myself and my fellow Lucky Dog workers.

"Let's go this way," I said to Justin.

"Sorry, I can't. I need to get Killer home and return to the station. But I just wanted . . . Rory, you know I care about you. And worry."

He'd made that clear last night, and not for the first time. I went all melty inside. Again.

We were facing one another now, and the expression on his wonderfully handsome face as he looked down at me made me want to reach up and pull his lips to mine. But we couldn't do that till I was officially cleared as a murder suspect. Still, walking our dogs together must be at least somewhat okay. Kissing, less so.

"Thanks." My voice came out as a croak. "I care — and worry — about you, too. But please hurry your investigation along and find the real killer fast." I smiled as Killer looked up, having heard his name as I spoke. "Not you, sweetheart," I said.

"I'm doing my damnedest to step things up," Justin said. "And I know you'll keep doing your own investigating no matter what I say. So, like I said before, stay safe."

"I will," I said, crossing my fingers behind my back.

That walk and conversation made me want to step up my own investigation. When Justin and Killer headed back down Destiny Boulevard in the direction of the police station, leaving Pluckie and me at the corner, we turned and walked along Fate Street toward Wishbones-to-Go.

I was getting hungry, yes. But I also realized there might be something else I could accomplish at the restaurant besides bringing lunch back to the store.

When Pluckie and I first walked in, there was a line at the order counter, as always. Arlen's bosses were there: Evonne Albing, owner of Destiny's Luckiest Tours, and the manager, Mike Eberhart. I saw them at this place often. They'd already reached the counter, and I waved hello to them a minute later as they left with bags in their hands.

That was good. I didn't need to hold a conversation with them.

A few of the others in line in front of me looked familiar, but most didn't. I believed they all were tourists.

I wouldn't be able to sit down inside this place with Pluckie, even if I wanted to, but the owners seemed fairly relaxed about people coming in to order with their dogs along, probably because to do otherwise would turn off at least some of the tourist business. If it was against local sanitation laws, whoever enforced those apparently turned a blind eye.

I knew the menu, which was displayed above the counter, fairly well, so I didn't have to stare at it to figure out what to order today. They always had chicken and turkey sandwiches as well as burgers, and they acquired a lot of turkey wishbones and handed them out with the meals.

Not having my attention distracted was a good thing. I noticed the owner, John O'Rourke, behind the counter talking with one of his staff. I knew who he was, had met him before, and saw him here often, but as was the case with Padraic, we'd hardly spoken over the few months I'd lived in Destiny.

I'd lose my place if I went over to talk to him now, but that was okay. "Excuse me," I said to the many people already in line behind me as I moved up along the side of the counter. I waited quietly off to the side until John had finished his conversation, then called out, "Hi, John. Have a minute to talk?"

John O'Rourke was on the list of shop-owners I wanted Celia to interview, since Carolyn had named Wishbones-to-Go as one of the victims of Flora's vandalism. I didn't think Celia had come in here yet, but I figured I might as well take advantage of seeing John now.

At my call, he turned to look at me. He was in his fifties, with hair that appeared thick but had started to gray at the temples.

Surprisingly, he hadn't overindulged in the good food he sold here. Or maybe he'd wished on an abundance of wishbones to stay slender, and it had worked.

Now, he stared at me through his thick glasses, as if assessing who I was and whether he wanted to respond.

"Hi," I said again, smiling and gesturing with my head sideways, slightly, to indicate that I wanted us to step aside to talk.

Fortunately, he agreed. "Hello, Rory," he said, proceeding to walk the length of the counter and come around the far end toward me. Pluckie and I joined him there. He looked down at my dog and said, "Let's go outside."

"Sure."

In a minute, we were on the patio at the front of the restaurant. Like the inside, it was furnished with a few small bedraggled tables with uncomfortable chairs. Wishbones-to-Go was designed to be mostly a takeout place, not a full-service restaurant.

John led me to the far outside corner of the building. "How are you, Rory?" His tone suggested he was just being polite and didn't really care.

"I've been better." I tried to make it sound as if I preferred not to answer. "And you? I mean — well, I understand that your place was broken into and trashed, like the Lucky Dog was." I glanced tellingly toward the window into Wishbones.

"Yeah, it was." The lines in his thin face deepened as he frowned down at me through his glasses. "And I heard all about how Flora Curtival chewed out everyone in town at the end of the Destiny Welcome on Friday, saying she'd done all this damage in retaliation for our good luck superstitions not fixing her marriage during her earlier visit with her husband. What an idiotic idea, even for Destiny. But I supposed her anger must have included me, since my place was vandalized."

I hadn't noticed John that night at the Welcome, and I gathered from what he was saying now that he hadn't been there.

Which hadn't kept him from hearing what had happened, of course, despite it supposedly being bad luck to talk about it. Or maybe after Flora's outburst, people weren't worried anymore about talking about it.

"Her anger definitely included me, too," I rasped, drawing my gaze down to our feet. John wore comfortable looking athletic shoes and clean white slacks. His shirt was white, too — apparently this was part of his uniform as the owner of a place that sold food.

Had he worn white when he'd killed Flora and stuffed a Richy the Rabbit's foot in her mouth? He certainly appeared strong enough to have hit her in the head and then smother her, the way she'd apparently been murdered.

Startled by my own thoughts, I looked up at John again. Of all the people I'd spoken with, he was the first one that my subconscious thoughts had begun to imagine as a possible killer.

Why? His attitude didn't seem particularly bad. But there was something I couldn't explain — yet — that dug at me.

I decided right there to make sure Celia not only interviewed him quickly but that she brought Derek along. I suddenly didn't trust this guy, although I couldn't say exactly why. I definitely wanted their impressions of him, too.

But of course my impression of him, and theirs, wouldn't be enough to sic Justin and the police department on his tail. Not without evidence.

"So how did you kill our friend Flora?" John asked, in a voice full of both irony and accusation. "She accused you of setting the cops on her before you got to her, I heard."

Startled, I felt my head shake as I looked up at him. He believed I was the killer.

Or was he taking that position to protect himself? Maybe that's what I was sensing.

"Yes, she did," I responded in a low voice. "And that's a good reason for me *not* to have hurt her, since I'd be so obvious a suspect."

"Well, aren't you the obvious suspect?" John hurled back at me. "And aren't you not under arrest because you're putting out for our police chief?"

I gasped, stepped back, and glared, feeling my right hand clench and release as if it couldn't decide whether to slap or punch him. Pluckie, standing at my feet, obviously sensed my anger and started to growl.

"Shut that creature up before I kick it out of here," John said, loudly enough that a couple of people at nearby patio tables glanced at us.

"You will not kick my dog," I hissed at him. "And you will not get away with murder." I straightened my shoulders. "You know, I came here to buy lunch for myself and several others, which I still intend to do even though I hate the idea that you'll derive profit from it. But you are not going to ruin my lunch, no matter how much of a murderous lunatic you are."

I pivoted away from him, realizing that I was shaking. And he hadn't even admitted to murder. Far from it. Instead, he'd accused me of it.

Yet his sometimes-restrained, sometimes-belligerent manner? I could see him killing a person that he wanted to retaliate against.

But how on earth would I ever prove it?

I ignored him and everyone else as Pluckie and I reentered the restaurant and I got at the back of the line, still trembling.

That's when I noticed who was standing right in front of us: Brad Nereida, of the Wish-on-a-Star children's shop — the other person Celia had interviewed yesterday, who I was supposed to talk to today in order to determine if he was a viable murder suspect.

Heavens. This was a regular Wednesday, but my luck today was very good. One way or another, I was about to engage in my fourth interview, with yet another person on my suspect list.

I saw John pass me on his way back behind the counter. Fortunately for him, he wasn't near enough for me to trip him.

Instead, I moved around just a little in the line and said to the man in front of me, "Oh, hi, Brad. How are you?"

And what did you tell Celia Vardox? Something that indicates you're a viable murder suspect?

Twenty-Three

I didn't ask him that, though. At least not yet.

"Fine," he said. "And you?"

"Fine, too." Was Brad's response as potentially false as mine? Not likely. And really, I was fine. At least for now, while I remained free and not under arrest, although I wished all the suspicions of me were eradicated and the real culprit caught. "Grabbing a little lunch here?" Boy, was my end of this conversation exciting. I wanted it to lead to more, assuming I had the time and felt comfortable that no one was listening in. But I wanted what I said to sound perfectly innocent.

"Yes, for myself and my staff," Brad said. As usual, he looked and sounded a bit tired.

"Too bad we didn't contact each other." I had to raise my voice a little since the crowd here was growing, both in size and noise level. "I'm here to get lunch for my helpers at the Lucky Dog, too. Maybe we could have coordinated things so just one of us had to come out here."

His face seemed to brighten a little. "That would be a good thing to do in the future. We're busy at Wish-on-a-Star, and though I've left my couple of employees on their own before, it always helps for me to be there with them."

"I hope they're doing a great job," I said, then added, "Are Lorraine and the kids back yet?" If so, he might not need both of those helpers for long, since his wife helped him run the store when his kids were in school. But since he was here, I figured I knew the answer.

"No." He paused, and his smile looked rather lonely to me. "Her mom is a little worse, so they're staying in San Diego for a while longer."

"Oh. Sorry to hear that. Was that why they went now, because her mother's ill?"

"Unfortunately, yes."

I glanced over his shoulder as another customer picked up his meal. Brad looked around, too, and we were able to move up a little, Pluckie staying right with me.

"Well, I hope your mother-in-law gets well fast," I said. I searched my mind for how to address the vandalism at his shop while standing here in this crowd of people who might eavesdrop — and came up with nothing except, "Hey, you know, I've got some other ideas of things we might be able to do together to help both of our shops." Like I could let him buy some of the toys I'd designed; a few might work for kids as well as dogs. Or so I'd tell him. "If you don't mind waiting for a couple of extra minutes after you get your food, let's walk back together."

Brad didn't look exactly thrilled, but I added, "Please? I really think if we retailers here in Destiny combine our ideas and resources, we'd all make a lot more money. And I do have some ideas. Okay?"

"Well, okay."

I ignored the reluctance in his voice and said, "Great!"

It took only about five minutes till we'd both given our orders and been handed our bags of sandwiches and wishbones. By the time I got mine, Brad stood near the door beyond the still-growing line of customers. Pluckie sat right beside me, nose in the air as she sniffed the smells of sandwiches being made and wishbones being given out.

I glanced around once more before leaving the cash register area, looking for John. I glimpsed him through the open window to the kitchen. No way could I call out to him that I wished he'd just come clean and confess to killing Flora. Instead, I waited till he appeared to look out at the burgeoning group of hungry clients, and I smiled and waved.

He only scowled back. Not exactly a sign of guilt, but neither was it proof of his innocence.

Then, pulling Pluckie's leash slightly so she'd keep up with me, I scurried as quickly as I could past the line of people till I reached Brad at the door. I still couldn't believe my luck, getting this opportunity to talk to four people who might have had a reason to kill Flora. "Might," of course, being the operative word. Considering John's attitude, maybe "might" would become "did" — although his having a motive, or even acting like he did, wasn't enough to prove him guilty.

I'd have to reassess Brad, though, now that I was considering him a suspect. And I was about to have an opportunity to question him, it seemed.

"Sorry," I said as I reached him, without saying what I was sorry for. He could take it to mean I felt bad about delaying him, if he wanted. One thing it wasn't was an apology for the conversation I hoped to have

286

with him on the way back to our shops.

We set off. I nearly tripped over a tourist who was bending to pick up one of the heads-up pennies with which the sidewalk here, too, was seeded. I caught myself, said "Excuse me," and with sweet and concerned Pluckie still at my side, hurried to catch up with Brad. He hadn't stopped even to be polite and wait for me, let alone make sure I wasn't hurt.

Well, I didn't have to like his ungentle-manliness to keep on talking to him.

"Okay," I said, "I wanted to let you know a little about the dog toys I've designed and manufactured. Some may be cute enough for kids, too, so you might want to look at them and consider them for your shop."

"Like the stuffed rabbit with the large rabbit's foot?" His tone sounded so wry that I turned to stare up at his face as we walked.

"Then you heard . . ." I chose not to finish, hoping he'd do it for me.

"That Flora was found with that foot in her mouth? Yeah."

"I guess word's getting around." Hey, as much as I hated realizing that maybe the whole town was learning that ugly little fact, maybe I could use it in my favor now. "I didn't kill her, Brad. Honest. Yes, I was irritated with her after she announced she'd

been the one to vandalize all our shops —
and steal nearly all the toys I'd designed, by
the way, including that particular one. It's
no surprise she had it with her when she
was killed. Given her rant at the end of the
Welcome, I figure the real killer jumped on
the opportunity to use the toys, especially
that rabbit foot, to try to frame me."

"Mmm-hmm." It wasn't easy for me to
hear his ironic mumble with the usual
sidewalk conversations and other noises going on around us.

But I figured I could use his apparent
dubiousness in my favor, somewhat, at least.
"You sound as convinced as Celia Vardox
did when she interviewed me. Did she
interview you? I gathered she and her
brother are trying to talk to everyone whose
shops Flora trashed for a series of articles
they plan to write for the *Star.*"

"Yes, Celia talked to me yesterday," Brad
replied. "Not sure I'd call it an interview,
exactly. More like an accusation."

"Sounds familiar," I said.

We'd crossed the street and were now
walking north on Fate Street. We weren't
far now from the Lucky Dog, but I didn't
want to end this conversation.

Accordingly, I added, "Look, you already
know I'm considered one of the top sus-

pects. Maybe *the* top suspect." I half waited for him to say something acknowledging this, but then went on. "Flora damaged your shop, too. If I go there now, can you show me what she did and where? I assume you've fixed it up by now, but I'm still trying to learn all I can in case it somehow helps me to clear myself."

"Sure, come on," he said, not sounding at all thrilled about the idea. As a result, Pluckie and I crossed Destiny Boulevard with him.

"How long ago did she vandalize your place?" I continued. No one crossed with us, so I wasn't too concerned about any eavesdropping.

"A couple of weeks," Brad said.

"Oh, then your wife was still in town then?"

"No, she and the kids left before that."

"Then your poor mother-in-law has been ill for a long time. That's a shame."

He came up with another "Mmm-hmmm."

We reached the Wish-on-a-Star shop and its quaint Gold Rush architecture. I recalled having wished on the display in the front window right after I'd reached Destiny a few months earlier — a large star-shaped light that zoomed across the top of the window like a shooting star. The window also displayed good-luck-themed children's items, mainly toys and clothes.

I considered stopping to wish on the star again, just in case it actually did produce good results — like getting an innocent person out of the spotlight of being a murder suspect. Previously, I'd wished on it to help me make the decision about whether to stay in Destiny. I'd decided to stay, and until recently I'd believed it had been the right decision.

Not so much now.

Instead, I decided I'd better try to ask Brad my last question, since talking in front of his staff wouldn't be a good idea. "Just one thing," I said to him, maneuvering a bit so I stood in front of him at the door. "I'll want you to point out what Flora did, like I said. But I'm also trying to figure out why she chose only particular shops to vandalize. Had you met her before?"

He glared at me, then looked down at the bag of food in his hand and back up at my face, clearly trying to convey that he wanted to get inside and feed his staff. But I just stood there, an expectant smile on my face. Or maybe, in fact, it was just a hopeful smile. He might choose not to respond.

"Sure I'd met her," he said after another

beat. "She came to my shop in her real estate guise, trying to get me to list this property with her. Of course I said no. Wish-on-a-Star isn't for sale, period. I assumed, when she admitted she was the person who'd trashed the place, that that was the reason why — revenge for my not wanting to sell it and give her a commission."

That made sense, I figured. Or as much sense as anything else about why Flora chose to exact her revenge on some shopowners in Destiny but not others.

"I see," I said. When I moved out of the way, he held the door open for Pluckie and me.

There were only a few customers in the shop and none of them appeared ready to decide what they wanted. They browsed along shelves that, like mine, held a variety of toys, but unlike mine had games and many kinds of clothing — all for kids. Brad distributed the sandwiches and wishbones to his helpers, a guy and girl who both appeared college-aged. Maybe they were here visiting Destiny to do research for school papers and happened to want jobs while they were in town. Or maybe they'd just fallen in love with the place and decided to move here. Or maybe none of the above; I might just be allowing my imagination to run wild.

When the assistants walked off behind some of the tall shelves, most likely to eat their lunches, I looked at Brad. "Tell me about the vandalism," I said, and he did. Some of the wooden shelves had been thrown to the floor, scattering children's toys such as several board games of tic-tac-toe, where the pieces to be placed on the board consisted of green shamrocks and white horseshoes.

"They were all salvageable, fortunately," Brad said. "So were the T-shirts and luck-themed baseball caps, which were tossed all over the place."

"And was anything unlucky left on the floor?"

"Yes." It turned out to be the standard broken mirror pieces and salt.

"Did you have any idea, at first, who did it?" I couldn't help asking.

"If what you really want to know is whether I killed Flora for doing it, do you think I would tell you that?" His expression looked both wry and irritated.

"I think that would be a no," I said, and he nodded.

TWENTY-FOUR

I didn't stay much longer in Wish-on-a-Star. I'd gotten what I needed to — more knowledge about the damage Flora had inflicted and why she might have chosen Brad's shop.

Although trashing it because she wasn't hired to sell it seemed a bit much, so did her apparent reason for vandalizing the other shops. The fact that I'd told the cops about a threat she'd made against Destiny was evidently her reason for hating me at the end, according to her tirade, but why had she hated me before? Just because I didn't want to buy or lease property she represented? And what about everyone else? Because she blamed them for not changing her luck a year ago? Just how had she expected them to do that, even though this was Destiny?

Had she simply been crazy?

No matter. She was dead, the victim of a

homicide, and someone needed to pay for that.

The guilty party, whoever that might be. Not me.

I sighed as I rearranged the bag of food in my hand and opened the door to the Lucky Dog. I let Pluckie enter ahead of me.

The place was busy, which made me smile. Everyone — Martha, Jeri, and Millie — were all waiting on customers who were mostly accompanied by dogs, and there were others who appeared as though they, too, might need help. I hurried to put the bag on the counter. I'd jump in and take care of at least one of these people right away.

Later, we might need to take turns eating our lunches.

The person nearest the door was an older gentleman holding a Jack Russell Terrier. My first, silent reaction was to wonder whether this older gentleman had enough energy to keep up with a Jack Russell. On the other hand, they were together and I'd no reason to believe they weren't compatible, especially when the dog saw me looking at him and wagged his tail.

Pluckie, who stayed at my side, started to stand on her hind legs to greet the other dog. I didn't know what the man might think about that so I said, "Sit, Pluckie."

"Cute dog," he said. Then, grinning at me, he continued. "So tell me what superstitions there are about dogs. Is my dog lucky or unlucky? If she's unlucky, what can I buy her here to change that?"

"For one thing, black dogs are lucky, and those with white on them, like my Pluckie, are particularly good luck if you're on your way to a business meeting."

"Well, I suspect the same goes for white-and-brown dogs like mine," the man said. "I'm in the tech industry and take Wiffle to work with me, and I have to say I'm pretty lucky."

"Wonderful!" I said, and I meant it. That indicated he might have a lot of money to spend on stuff for his beloved Wiffle.

And in fact, Wiffle got a new collar and leash, both decorated with outlines of crossed fingers, as well as a variety of fun toys — including one of my Richy the Rabbits. I proudly told the customer that these were new and that I'd designed them.

I didn't mention that one had been left at a crime scene in a compromising position.

They soon left, with Wiffle wearing his new collar and leash and walking proudly beside the man. I'd already hooked Pluckie to the counter, so I was ready to help the next customer, and there still were enough of them that I didn't want to break for lunch.

I had urged Martha to head upstairs to eat, though, and Millie had gone with her, carrying their sandwiches and wishbones and leaving Jeri to help me in the shop for now.

When Millie returned a while later, I figured it was time to let Jeri go eat — but then I noticed who was walking in the door.

I certainly hadn't anticipated Celia Vardox coming here. She rarely did, and now that she and I were sort of conspiring together in an attempt to find Flora's killer, I definitely didn't want us seen together.

She must have anticipated that. She made her way around the nearest shelves and the customers oohing and aahing over some more cute dog toys and approached me.

"Hi, Rory," she said stiffly. "I'd like to ask you a few questions regarding some matters that have gone on around here."

"You want to interview me for a story?" I asked incredulously.

Glancing around, she seemed to make sure no one was close to us and gave a quick wink. "That's right." She wore a long blue dress today that was belted at the waist and, as always, held a pad of paper and a pen.

The edge of a tablet computer extended from a pocket in the bag she carried over her shoulder. If she wasn't here in her usual role of reporter, she certainly was giving that impression.

"Well . . ." I began.

It turned out that Jeri wasn't very far away. She must have overheard Celia's request for an interview and sidled up to me. "Not a good idea," she sang very softly.

"I get it," I murmured back. "But —" I looked at Celia. "Look, I can guess what you want to ask me, and the answer is no." I scanned the area near us.

She followed my lead. "I'm not about to accuse you of a crime, Rory. I simply want your perspective on some information I've gotten from our police department."

Her grin told me what this would be about if she were actually serious: Could I prove that I didn't kill Flora, since they were certain I had?

Okay, if I was right about things, she was joking. But whatever her real reason for coming here, I did need to talk to her. Had any of her probing interviews given her enough knowledge, maybe even evidence, for us to start going after one particular person?

Or was she simply getting frustrated with

what we'd been up to and wanting to either rev it up — or tone it down?

Whichever, I needed to find out.

A few minutes later we sat in the back storeroom on a couple of folding chairs near the card table, which was laden with merchandise that hadn't yet been shelved in the store for sale. We huddled close together as if we'd previously agreed on how to proceed with this conversation, which we hadn't.

"So what's up, Celia?" I asked softly.

She leaned even closer toward me, close enough that I figured if I inhaled deeply I might be able to figure out what she'd had for lunch. I didn't, of course, although I did sense some soft floral cologne.

"I just want you to fill me in on what you've learned so far," she said.

"Sure, if you'll do the same for me."

We both seemed to hesitate for a few moments, as if neither wanted to go first. A silly kind of standoff, I thought. We were aiming for the same goal, even if it was for different reasons. And we'd already discussed how to work together.

It even seemed to be succeeding . . . didn't it?

"I've spoken with most of the people we've talked about, and probably even more than you've interviewed," I began. "The ones who have talked with you seemed to feel you were accusing them of murder."

"That's the whole point, isn't it?" Celia interrupted, an expression of satisfaction on her attractive and perceptive face.

"Exactly. And it's been working out pretty well. I'm commiserating with them, since we're supposedly in the same position — being accused by you. Lots of empathy in those conversations. I'd like to get your impressions on a couple of them, actually."

"That's nice. But here's what I really want to know." Celia leaned even closer toward me. "Are you zeroing in on any particular person as the most likely killer yet? I'd love to focus on that person, do a surreptitious background check, then be ready to pounce with a great reveal-all article" — at my glare, she backed down just a little — "but only when you and I agree. Or," she added with more of a conniving cat's smile, "when it's clear the cops are ready to make an arrest."

"And you have a contact at the department who'll let you know that?" It wouldn't be Justin, I was sure of that. But he might want to know who on his staff Celia could be referring to.

She was too smart to make that revelation. "Well, sure, I've got a few connections," she said, the epitome of innocence in her slight grin.

Was it true? And if so, who was she alluding to?

And should I at least hint about it to Justin?

Not yet. Maybe not at all. I didn't have enough to go on, even for this.

And what if Celia was just exaggerating, or simply trying to fool me about her insider access to the police department? Or perhaps indulging in wishful thinking?

Well, I'd play along for now, act as if I fully believed her.

"Great!" I said. "Please let me know when one or more of the cops tells you I'm finally about to be let off the hook — which is the correct result of all this, of course."

"Of course." But her tone was wry, as if she was humoring me.

Was that what this was all about for her — a way to stay close enough to me to check out how I was doing and keep tabs on when I'd actually be arrested? Horror flowed through me, but I quickly got it under control. I needed to continue as if all was well between us and we were actually making progress to clear my name.

In fact, that still appeared to be a good

potential outcome of our inquiries.

"In the meantime, though," Celia continued, "I'd really like to know what your thoughts are. Who you're really suspicious of at this point."

I wasn't about to tell her that now. "Not sure," I said. "I haven't really zeroed in on any of them. Nor have I eliminated any." I didn't choose to share that the person on the list with the worst attitude was John O'Rourke of Wishbones-to-Go, or that he was my number one suspect because of it. I wasn't even about to tell her the order in which I was considering people as viable suspects.

"That's too bad," she said. "Even so, I'd like your thoughts on each of them."

I hesitated, but only for a moment. "Okay, I'll tell you, but I'll want to hear your suspicions, too. Maybe we should both write down who we think is most likely to have done it."

Celia's expression changed from innocent and interested to disgusted. "I don't think we're going to get over this 'you show me yours, then I'll show you mine' mentality, are we?"

I shrugged. "Maybe not."

"Wonderful. Well, are there any people on our list that you haven't talked to yet?"

"I don't think so. Are there any new suspects you've added to our list?"

"Nope." She didn't elaborate on her response and I believed her . . . kind of.

I sighed. "Okay, here are the people I've talked to so far, each the day after you confronted them." I pondered the order for a moment, then told how yesterday I'd pretended to sympathize with Padraic Hassler of the Shamrock Steakhouse, and today I'd met with Kiara Mardeer of Heads-Up Penny Gift Shop, John O'Rourke of Wishbones-to-Go, and Brad Nereida of Wish-On-A-Star Children's Shop. I didn't mention Serina of the Rainbow B&B or Carolyn Innes of Buttons of Fortune, partly because they were my friends, but also because Celia hadn't had them on her list to interview. I'd spoken with them more informally than the others, or at least that's the way I considered it.

"So who do you think is guilty?" Celia's expression was once more the picture of innocence.

"Why don't you tell me your thoughts about it first?" I said.

She laughed. "Okay, Rory," she said. "We already went through all of this when we decided to work together, didn't we? Well, I can tell you this: so far, no one seems to stand out to me as being the clear guilty party. Their attitudes were similar about not really wanting to go on the record in an article I was writing, but they all denied doing anything to Flora no matter how angry they might have been with her." She paused. "And they got angry with me for pushing them, which actually was fun."

"It certainly seemed to encourage them to talk to me," I said. "Although part of that appeared to not entirely be sympathy, but maybe attempts to get me to reveal things to them."

"Like admit you did it?" Celia grinned.

"Right," I agreed glumly.

"Okay. I'm not sure any of this is actually getting us anywhere," she said.

"I'm not sure either."

Even though our conversation hadn't led to anything I could pursue as evidence, at least not yet, I figured it would be good to complete this non-investigation of everyone we deemed possible suspects, and then decide what to do after that.

Perhaps I would even share whatever suspicions I had, so that Celia could use her media resources to push a bit harder for the truth.

"Well," Celia said, "I'm planning to go grab some coffee early tomorrow at Beware-of-Bubbles, when both Marypat and Dan Dresdan are likely to be there. I'll put my pushiest and most accusatory demeanor on and see where that gets us."

"And I'm sure I'm going to need a cup of coffee soon after so I can ask how they're doing," I said.

TWENTY-FIVE

The rest of the day at the Lucky Dog was lots of fun, as it turned out. By the time Celia and I exited the back room, a whole pack of dogs was in the shop, several of them playing ball and keep-away with Pluckie. Their owners were with them, too, of course — a van-load of tourists in their twenties taking a tour of this part of California with their canine families.

They sounded fascinated by superstitions and obsessed with dogs — my kind of people.

At my suggestion, we locked the shop doors temporarily and loosed the hounds for a ten minute romp, which everyone appeared to enjoy, especially the dogs.

The event resulted in our sale of a lot of the toys they played with: balls of many sizes decorated with symbols of good luck as well as stuffed toys and even lucky-symbol dog treats.

"This was fantastic," said a girl who'd already acquired a Destiny sweatshirt somewhere and who now bought a dog sweater that almost matched it for her Bichon Frise — as well as one of my Richy the Rabbits. "Candy and I will definitely be back here again. Soon. With or without our friends."

I smiled and encouraged her, holding up my hand with my fingers crossed. "Pluckie and I certainly hope so."

Martha, Millie, and Jeri also gathered around grinning, and we were all sorry to see this group leave. On the other hand, some other intrigued tourists were waiting outside. When we'd informed the group on the sidewalk that our closure was very temporary, that had apparently acted as a magnet to draw other people, whether their pets were with them or not, to come in and buy stuff.

As the afternoon drew to a close and the number of customers wound down, I sneaked off temporarily with Martha so we could review the day's receipts. They were substantial. And she was clearly happy about it.

Me too.

"This place has continued to do so well since you took over as manager," my boss and senior friend gushed. "I wish you'd come here ages ago."

Was this a time to ask how long she intended to remain active in its management — or whether she might be interested, ultimately, in selling? I'd hinted at the possibility of my future purchase before, and she'd not really responded much, probably by design rather than due to lack of understanding of what I was driving at.

"I'm just delighted I'm here now," was all I said. Martha's health had improved since I'd first met her, and as long as that continued, I'd most likely hold back on proposing any long-term changes.

She headed upstairs at her usual time, Millie accompanying her at first while I got ready to close the store and Jeri headed to her family's shop. As always, I was glad that Martha's need to use a wheelchair was limited to times when she needed to go a few blocks away, like to a Destiny Welcome; she needed no major help on her own stairway.

I wasn't surprised when Gemma showed up, since we'd already talked about the possibility of grabbing dinner together, and perhaps I shouldn't have been surprised that Stuart and Justin soon joined her inside the Lucky Dog. In fact, I'd anticipated Stuart — but not Justin. Nor Killer, who was with him. He'd apparently taken the time to go home for his dog.

We decided to eat at the Shamrock Steakhouse, since it was good and close and a place we'd been together before. Gemma and Stuart had even been with me when I'd gone off to have my chat with Padraic about Celia, the *Destiny Star* . . . and Flora's murder. I didn't consider him the most viable murder suspect and hoped he now thought the same of me, too, despite his accusations that day.

Pluckie and I walked beside Justin and Killer, following Gemma and Stuart. "So how's your murder investigation going now?" Justin asked, checking in as usual.

I rolled my eyes, not easy to do since I was also watching for sidewalk cracks to avoid. "Still fine," I finally said, brightly. "And yours?"

I liked the sound of his laugh, as always. I also liked that he reached over to give me a slight hug that brought me against his hard cop's body. "Okay, Rory," he said. "Truce, at least for tonight. But I'm still counting on you to be careful. And also to let me know if you ever get to the point that you have a real suspect and why you feel that way, so I can make sure our official investigation heads that direction, too."

"And if you ever get to the point where those around you buy into the idea of my innocence, I hope you'll let me know that as well."

"If and when I can," he said.

"And I'm supposed to feel reassured?"

"As reassured as I can promise at the moment." He didn't sound happy about that, and I certainly wasn't.

While we were waiting to be seated, Gemma's phone rang. She moved off to the side to take the call but kept an eye on us and followed us out to the patio. There, one of the many wait staff dressed in blarney green showed us to a table beneath a heat lamp, a good thing on this nippy November night.

I ordered a salad, and so did Gemma. The guys both ordered steaks, and I made them promise to save some for the dogs.

Then, when I saw Gemma give me a slight nod, I excused myself to head to the restroom, and so did she. I ordered Justin and Stuart to keep an eye on Pluckie.

"I just wanted to let you know it was Brie on the phone," Gemma said as we made our ways around the outside tables and entered the restaurant door. The restroom hallway was in front of us. "She has a couple of rental places to show us and she said one of them has a number of interested people already. She wants to schedule our visit for tomorrow, but the owners of the Broken Mirror are coming in and I won't be able to get away. Can you check it out?"

"Sure," I said. I'd work it in somehow. I had no idea what made an apartment that popular in Destiny unless it had some good luck tied into it — or at least that was what its owner or real estate agent maintained. I wasn't sure I'd believe it if Brie said so, but, in case it turned out to be perfect enough to convince Gemma and me to move now, I'd hate to let a really good place slip through our fingers.

"Great. How about if you call her and tell her?" Gemma checked her phone for the number that had just called and I pressed it into mine.

In a minute, I'd scheduled a time the next day to meet Brie at her office. She'd take me to see the rental unit, supposedly a gorgeous condo in the town's main residential area. Its address? Unit seven at 7 Ladybug Lane, and of course seven was supposed to be a lucky number. Plus, ladybugs were reputed to be lucky, and there was even a song called "Lucky Ladybug."

I wasn't sure if this would make Gemma and me jump on it, but it wouldn't hurt to go check it out.

And use the opportunity to ask Brie some more questions.

As I headed again for the ladies room, I spotted Padraic talking to one of the servers just outside the kitchen. I'd been hoping to run into him so I could do a brief follow-up of our prior conversation. Did I have any more reason to suspect him now than I had before? Only perhaps because I hadn't found the real killer for certain, despite my suspicions of John O'Rourke. I couldn't resist joining the group.

"Hi, Padraic."

The male server he'd been talking to slipped away as the boss turned to face me.

"Hello, Rory. Are you here for dinner or to discuss murder?" His big smile beneath his silvery hair told me he was joking.

"Oh, murder, of course," I said in a low voice, sidling up closer to him. At his wide-eyed look of panic, I was the one to smile. "Or just to have one heck of a great Shamrock Steakhouse salad. Which do you think?"

He appeared relieved and managed a laugh. "I think a salad's a good idea."

"Me too." But I took yet another step closer. "Especially if you happen to have thought of someone you think should con-

311

fess to the murder instead of me." I doubted I'd ever forget how he'd told me to confess to save himself from being questioned by the cops.

"If I did, I'd have let your friend the police chief over there" — he gestured with his shoulder toward the windows to the patio — "know who and why."

"Sounds good," I said as his attention was once more distracted, this time by a guy in a white chef's hat.

I still couldn't really pounce on Padraic as being the main suspect in my amateur investigation — unless, of course, he happened to be one heck of an actor as well as a leprechaun-like restaurant owner. I hadn't erased him from my mental list of suspects, but neither was he a major player there.

I headed at last to the restroom. Gemma was near the door but said she'd wait for me. We soon returned to our table. Dinner was enjoyable, and so was the company. The dogs got their tastes of steak, and I got my Justin fix.

Later, he and I again walked side by side back to the B&B, following Gemma and Stuart. They'd both dressed in blue business-casual that evening, Stuart in a navy button-down shirt and slacks, and Gemma in a knee-length dress. They looked, and acted, like they belonged together, but Stuart was leaving the next day to return to his editor's job.

I wondered if they would ever commit to one another, or if this sometimes remote, sometimes close-up relationship was what they really wanted.

And if whoever it was that Gemma had seen in the mirror was a better choice for her.

Me? Interestingly enough, although I still missed my Warren, I was beginning to feel pretty close to Justin — despite how much his attitude about me as a murder suspect and detective bothered me right now.

"I don't suppose you'd like to bring me up to date on what you're doing and who you're talking to," he said as we stopped to let Killer raise his leg on a tree trunk.

"You're right," I said. "But before you warn me again, yes, I'm being careful. And yes, I'll let you know if anyone starts to stand out and I get any evidence against them." Just because John O'Rourke's attitude had, in fact, made him stand out in my mind, I couldn't really justify siccing the cops on him . . . not yet, at least.

"Thanks, Rory."

His tone sounded so serious that I pivoted to look up at him. He in turn stared down

313

at me with an expression on his face that I wasn't sure I could interpret — but it appeared to be so full of love that I started shaking.

Not for long, though. He pulled me into his arms, which caused our dogs' leashes to tangle a bit.

Our kiss wasn't full of heat and sex but soft and sweet and ongoing, as if it was to cement some kind of commitment we'd just made. But we hadn't.

Had we?

"When this is over, Rory," Justin said in a husky voice as he pulled away, "I have something important to ask you."

Oh, heavens. Was he going to ask me to marry him?

If so, how would I respond?

Yes, yes, yes, shouted something inside me. I almost repeated it aloud but didn't. And something else inside me apologized to Warren, one final time, I hoped, for the thought.

Besides, what he had in mind could be something altogether different — taking a trip together or even just agreeing to a weekly dog-walking date.

We continued walking and soon reached the B&B.

Gemma and Stuart were already inside.

Justin and I and the dogs strolled over to the lawn beside the parking area and I let Pluckie conduct her final business of the night.

"What's on your agenda for tomorrow?" Justin asked.

"Why do you ask — so you can be there giving me orders if I'm throwing questions out to possible murder suspects?" I kept my tone light.

"Of course." His voice, too, didn't sound quite serious, even though we both were.

"Well, you can feel pretty reassured, since I'm just going to go look at a potential rental unit for Gemma and me."

I didn't tell him that I planned to follow up with the Dresdans after Celia confronted them, as she'd done with our other suspects.

And I didn't know, just then, how tomorrow's activities would lead me in a whole different direction.

TWENTY-SIX

The next morning, I felt rather restless even after Pluckie and I had gotten to the Lucky Dog.

Would I like the rental unit Brie intended to show me that afternoon?

Would I be able to pounce on it if I did like it, or would someone else who'd expressed interest get it first?

And what about Gemma? If I liked it, could I be sure she would, too? Most likely, yes. We'd been friends long enough for me to feel fairly certain I knew her tastes as well as my own.

Did I care that the number seven was so associated with the place? Not really, I told myself. Not this superstition agnostic. And Gemma wasn't any more sure of the reality of superstitions than I was.

Even so . . .

As usual, first thing before the store opened, I called Martha to make sure she was okay and that she'd be downstairs on time. Then I checked shelves and restocked those that needed it. I did a quick computer scan of what we'd sold yesterday and confirmed that all credit card purchases had gone through.

Millie came in a short while before we opened at ten. She headed upstairs to help Martha, as she often did. I waited for them to return and, once they did, I took their coffee orders.

I was going to Beware-of-Bubbles Coffee Shop — both because I wanted coffee and because I needed to take a walk.

And if I happened to run into Celia there interviewing the owners? That wasn't my intention — not really — but it wouldn't hurt.

I'd considered calling Celia to ask when exactly she was heading to the shop and whether she'd made an official appointment to talk with the Dresdans, but decided not to. I was stopping by there anyway. If she was there for her interview, I'd stay out of her way unless she indicated in some manner that she wanted me to join her.

And it might actually be a good thing if innocent little me happened to be there while nasty reporter Celia was browbeating the shop owners. My role as empathizer might appear even more natural than it had in some of the other instances.

Pluckie seemed overjoyed when I unhooked her leash from the counter. Her company on this walk would help me to chill out a bit — I hoped. The day was unusually warm for this time of year, but I wore a jacket over my Lucky Dog aqua knit shirt nonetheless. I figured I'd take it off soon.

The usual Destiny crowd populated the sidewalk, which was fine with me. Better than fine. Maybe some would be shoppers for their pets. And having them prolong my walk to the coffee shop was also fine with me.

Of course Pluckie added to the time, as usual, as she sniffed the ground and other dogs' noses and butts and squatted once or twice.

But very soon, we were there.

I looked around first thing as I walked in and wasn't at all surprised to see Celia sitting at a table in the corner with Marypat Dresdan across from her. Was she interviewing just the wife without the husband? Were they taking turns?

I'd find out later. Right now, I moseyed to the end of the usual line with Pluckie. No one I knew was ahead of me, which meant I didn't have anyone to talk to, at least not immediately. I soon noticed Dan Dresdan storming his way through the seating area toward his wife. He immediately pulled another chair over to the small table where the two women sat.

That was when Celia looked up toward me, shook her head slightly in a negative manner, then got back to talking to Marypat as Dan joined them.

She didn't want me butting in now. I'd find out from her later, though, what had gone on in this conversation.

And I definitely was intrigued.

I carried one of those small cardboard trays to the Lucky Dog, since I had not only my drink to transport but some for each of the others. When I got back to my shop, I was pleased to see it was crowded.

It was probably a good thing that I hadn't joined Celia during her interrogation/ interview. I would just return later to do my now-habitual commiseration with Celia's targets, this time the owners of Beware-of-Bubbles.

I did get a call from Celia about a half hour later. Fortunately, I was in the storeroom again, alone, so I could talk.

"What the heck were you doing there?"

she stormed over the phone. "You could have ruined everything."

"How? Were you showing them sympathy for the vandalism Flora caused and indicating you believed I was the killer?" My own temper was a bit stoked.

"Not at all. I was pushing them. Demanding answers to stuff the police probably already asked them, like where they were the night Flora was killed, and had they recognized any merchandise from your shop that Flora had apparently stolen — without mentioning why I asked that. But they'd already heard about the toy rabbit's foot in her mouth."

"And what did they say? What did they do?"

"Nothing unusual. They got aggravated that I'd dare ask them questions and consider including them in an article about a murder when they'd had nothing to do with it except for being vandalism victims of the murder victim. They're innocent, or so they proclaimed over and over, especially when I kept suggesting that they had as much reason to kill Flora as anyone else. They did, in fact, point out and describe where she'd vandalized their place — it was right inside the area where drinks are brewed."

"How did they react as they talked about

it?" I could guess. What victim of this kind of crime could simply describe it with no emotion?

"Angrily, but they did keep it under control — and kept assuring me that it would take more than that, even peppered with broken mirror pieces and lots of grains of salt, to make either of them decide to harm anyone physically. Call the cops, yes. Kill a person, even Flora? No."

"Did you believe them?" I had to ask, even though I figured I knew this answer too.

"Yeah, I did. And guess who they suggested I might want to interview next as a possible suspect?"

That had to be me. "Do you think they'll be empathetic with me despite their supposed suspicions against me?"

Celia's response didn't really matter. It was the pattern we'd established. I'd have to at least try talking to them.

"They seemed like nice enough people. Maybe they'll just figure I told you what they said so you felt you had to convince them of your innocence. But, yeah, might as well talk to them too."

I decided that wouldn't happen until tomorrow.

First of all, the established pattern required me to wait a day, and I really should stick to the established pattern.

Second, I didn't feel in the mood to stave off the Dresdans' accusations, or even pretend that I didn't know how they felt.

Most importantly, I told myself, I'd already made an appointment to talk with Brie Timons about the possible new home for Gemma and me. And I intended to keep it.

After my call with Celia ended, I walked back into the store and blinked, trying to get my mind back on track.

I had pet items to sell. And there were, as was usually the case, a lot of customers here, some who looked like they needed assistance.

I complied after placing my coffee cup on a shelf under the sales counter. My mood lightened quite a bit as I introduced a couple of Chihuahua mixes to Pluckie. Their owners, a young couple, bought not only some dog toys but also a lucky hematite amulet, similar to my dog-face one, and the man presented it to the lady — his fiancée, they informed me.

The rest of the morning progressed similarly. Jeri had to leave to go help out at the Heads-Up Penny, and Martha took an early lunch break, possibly because she was tired.

I was just happy to see her taking care of herself and relaxing for a while. She promised to be back downstairs from her apartment by one-thirty, though. I'd already told her about my two o'clock appointment with Brie, and she'd been delighted. It was, after all, another indication that I'd be staying in Destiny longer — even if we never talked much, or at all, about the possibility of my taking over the store someday.

Things didn't really slow down at noon, but I nevertheless encouraged Millie to go out and pick up sandwiches for herself, Martha, and me.

She soon returned with a bag of food from Wishbones-to-Go, which was what I'd anticipated — as well as three wishbones. I let her go upstairs to eat with Martha as well as break a couple of those wishbones together. I'd save my wishbone but took some surreptitious bites of sandwich behind the counter while some of my customers made decisions on what to buy.

Millie soon rejoined me and helped out with our now slightly smaller client group. Martha arrived back downstairs right on time at one-thirty.

It was time for me to go.

I thought about calling Gemma to go over any specific thoughts she had about what I should look for in this supposedly special rental, but I decided not to. For one thing, I might wind up looking at more than one possibility today, and I most likely wouldn't sign a lease without Gemma with me anyway. Although if I fell in love with the apartment associated with lucky number seven and had to jump on it right away, I might go ahead and do that and hope Gemma ultimately agreed with me.

I took Pluckie along, both for company and luck. As we went out the door she saw those two Chihuahuas walking by, and that delayed us just a little as the dogs all traded nose and butt sniffs again.

Pluckie also needed to make a couple of stops along the way. She'd been a very good girl, as always, but I hadn't had a lot of opportunity to take her out after our return from Beware-of-Bubbles.

We soon made our way from Destiny Boulevard onto Fate Street, then west on Luck Street, and down a few blocks till we were outside the charming old-style offices of Rising Moon Realty. Pluckie and I walked up the six wide outside steps and through the door. Like the last time, when I'd been here with Gemma, only two of the four inside desks were occupied, and both occupants, the same man and woman, were on their phones.

I glanced around. As far as I could tell, the photos of houses and apartments and townhouses were the same as when I'd been here before, and I gathered they were for decoration rather than to demonstrate available places.

I figured I'd have to wait for someone to let Brie know I was here, but she came through the door at the back of the large room as if fully aware I'd arrived. Hey, she was into real estate–related stuff, so maybe she had a camera aimed at the front door so she could monitor who came in on a screen in her office.

She wore a robin's egg blue pantsuit today with a navy blouse, and her graying hair looked tamed behind a blue headband. "Rory!" she exclaimed. "So glad you're here. Gemma said she'd rely on you to look at the property to determine if it's right for the two of you."

"That's right," I said.

She gave Pluckie a quizzical glance, as if wondering if my dog would behave herself, but she didn't ask. Instead, she motioned for me to follow her out the front door. "My car's outside in the parking lot," she said.

Her car turned out to be an upscale, new-model Mercedes Benz. The real estate business must pay well, I thought. Either that or wealth was the impression Brie wanted to convey, whether or not she could actually afford this car.

She opened the doors and motioned for me to put Pluckie in the backseat, and then I got into the passenger side. "It isn't far," Brie said.

As she drove through town, past some shops and toward the main residential district, we chatted a little. I asked her how long she'd lived in Destiny as well as how long she had run Rising Moon Realty.

Both were about four years. Before that, she'd lived in San Bernardino, which was where she'd obtained her real estate license and become not just a salesperson but a broker, too.

"I'd imagine that people with businesses here aren't inclined to sell them, at least not very often. Do you make as much money from sales or rentals of commercial property as residential?"

Okay, I was being nosy. But she'd sort of asked about my salary, so it was fair to be inquisitive about her income. Or so I thought.

"Oh, I'm only in residential." We'd reached a stop sign and she looked briefly toward me. "Commercial property is a whole other ballgame around here, and you're right. It seldom comes on the market. There are a couple of other real estate companies with offices in town and they take care of them when anyone's ready to deal in commercial."

As we started off again, I continued to look at her, feeling a bit puzzled. "But I understood that Flora was talking to at least one business owner in town about either buying or selling commercial property." I could have been mistaken, but I was fairly certain that Brad Nereida had mentioned that. Not that I'd tell Brie, or she might start bothering Brad about it, too.

"No, she couldn't have." Brie shot a quick glare at me now, her light brown eyes fiery. "You must be mistaken."

"I don't think so," I said.

"She was my employee." Brie's voice was loud and shrill in the car, and her hands gripped the steering wheel tightly. "I was training her. We talked about that, and she — never mind. She's gone now."

She seemed to have almost gone ballistic for a minute, but then calmed almost immediately. Or was she? I didn't know what Brie was thinking, but her eyes stared fixedly at the road.

I wondered, then. I hadn't focused much

on Brie as a possible murder suspect, but she had certainly known Flora, perhaps better than anyone else around here, and she had even seen the body. She'd certainly gotten emotional at my suggestion that her former employee had done something she hadn't approved of.

It might have been a stretch to speculate about it, but what if Flora had wanted to go to work for one of those other real estate brokers in town — one dealing with commercial property? Or maybe even open up her own office, although from the little I knew about her, she seemed only recently to have gotten into the real estate business and might not have been qualified.

In any event, had Brie learned about Flora's ambitions and gotten so upset about it that she'd killed her employee?

Hardly likely.

Yet my mind kept sliding around the possibility that Brie was a better murder suspect than anyone else I'd chatted with so far.

TWENTY-SEVEN

All I talked about after that, though, was how eager I was to see the rental unit that was all about the lucky number seven. I even joked a bit, asking if the song "Lucky Ladybug" was piped into the air around it every day.

"So you're a real superstition lover," Brie commented mildly when I stopped to take a breath.

"Well . . . I do live in Destiny. And I came here to learn the truth about superstitions."

"So do you think they are true?"

"Sometimes." Maybe. After all, some appeared to come true. But others . . .

We were just turning the corner onto Ladybug Lane. Brie slammed on her brakes, and I bent forward against my seat belt. I immediately turned to check on Pluckie. She'd slipped onto the floor of the backseat but appeared fine.

"What — ?" I began asking as I turned

around again, but I didn't need to finish my question.

A black cat was just stepping elegantly onto the curb at our side of the street. Catrice, the cat lady, was there in the shadows near a building, apparently waiting for her charge. Fortunately, the cat looked unharmed.

My nerves were another story.

"We'd better get to that good luck property soon," Brie said. "We need to counter this possible bad luck."

I just hoped the possible bad luck on my part wouldn't be an attack from Brie, if she happened to be Flora's killer.

Well, I'd be careful. Gemma knew where I was going and who I was with. I could always remind Brie of that.

She drove slowly for about a block. I studied the apartment buildings along the street. It was a charming neighborhood. The structures had the aura of Gold Rush days about them, but they appeared a whole lot newer than that.

Brie soon parked in front of a development of townhomes — connected units with two stories each, in similar style. This had to be 7 Ladybug Lane. It didn't take me long to spot unit number seven.

My first impression was that it appeared

inviting. Should I hope I hated the inside? Otherwise, I might wind up doing business with this woman who I suspected could be a murderer.

Fortunately or not, as it turned out, what I thought of the place wouldn't matter. We got out of Brie's car and walked up the narrow path through a rock garden that Pluckie immediately started sniffing. I let her for a minute, then we continued till we reached the entrance. The door opened and several people walked out.

"Well, hello, Brie," said a woman who dressed as businesslike as Brie did. "My clients here have just signed a lease on this place. You can show it as an example of this development, but unfortunately it's no longer available." The couple with her were beaming. Obviously this was about to become their home.

Mixed emotions passed through me.

I did let Brie show Pluckie and me around the inside on a brief tour. Had the place still been available, I wasn't sure what I'd have done. I liked it and would have recommended it to Gemma, had it been available.

According to Brie, it was the only unit here that was currently up for rent, and it was certainly the only unit number seven, although, thanks to the rest of the address, maybe the other units could be claimed to be somewhat lucky too. In any event, Gemma and I weren't moving yet — and one good thing about it was that I wouldn't have to do business with Brie.

Her attitude about the situation was surprisingly good. Or maybe she was just a seasoned enough real estate broker not to get upset if she lost out on a transaction, especially if she thought she still had potential clients on the hook if she found something else for them.

She certainly was acting differently now from the moments after I'd suggested Flora was getting involved in real estate transactions that Brie's office didn't handle.

Which relieved me a little. No matter what my concerns were regarding Brie, I didn't feel I had to run to Justin or anyone else to let them know my suspicions . . . yet. I hadn't gotten any sense, either, that the life of the landlord's realtor was in danger from Brie, which was a very good thing.

But that still didn't remove my suspicions of her in relation to Flora's death.

On the ride back to Rising Moon Realty, Brie's attitude remained stable and friendly as she told me she was putting together some other listings for us. I said nothing that would allow her to believe I didn't trust her in any respect. Even so, Gemma and I wouldn't have to work with her any longer if we didn't choose to.

Maybe that black cat crossing our path had been an omen of good, not bad, luck.

Or so I thought was possible . . . at first.

Getting out of the car, I said a quick goodbye to Brie before Pluckie and I set off at a brisk walk back to the store. I breathed more naturally on the way and found myself smiling as, once we reached Destiny Boulevard, the typical crowd of tourists sauntered along the sidewalks, avoiding cracks and picking up heads-up pennies.

When I opened the door to the Lucky Dog, I let Pluckie in first. Then I swallowed hard.

Detective Richard Choye stood there talking with Martha near one of the tall shelf sets full of dog toys. She must have glanced toward me, since he turned and aimed a big, snide smile at me.

Whatever good mood I'd been in immediately evaporated.

I hadn't wanted to be alone with Choye, but he suggested it, and it was probably better than remaining in front of my fellow Lucky Dog staff and our customers, since I didn't know why he was at my shop.

Of course, I realized he was there to talk about Flora's murder, but was he going to tell me they'd caught the perpetrator and I was off the hook?

Not likely. And especially not since I now thought the person who'd done it had been in my company a lot of this afternoon.

So was he here to arrest me?

I kept Pluckie with me for moral support as we went into the rear storeroom and I waved Choye toward one of the chairs around the card table.

As usual, he wore a detective-serious suit, black this time. "Thanks, Rory," he said as he sat down. His politeness didn't fool me, but his sitting made me feel slightly better. At least he wasn't whipping out handcuffs and pulling my hands behind my back.

Where was Justin? Did he know about this visit?

I thought about acting like the perfect hostess, offering to brew coffee or even give him a dog treat. Or I could always run out to buy something to give him . . . and not come back.

Instead, I said nothing and offered no refreshments, just waited for him to begin.

"I'm here today because I spoke earlier with Celia and Derek Vardox."

My heart began racing immediately. I

knew Celia still considered me a suspect despite the little game we were playing. Did her brother? Had they made accusations about me to Choye?

"I've spoken with Celia now and then recently," I said truthfully. We might have been seen together occasionally, so that wouldn't be much of a surprise. "I think she's working on a story about Flora Curtival and what happened to her."

"Exactly. I've had to tell the two of them to back off, since they've apparently been getting pushy with a number of locals we're considering as possible suspects." He paused, aiming his dark eyes toward me in an inquisitive stare. "Has she been pushy with you, too?"

"Not too bad," I said. I didn't want to get into the nature of any of our conversations in case he was just bent out of shape by the reporters talking to so many suspects, and even possibly accusing them. At least a reporter on a story had an ostensible reason to talk to people.

A suspect like me also had a reason, but it might not be acceptable to the cops.

Should I tell him my suspicions about Brie? I had nothing to back them up. And she'd certainly not shown any indication of a bad temper after potentially losing a commission for that residential unit.

It had only been earlier, when we'd talked about Flora . . .

Choye was still speaking. "Well, before I told them to back off, I asked their opinion about who's their most likely suspect and why. And guess who was at the top of their list."

I suddenly wanted to confront Celia and tell her once more that I was being framed.

Or maybe I was just the easiest person for her to suggest while she conducted her interviews and looked for answers.

Could she have considered the possibility of Brie? If so, why?

"Since you're here, I can guess," I replied drolly, trying not to let my nervousness show too much. "But I'll tell you once again that I didn't do it. The fact that Flora stole some of my dog toys doesn't mean I'd kill her, and I'd have had to be pretty stupid to use one of those toys as a symbol. If you think you have any other evidence against me, tell me what it is and I'll let you know my opinion."

"Oh, you've played games with detective work long enough to realize I can't tell you anything like that. Just be careful, Ms. Chasen." He stared at me once more, then smiled again. "I think you know enough to do that, at least. And in case you're wondering, Chief Halbertson didn't know I was coming here today. But I'll let him know I saw you — and that although you didn't immediately jump up and confess, I didn't see any reason to aim our investigation elsewhere, either."

He stood up and, without another word to me, strode out of the storeroom, leaving me there staring after him.

What was that really all about? I couldn't exactly run after him and ask him.

Was he trying to make me so nervous that I'd jump up and confess, as he'd described it?

Or was there something else on his mind?

I didn't leave the storeroom right away. Maybe I wasn't under arrest yet, but I was clearly not off the hook. In fact, maybe I was on the hook and the line was being drawn tighter and tighter before I was reeled in and arrested.

One option for protecting myself was to call an attorney. I'd not been read my Miranda rights, since I wasn't under arrest, but talking to someone who knew the law sounded darned good.

I looked up her number on my smart phone and called Attorney Emily Rasmuten. She was Martha's lawyer for business-related things, but I knew she and her firm also did criminal work.

"I'm booked up for the rest of today, Rory," she told me. "Can you wait till tomorrow morning?"

Could I? I certainly hoped so. We agreed on a time and I crossed my fingers that waiting wasn't a mistake.

I sat at the table a little longer, stroking Pluckie's head and calming myself. Then we went back into the store.

I tried to maintain a cheerful front, although I did get some quizzical and sympathetic glances from Martha and our assistants.

What had Choye said to them before I returned? As he was leaving?

Did they believe I could have killed Flora?

Should I have told Choye about my latest suspicions about Brie? That was purely speculation on my part. I certainly had no evidence against her.

No, I shouldn't have told Choye.

But I knew who I should tell.

Justin offered to pick me up, but I told him no, and explained why. No matter what his justifications were to his staff and others, it would be better for us not to be seen together right now.

I'd called him while out walking Pluckie. We'd headed past the Broken Mirror Bookstore, which had a crowd. It wasn't a good time for me to talk to Gemma. Or really anyone. My mind was a morass of worry about all that had happened, or not happened, that day, and what I should do next.

Waiting until the following morning to talk to the lawyer might not be the best way to straighten things out. Maybe Justin could help.

We decided to meet at a fast food restaurant in a small town about ten miles down the road from Destiny. Might we be seen there by someone who'd recognize us? Possibly, but it wasn't too likely.

And if we were, I knew Justin wouldn't hide anything. Neither would I.

So, about an hour and a half after my call, once the shop was closed and Pluckie and I had returned to the B&B and gotten my car, we met Justin and Killer inside the restaurant. I wasn't especially hungry, but meeting there worked out fine. Justin had arrived first and he and Killer had gotten their meals but hadn't eaten yet. I ordered a salad for me and burger for Pluckie, and then we joined them at a table in a far corner.

"I'll check with Choye tomorrow," Justin

began, "but I want to hear exactly what he said to you."

He was in one of his traditional blue button-down shirts, and the tenseness of his shoulders was apparent. His handsome face, too, looked strained. I hated to be putting him in such a difficult position, between his job as the highest ranking police official of a very special town . . . and me.

I went over what Choye had said and more than hinted at. "Part of it was because of his conversations with the Vardoxes," I said. "And . . . well, Celia and I are helping one another in this," I explained.

"Damn it, Rory," Justin growled when I was done. At least his voice wasn't very raised here, although with the noisy conversations around us I wasn't sure it would have mattered. "I thought you at least promised to keep me informed about what you were doing — and to stay safe."

"I'm doing my best to live up to the latter," I said, realizing the word "live" was highly appropriate. "And . . . well, I'll try to do a better job of keeping you informed, too. That means there's something I want to tell you."

"What?" He looked at me with some suspicion and some amusement.

"Well, it's probably nothing, but I spent

some time with Brie Timons today looking for a place for Gemma and me to move to. I told her that one of the shopowners I'd been speaking with lately said Flora asked for a listing to sell the shop. Brie got really upset and said they only deal in residential property, not commercial. But what if Flora was acting on her own or looking for a job with another real estate broker? With Brie's attitude —"

"— you think she could have been angry enough to kill? Seems a bit far-fetched."

"I realize that. And she didn't seem to get upset later when she learned that someone else had signed a lease for the place she'd wanted to show Gemma and me. So maybe her earlier blow-up meant nothing."

"Probably, but I'm glad you let me know. I'll look into it. I promise. And although the whole department has been working on this and I keep pushing them, I'll try to get the investigation stepped up even more. You've suffered with this suspicion long enough."

"Thank you." My tone was hoarse but heartfelt.

The expression on his face was softer now, his gaze on me filled with . . . well, caring.

Love?

I felt my eyes well up a bit. If we hadn't been in public like this, I'd have thrown my arms around him.

Kissed him, and probably more.

"I'd like for you to come home with me tonight," he said softly.

"I'd like it, too, but I won't. Until this situation is resolved I think this is the only way we should be anywhere alone, and even this may be stretching it. I don't want you or your position compromised."

"And I hate that you — well, I appreciate that, Rory. And even if we can only be seen in public together, for the most part, I'll be there for you as much as I can."

We couldn't seal that bargain right away, but after we were done eating Justin and Killer walked Pluckie and me to our car.

There, observers or not, we shared one heck of a good-night kiss.

"Good night, Rory," Justin said in a low voice. As I opened my mouth to tell him good night, too, he planted another kiss on it. When he pulled away, he said, "You know I love you, don't you?"

But before I could respond to that, he and Killer walked away.

TWENTY-EIGHT

I talked a lot to Pluckie on our way back to the B&B. I had her in a safety harness on the passenger seat behind me, and I adored how she just sat there and looked at me each time I was able to glance back in her direction. Sometimes she cocked her head so that her long black ears hung first more to one side, then to the other.

"Love," I said to her. "Justin said he loves me. I didn't really have time to respond, but what would I have said if he'd stayed?"

I managed a brief look toward my interested pup and she cocked her head once more.

"You're probably right," I said. "I think I love him, too. Sorry, Warren," I added immediately, addressing my deceased fiancé as if he was there. "I hope I'm approaching this right." I let go of the steering wheel briefly with one hand and crossed my fingers. "But the timing — I could be

343

Justin's worst nightmare. What if I'm arrested, especially by people in his own department?"

I knew, with Justin as their boss, the detectives must all be attempting to do a good job solving the murder of Flora Curtival. He would require it of them. Yet they were taking the easy route, jumping onto someone just a bit too obvious — thanks to physical circumstantial evidence as well as an argument with the victim by the suspect . . . me. But I'd learned in my own unofficial investigations, not to mention from TV shows and movies, that the most obvious suspect isn't always the guilty party. Like now. Surely they were smart enough to realize that.

Although in the other two situations, they'd needed some help . . .

We'd reached the B&B. I parked in the front lot and gave Plucky her last walk of the evening before we entered beneath the prongs-up horseshoe. I crossed my fingers and aimed a quick wish up at it: *let this all get resolved accurately and fast.*

Once we were in the lobby, I called Gemma. I'd already let her know how we'd lost out on unit seven at 7 Ladybug Lane, but I hadn't told her about my conversations with Brie — and my resulting suspicions.

"Oh, Rory," she said immediately as she answered the call. "Sorry. I meant to let you know, but I'm not staying at the B&B tonight. I'll be back to open the store early tomorrow, but Stuart and I are hanging out in Santa Barbara together tonight."

I decided not to bother her with my thoughts about Brie. She and Stuart were having a romantic evening, I was sure. Well, good for them. Maybe Gemma had made her decision, that face in the mirror notwithstanding.

Under other, better circumstances, I'd be having a romantic evening as well, with the guy I loved.

Yes, I was admitting it to myself. And given the right circumstances, I'd admit it to Justin, too.

I crossed my fingers that those circumstances would occur soon. For now, Pluckie and I started up the stairs toward our room and I finished my conversation with Gemma. "Well, I'm sure I don't have to tell you to have a good time, but I will anyway. Enjoy yourself."

She deserved it. After all, in addition to being my good friend, she'd been a murder suspect at one time, too. She knew what I was going through.

And I could only hope that the resolution of my situation would happen quickly and with as good an outcome as hers.

After I was ready for bed and Pluckie lay on the floor beside me, I picked up my cell phone, which was on its charger. Should I call Justin?

If I did, what would I say to him?

When I got to the point where I was ready to tell him what I really thought of him, it had to be in person, not over the phone.

In any event, it couldn't be before this murder situation was resolved. Favorably.

Which simply had to happen, and soon.

I'd ask Emily Rasmuten tomorrow for any suggestions, but I doubted there were any real answers till the actual killer was caught. Which meant I had to step up my efforts to find that person and the evidence against her. Yes, her. I believed that the likely person was Brie.

Of course, I'd had a different primary suspect yesterday, John O'Rourke. How much evidence could I turn over to Justin against either of them?

Zilch.

I shook my head and put my phone back down, just as it started to ring. I looked at the caller ID. It was Justin.

I smiled at the thought that he must be thinking about me, too.

Or was he calling to let me know that tomorrow was D-Day, when I'd finally be arrested?

We'd last seen each other less than an hour before, so surely that wasn't it. I swiped the button to answer and held the phone to my ear. "Hi, Justin."

"Hi, Rory," he said.

I wondered if he'd say anything further about his feelings, but he obviously was focused on our immediate problems right now.

"Look, I'm thinking that tomorrow we should hold a meeting at the department with Detectives Choye and Fidelio," he began. "We'll go over your ideas about who could have killed Flora and why. Nothing formal, of course, but I'll let them ask you non-accusatory questions and maybe something will come out that will help them turn in another, more credible direction. Okay?"

I sighed. "Okay," I said. "But it'll have to be in the afternoon, and I'll need to check whether Emily Rasmuten has time to participate."

"The lawyer?"

I nodded, though he of course couldn't

see it. "Yes. She and I are talking tomorrow morning, and I'm likely to hire her."

He paused. "That's probably a good idea. At least it shouldn't hurt. But . . ."

"But what?"

"But she'll probably advise you not to see me socially or any other way for now."

I sighed. "Maybe so."

Neither one of us said anything for a minute. Then we both began speaking at once.

"Maybe tomorrow morning —" I began.

"I can stop at your shop first thing when you open tomorrow," Justin said.

We both stopped and laughed. "I think we're on the same page, or close to it," I said.

"I agree. Anyway, I'll pop over when you first open so there'll be other people around who'd be able to vouch for the fact that nothing about the murder was mentioned between us." He paused. "And after that I think we'd better hold off even talking to each other for a while, aside from at the station, to make sure your legal representation works out okay and no one can claim that either of us is being compromised by staying in touch with the other. For now."

"For now," I agreed.

We continued to talk very briefly but

didn't say anything much. And then Justin said, "I'll see you tomorrow, Rory. Good night."

"Good night," I parroted, but by the time I finished, he was no longer on the line.

Gemma wasn't around the next morning in the Rainbow B&B breakfast room, of course, which was probably just as well. She'd always been fairly honest with me, and since I undoubtedly looked like crap, she would tell me so. I'd barely slept that night. I was too worried about what today would bring.

Would Emily agree to represent me after we talked? Probably. Would she agree to the kind of police discussion Justin had suggested? That was unknown. She'd have to feel comfortable that I wouldn't say anything that could be used against me, and since she was just jumping into the case — maybe — she wasn't likely to champion the idea, even if the reason for the meeting was for me to give the police my insights into who else was a more logical murder suspect than me.

Plus, I was going to see Justin again. With people around, sure. But this would be the first time since last night, when he'd said he loved me. And neither early in the day, when he popped into the store, nor later, if our meeting at his department occurred, would there be an opportunity for me to respond — even if I'd figured out the best way to do so.

Pluckie had awakened me to go outside, so I'd dressed quickly, then returned to my room to shower and change into something more fitting for the day at the store — a green Lucky Dog knit shirt and slacks. I ate a breakfast consisting of Serina's great food in her usual dining room, sitting alone with Pluckie at my feet. I could have joined other people who'd lived here for a while, or others I'd just met, but I wanted to be alone.

Besides, I hardly ate. Pluckie and I left for the shop soon.

I had things to do before opening that day. Or so I told myself. What could I do to prepare for Justin's early arrival? Straighten the merchandise on our shelves? Restock some of those shelves from the storeroom? Breathe a lot to try to calm my nerves once more? Take a nap to make up for the sleep I lost last night — assuming I'd be able to sleep better here? Hah.

I did accomplish some of the former, at first, and it took me till less than half an hour before we were scheduled to open. Good. Martha would come downstairs around ten, and Millie, due to arrive then also, would be the one to help her.

I'd just hang out in the store, waiting on customers and looking busy till Justin arrived — although he tended to be pretty prompt. He'd said he would arrive around when we opened, so I expected he'd be there at ten.

I decided that right now was a good time to seed the sidewalk in front of the Lucky Dog with heads-up pennies. I hooked Pluckie up to the counter, pulled the stash of shiny pennies I saved in a plastic bag out of a drawer near our store computer, and walked outside.

I first walked in front of our window, making sure the display of dog toys and lucky superstition symbols looked well organized and attractive, which it did. Then I began placing pennies on the cracked sidewalk here and there. Some visitors had already arrived in the area, so a few pennies got picked up almost as quickly as I put them down. Not all of them, though. Maybe I was just too fast for this group.

"Good luck to all you visitors to Destiny," I called, waving my hand, with crossed fingers, toward them.

As I moved around, I noticed that Brad Nereida had just arrived at the Wish-on-a-

Star store across the street. He was the one who'd told me Flora was trying to list commercial real estate for sale. Maybe a conversation they'd had had given her that idea.

Brie had overreacted when I'd told her, but had she known about the possibility of this already? The more I thought about it, the more it seemed so. She'd said something about talking with Flora about it, then cut herself off.

Would Brad know anything about Brie's knowledge? Might Flora have mentioned Brie? I wasn't sure whether the information, if I got hold of it, would help or hurt in trying to get Justin's police department heading in the same direction as I was now, but I needed to find out.

I opened my shop door and slipped my head in. "Be back soon," I called to Pluckie. Millie had a key to get in, so she could help Martha with customers if she happened to get here before I returned, but that shouldn't be a problem.

I walked past the Broken Mirror Bookstore, but it remained closed and I didn't see Gemma inside. Was she still saying goodbye to Stuart somewhere? I'd have to talk to her later to find out what was going on.

When I reached the corner where Fate

Street met Destiny Boulevard, I crossed to the other side of the street. I headed back toward Wish-on-a-Star and glanced at the window. The sign with the shooting star made out of neon lights was turned on, as it usually was, even when the shop was closed. I couldn't help it — I made another wish: that all would go well today and Justin's subordinate cops would buy into the idea that there were other suspects much more viable than me. Then I watched the light descend quickly, as if it were a falling star.

I glanced up at the actual sky. It was a little overcast today, but there was no rain in the forecast. Plus, it was daytime, so I'd not be able to see a genuine falling star even if there were any.

Would this wish come true? The last one, about determining whether I should stay in Destiny, seemed to. I'd stayed and been happy here.

Till recently.

Time to see if I could learn anything here. I approached the shop's door, but when I tried pulling it open, it was locked.

I looked through the window and saw Brad's shadow in the distance behind some shelves of children's clothing. I knocked on the glass and he looked up, startled.

I gestured to him to open the door. I

couldn't really see his expression, but his slowness suggested he wasn't pleased I was here, at least not now. Nevertheless, he did come and let me in.

"Hi, Rory." His tone wasn't extremely welcoming either. I was used to seeing him looking tired, but this morning he appeared well rested. He wore a sweatshirt over jeans, and the shirt was snug enough to suggest that this average-appearing guy might actually have a body beneath his clothes.

"Hi, Brad," I said. "Hope you don't mind my coming in, but I have a few questions for you."

"About what?" His light brown eyes scowled, again breaking with his tradition of appearing ordinary and fairly emotionless.

I smiled at him nonetheless. "This place," I said, gesturing around his shop. "I know you said it wasn't for sale when Flora Curtival asked you about it. Did she indicate at all why she was interested — like whether she was opening her own real estate business or working for someone else, or anything at all?" I'd start there, then work into whether Flora had also happened to mention to him, during that probably brief meeting, that she'd discussed the possible listing with her boss.

"I think she was interested in opening her

own real estate business," he said.

"What did she say about that?" I pressed, since I'd gathered Flora probably didn't have enough experience to get the right kind of license for it.

"Not much. She just talked about it now and then."

Now and then? I'd thought she'd just come to his shop once before she'd trashed it.

Even if there were more visits, it had to have been after she'd moved here, not a year ago, since she was working as a real estate agent in town. It was therefore after her divorce. But why would she have been zeroing in on this Wish-on-a-Star?

Or was she?

I noticed then that Brad seemed to be breathing heavily as he lifted some small-sized shirts from a shelf and began refolding them. They'd appeared fine to me before he started, and it seemed as if he was using that as an excuse not to look at me. Or was I imagining that?

An odd thought suddenly struck me. Brad and Flora had spoken several times. Together? Alone?

"Do you know if Flora also asked your wife about selling the shop?" Maybe she had, and it had caused dissension between the married couple.

"No! My wife had nothing to do with —"
He had rounded on me and no longer
looked average, but angry.

I swallowed hard. I was afraid I might now
have the real answer about who'd killed
Flora, without really knowing why.

"Of course not," I soothed. "I hope your
wife's mother is doing better and that she
comes home soon. Anyway, it's time for me
to go open my shop." I shot him a smile
and headed for the door.

He grabbed my arm. "No, you'll stay
here." He pulled me farther into his shop,
too strong for me to resist.

I glanced toward the window. Was anyone
looking in, past the display of the falling
star, which shielded most of the glass? I
didn't see anyone.

And I suddenly wondered whether I was
going to meet a similar fate as Flora.

TWENTY-NINE

He forced me to sit down on a chair in his office. I tried not to show that I was scared.

I wondered if Justin would really arrive at the Lucky Dog within the next ten or fifteen minutes, after it opened. But as long as Brad was right here with me I couldn't pull my phone from my pocket and call. Justin was the last person I'd spoken with, though, so maybe I'd be able to somehow just push a button to contact him.

But not at this moment.

And as it turned out, Brad had a gun. He'd pulled it out of the drawer of his modern-day metal desk and aimed it at me. It was small, but undoubtedly lethal as any other weapon of that kind.

Now he still held it but was pacing at the other side of the room, obviously agitated.

Is that how he'd been when he'd murdered Flora?

Why had he murdered her?

Maybe I could find that out, at least. I decided to play this very sympathetically.

"I don't understand, Brad," I said softly. "Was Flora being too pushy about trying to get you to sell your store?"

He pivoted quickly to face me again. "No, the bitch was taunting me about my wife."

I shook my head. "What about your wife?"

"You want to know? You really want to know?" He leaned over his desk toward me, saliva dripping from one corner of his mouth. The guy was definitely emotional. And murderous. Was I going to survive this?

I had to. Justin just said he loved me . . .

"Yes, please tell me," I said. "I know Flora could really be a terrible person. What did she do?"

"I was one of her first victims when she came back to Destiny seeking revenge for not getting enough good luck here to keep her marriage together." Brad practically spat at me as he related how he'd vaguely re-called her visiting the first time, with her husband. They'd come into this shop and Flora had shown her husband some of the cute kids' clothes decorated with supersti-tion symbols. "She was trying to convince him they'd have kids soon if they stayed together. I didn't remember that — if I'd known it in the first place — but she told me about it later. After she'd told my wife that I'd seduced her and she was now in love with me."

"What!" My mind raced around that. Apparently seduction must have been part of Flora's plans — that and making sure Brad's marriage crumbled as hers had done. What a flimsy reason for ruining someone else's marriage.

Flora hadn't exactly been sane, I'd already figured. This was just another piece of evidence that showed it.

"I didn't know at first that she'd done that, but my shop was near the top of her revenge list because of the having-kids thing. That's something else she told me later." Brad had tears in his eyes and in his voice. "When Lorraine packed up our kids and herself and told me she had to go help her sick mother, I believed her. After she was gone, Flora kept popping in here, trying to get me to go out with her, to visit her once she'd moved into her own apartment. The thing is, she kept threatening to tell Lorraine we'd had sex. I didn't know then that she'd already told Lorraine that, and it was why Lorraine left in the first place."

Okay, I had to know. "And had you had sex with her, before?"

He hung his head. "Yes. Once. The first

time she came on to me, I was flattered. And interested. And — well, damned naive. I didn't know she was really after revenge and would stop at nothing to get it."

"Oh." I recalled that the tack I was taking was to act sympathetic. "That was cruel of her." And not very bright on his part, I thought, although I wasn't about to say that.

"She let me know later that she'd come into the shop one day when I wasn't here and told Lorraine. She said she pretended to feel remorse — although she also told my wife she was still turned on by me and would love to do it again." He looked up at me again. "Yes, I'd behaved badly. I was stupid." Okay, he acknowledged that. Good. I'd be careful not to agree with him, though. "But I love my wife and my kids, and if I could take it all back, I would."

He practically sobbed at the end. If he felt that bad about it, maybe he would just let me go.

"I'm sure you would," I said soothingly, starting to rise.

"What are you doing?" His voice came out as a scream, and he raised his hand holding the gun.

"I . . . I just wanted to give you a hug," I lied. I'd rather have given him a sharp kick where it hurt and run out of there, but I didn't dare try — not with him holding a weapon. I sat back down and wondered what I should do next.

I could ask some more questions, at least — and I had plenty. "Why did you stick that rabbit's foot toy into Flora's mouth?" I swallowed and added, "Did you want to frame me?"

"She had a bunch of those toys with her. I had nothing against you in particular, but that helped to ensure she couldn't breathe, along with the area rug I used over her head after I hit her. It was a happy accident this pointed to someone else as the killer — you. I had no idea she'd stolen those things from you."

Okay, he hadn't meant at first to frame me. Not that it made much difference now.

I couldn't call for help. I wasn't sure how best to help myself.

Then a possibility came to me. This was Destiny, after all. "I wonder how long you'll have to suffer bad luck," I murmured, although loudly enough that he should be able to hear me.

"What do you mean?" he shot back immediately.

"Well, murdering someone brings bad luck to the killer. I learned that before and saw it, too, when I found out who really committed those two prior killings in Destiny."

"I knew that about the first killing and the second." Brad's voice was now a croak. "Even though no one was supposed to talk about them or they'd suffer bad luck, too. But with this third one?"

"Oh, yes," I said hastily. "I've heard some pretty bad stuff is happening to that murderer in jail." Just the fact that the killer wound up arrested was bad luck, wasn't it? I wasn't about to go into any other details with Brad — and actually I didn't know much, although it hadn't been long ago and a trial was still pending.

"And you're aware, of course, that things happen in threes," I added. "There was bound to be a third murder in Destiny, since one of those deaths wasn't a murder. You just had the bad luck to be the one to commit it."

"I just want my family back," Brad cried out. "My life back. Do you know of anything I can do to turn my luck around now?"

Really? He was asking the person he was currently holding hostage? Yeah, let me go and turn yourself in, I thought. But since I knew that wouldn't happen, I didn't even try saying it.

"I'm sure you'd be able to find something

here in Destiny. There's a lot of good luck here, not just bad."

"That's not what Flora said," Brad countered sadly. "And she was right. She may have come back here to turn things around, but instead she . . . she died."

She was murdered. By you. Once again I didn't say my thoughts aloud. "No, she came back here to get revenge. She even admitted it to the entire town in her rant at the Break-a-Leg Theater a week ago. The fact her bad luck didn't turn around was probably her own doing."

"And I added to it. Boy, did I add to it." Brad's expression was pitiful now. How had I ever thought he was just average looking? Now he looked like a sorrowful, dangerous killer — assuming I knew what one of those looked like. Dangerous killer, yes. But sorrowful?

"And she added to your bad luck," I said. "She can't change anything for herself now. But you can help yourself."

"How? My luck's so damned bad right now. And if I just let you go, you'll add to it. I don't want to end up in jail for the rest of my life."

That could definitely be a result of committing murder, I thought. And adding another person as your victim might not make the penalty any worse. He only had one life. He could either lose it or spend the rest of it in prison.

"I understand," I said. "And I can't promise a better outcome. But you know, you have one of the luckiest symbols right here in the Wish-on-a-Star shop. One that could turn your bad luck into good, if you gave it a try. It did for me not long after I first came here."

"Really? What?"

I told him about how I'd been at a crossroads in my life and didn't know whether it would be good luck or bad for me to stay in Destiny. I happened to be on Destiny Boulevard one evening and saw his display in the window of his store, and I wished on its falling star. "I wished I knew what the right decision was: should I stay or leave. And the next day, everything pointed me in the right direction. I stayed, and my luck has been really good."

"Till lately," he added. His expression changed to something I interpreted as both ironic and threatening.

Damn. Wasn't this going to work?

"That's right. I'd go wish on your falling star again, but I'm not sure how often it can provide good luck, and right now you need it even more than I do. Have you ever tried wishing on it?"

His eyes opened wide. "Not really. It was just a symbol, to bring tourists in to buy things. Lorraine . . . well, she was the one who really believed in superstitions. I just mostly went along with her."

"Well, maybe now's a good time for you to start. Tell you what. Why don't we go out on the sidewalk and you can make your wish. I'll stay right with you and you can even hold my hand. Keep your gun in your pocket so you can grab it if you think I'm about to run — which I won't. Then we'll come back in and you can lock up again."

Was this utterly foolish? Sure, but it was a chance for me to get out of this, possibly unharmed and alive.

Especially if Justin had arrived at my shop when he'd said he would. I couldn't be sure — but at least, yes, it was a chance.

If Justin wasn't there, I wouldn't come back into this shop with Brad. I wasn't sure how I'd handle it, since I'd do anything to prevent the people outside from getting hurt, but I had to try this anyway.

Brad hadn't acted particularly bright before. Would he continue that trend now?

"You know I'll shoot you if you try to get away," he said in a low voice. "If you leave and tell people what I've admitted to you, it's over for me anyway, so shooting you won't make things any worse."

"I understand." I wished I could hide the quaver in my voice, although maybe it was to my advantage if he thought I was terrified.

Which I actually was.

He raised his gun and gestured for me to stand. Nervously, I obeyed.

"You really think that wishing on my own store's fake falling star will bring me good luck?" he said as I started toward the door.

I turned back to him. "You've been a resident of Destiny longer than I have. Even if Lorraine was the real believer, you've got to have learned that there's a lot of power in superstitions, even though no one can guarantee anything. Isn't it worth trying, though?"

"I guess. And maybe if it works I can tell Lorraine and she'll understand and come back . . . Okay. Let's try it. But we'll come back in here afterward and wait till I either see some sign of my luck changing or decide what else to do. You got that?" His voice was hard again, his expression blank.

"Of course," is what I said. What I intended to do was different.

Would I survive?

As I preceded him toward the door, I felt

my fingers cross. Yes, I knew that crossed fingers never guaranteed good luck any more than most symbols — but it couldn't hurt.

When I reached the door, Brad reached around me to unlock it, then pushed it slightly. I continued the motion until the door was open enough for me to slide through.

Could I get out and run?

Too many people on the sidewalk. If I tried it, someone else could get hurt.

Instead, I walked slowly outside, my gaze across the street toward the Lucky Dog. A similar crowd filled the sidewalk there, and I couldn't see beyond its window, which reflected a bit of sunlight back toward me.

Maybe this was a horrible idea. But what else could I have done?

Oh, no. The crowd near us started to part a bit and I realized why nearly immediately. A black cat was strutting through them as though it hadn't a care in the world.

Then again, maybe it knew exactly the reaction humans would have to it in this town.

The cat was now in front of me. Crossing my path? Brad's? Both of ours? Not exactly, but close.

What would happen if we both experienced bad luck now? I hated to even consider it — but figured my presence here on earth might be limited. Hopefully it would only be me, though, and not any of these tourists. I crossed my fingers even tighter.

Fortunately, Brad's attention was more on making our way to his shop's window. As far as I could tell, he hadn't noticed the cat.

I looked around a bit more — including a glance across the street.

And then — I forced myself not to smile as Justin walked out the Lucky Dog's door and his eyes lit on me. He started to raise his arm as if to wave, and I quickly shook my head no. I forced myself to cough and bent my body forward quickly so Brad, behind me, hopefully wouldn't catch that I'd been attempting to communicate with someone.

"Sorry," I gasped. "I'm allergic to something in the air here." I continued to cough as I stood up again and sidled along the building to the window where the falling star sign reigned. "Here you are." I took another couple of steps farther and let Brad walk up to face the star. "You of all people know the drill."

The light of the mock shooting star wasn't on now, which was good. You were supposed to wish on a star the moment you saw it. A false one as much as a real one — a meteor or comet? Who knew?

Brad stood there staring at the sign. Colored lights shone around the perimeter of where the arc of the soon-to-be falling star was outlined. He'd grabbed my wrist in his left hand so I'd stay with him. He was right-handed, so I knew his gun was in his pocket on that side.

In moments, a light came on near the top left of the sign. It rose slowly along the marked arc. "Now!" I said.

"I wish —" Brad began, staring at it earnestly. "I can't say it aloud. That's bad luck."

"I can," I said. "I wish this was all over."

I felt pretty sure I was about to get my wish. As I glanced toward Brad again, I saw Justin approach. I started fake-coughing again and bent over, even as I made that cough start sounding like, "Killer, killer."

Justin got it. Before Brad could react, he'd been pushed to the ground, with his hands grabbed by Justin.

"Gun in his pocket," I said, and Justin immediately found it, pulled it out, and placed it on the ground as he started cuffing the writhing, shouting Brad and reciting his Miranda rights.

Sweet man that Justin was, he believed my story immediately, with no questions.

Or maybe the fact that Brad was armed had something to do with it.

And it helped that a cuffed Brad began cussing me and ruing aloud that he hadn't killed me, too, when he'd had the chance.

In moments, it was, in fact, over.

My second wish on that unreal falling star had also come true.

THIRTY

I did the appropriate thing, because of our sort-of alliance, and immediately called Celia Vardox as I stood off to the side while Justin's backup arrived to investigate the scene and take Brad away.

"Who? He what?" Celia's shrieks over the phone nearly deafened me, but I smiled.

"I'm sure I'll get in trouble if I give you any details," I said to her. "But if you want to try to interview anyone here at the crime scene — my crime scene, where I was a victim of sorts — you'd better get here fast."

Local shop owners from stores nearby were beginning to show up, populating the crowd along with the tourists. When Jeri arrived with her mother, I smiled in relief and asked her to go across the street, tell Martha and Millie what was going on, and let them know it would be a while before I could come in to work.

"I can help out there now," Jeri said,

glancing at Kiara, who smiled and nodded at her. "But what's really going on here?"

I didn't want to get into details since I wasn't sure whether my talking to anyone besides the police would taint my ability to testify against Brad. I just said, "Brad Nereida has some legal issues he needs to deal with."

Jeri, ever astute, opened her dark eyes wider in a shocked expression. "Did he kill Flora? Why?"

"Rory can't talk about it," said Celia, who'd just arrived. "But Derek and I will be interviewing everyone possible and putting the story up on our website even before a new edition of the *Star* comes out."

This was one of those times that I appreciated Celia — unlike some other times recently.

I asked Jeri to keep an eye on Pluckie, glad in many ways that my dog had remained safe in the shop while I experienced the ordeal. "I'll be there as soon as I can," I said.

Detectives Choye and Fidelio had been among the first cops to arrive. Choye had helped Brad into the back of a police vehicle that a uniformed officer was driving, and then they were gone. Some crime scene technicians remained around, and one asked me for my fingerprints since they would undoubtedly find some inside. I didn't see Justin and assumed he, too, was in the Wish-on-a-Star shop.

I had a real urge to cross the street to my store and get out of this area that still stoked my emotions. I even took a couple of steps through the crowd in that direction.

But before I got far, Justin exited the store and came up to me. "We need to get your statement, Rory," he said softly, and I heard caring and sympathy in his tone. "Detective Fidelio will take it, but I'll be there, too."

Shouldn't he be able to talk to me alone, be nice to me in front of crowds now, since I should no longer be considered a murder suspect?

Although that might still be premature until they conducted more of an investigation against Brad. And part of that investigation would be whatever I said against him.

"Of course," I said.

"Please come to the station, then. You and the detective can both ride with me."

Lura Fidelio had come up to us on the sidewalk and heard what Justin said. "Fine," she agreed, which I said as well. We crossed the street, since Justin's car was parked near the front of the Lucky Dog.

A black cat sat right in front of my shop.

The same one who'd been in front of Wish-on-a-Star before Brad had been taken into custody?

If so, whatever bad luck he'd provided by crossing someone's path had slammed into Brad, not me. Of course, in some cultures black cats were all good luck.

I decided that was true for me. After all, I loved all pets. Lots of people kept black cats as family members.

"Thanks," I whispered, smiling at the cat, who only lifted a front paw and began licking it.

I wondered if Catrice was anywhere around. She was hard to find, and almost impossible to talk to. But I hoped to be able to tell her about this . . . if she didn't already know.

I saw Gemma approaching from the Broken Mirror, along with Stuart. I excused myself before getting into Justin's car.

"What's going on?" Gemma demanded, looking over my shoulder with wide eyes toward the children's shop.

"I can't say much now," I told her, "but one good thing is that I'm no longer a murder suspect."

"Brad?" She looked amazed.

I nodded. "Tell you more later."

Gemma turned toward Stuart, who had

caught up with her, and he took her into his arms.

Hey, if anyone needed comfort it was me, and Justin had already gotten into the driver's seat of his car without giving me even a cool but kind hug.

But the worst was definitely over. I was fine. I'd tell the authorities all I knew — and call to cancel my appointment with Emily Rasmuten.

I no longer needed a lawyer.

I hoped.

The session did, in fact, go well. I answered Detective Fidelio's questions, and they all seemed logical. I explained first why I'd happened to go to the Wish-on-a-Star shop early that morning: to ask Brad more about his conversations with Flora about her possibly getting into commercial real estate.

"I have to admit," I said, knowing my expression looked sheepish, "that I had suspicions then that Flora's boss, Brie, had found out about her aspirations to be a commercial real estate agent and that she didn't want the woman she'd trained dumping her job and going into even remote competition with her."

"You thought she might have killed Flora because of that?" Lura asked.

Even though this was a follow-up interrogation of someone who should no longer be considered a murder suspect, the tall detective, as always clad in a dressy suit and serious demeanor, loomed over me where I sat at a table in a department conference room, as if menacing me to be sure to tell the truth.

And of course, I did. "Yes. Brie had given me the impression that she was really upset to hear that Flora had let clients know her aspirations, and I gathered she might have told Flora about her anger, too. Since Brad was the one who'd mentioned that Flora had talked to him about getting a listing on his shop, I decided to ask him about it when I saw him arrive early this morning."

I hadn't thought much about it before, but maybe I'd jumped to the conclusion about Brie and Flora since the accusation against Martha, when she was a murder suspect, had also peripherally involved whether she would be willing to sell the Lucky Dog property. Real estate in Destiny apparently had worth beyond normal property values — and it was superstition related, like everything else here.

"So what made you decide to change who you thought was the murderer?" Lura's tone was both interested and scornful, and I looked up at her and grinned ironically.

"Oh, maybe Brad's aiming a gun at me had something to do with that."

The interrogation didn't really last long, but I felt exhausted afterward.

But one really good thing was that Justin said he would drive me back to the Lucky Dog — without anyone else along.

Yes, he definitely could talk to me in public again.

Word had gotten out. In fact, I gathered that everyone had heard what had happened.

I hoped that Brad would get a fair trial, whenever that might be, since it was likely that around here, at least, people would already think they knew he was guilty.

Which he was, of course, but that didn't mean his trial shouldn't be conducted fairly.

All afternoon, people kept coming into the Lucky Dog, asking me questions. Even Arlen came in, after his aunt called him, to say he was glad the vandalism cases had been solved and the murderer of the woman who'd done it all had been found — and that I hadn't been the killer. Not that he'd thought I was . . . or so he claimed.

"But I'll bet one thing the cops won't be able to resolve, now that she's dead, is how

Flora committed all the mischief here, breaking into shops and ransacking and stealing and even turning the horseshoe at the Rainbow B&B upside down, without anyone catching her in the act. Or spilling salt on the floors of some of the places she'd vandalized, after what she'd left there before had already been cleaned up. Or how she heard a police radio and slipped into and out of the sound booth at the Break-a-Leg Theater without anyone catching her there either."

"Maybe she was just lucky," I speculated wryly, and Arlen smiled.

When appropriate, though, I might even run those questions by Justin.

When I took Pluckie out for her mandatory walks that day, there was no way to give her any privacy — not that she really cared.

At one point I ducked into the Broken Mirror with her, just to get away from the people hounding my dog and me. Gemma was there with Stuart, and although they had a number of customers, she was able to break away to say hi.

"You okay?" she asked me.

"I sure am," I fibbed. I didn't like this notoriety, even though it wasn't because people thought that I was a killer anymore.

"You know, stepping back to where we were before, it turns out it's a good thing that unit seven at 7 Ladybug Lane wasn't available."

I blinked as I looked at my long-time friend. Her lovely face was aglow with a big smile.

"And why is that?" I asked, thinking I might know the answer already. Stuart was helping some customers nearby. Was he the reason?

"Well . . . it's too soon for anything definitive," she said, "but I'm going to find a place where I'll stay by myself for now. Stuart's heading back to his job in New York City tomorrow, but he'll be back soon, and I'd like for us not to have to stay together in the bed and breakfast — or even with you around, I'm sorry to say."

"You're not sorry at all." I grinned. "This sounds serious."

She shrugged one of her narrow shoulders beneath the lacy white blouse she was wearing that day. "Could be."

I reached over and hugged her. "I hope so, if that's what you want."

"I want," she said, with a big smile that faded a bit almost at once. "Although I can't help thinking . . ."

"About that face in the mirror? I get it,

379

but so what if this is Destiny? It might just have been your imagination, and if it wasn't, well, not all superstitions are true."

"Of course. That's just silly. Stuart's the one for me." She smiled again.

I hoped she was right. But time would tell . . .

My feelings about superstitions were changing. As always. Now that I'd been in Destiny for a while, I'd come to believe that the validity of superstitions might partly depend on how you look at them, and how they treated you and you treated them.

As with my loss of Warren. He'd had the bad luck to walk under a ladder, which resulted in his death — definitely bad luck for him. And for me.

And yet it had led to a major change in my life as I tried to figure out superstitions and good luck, and now here I was, in Destiny, with a new life and new people . . .

I found myself smiling pensively as Pluckie and I made our way back to the Lucky Dog, through throngs of people.

Throngs. Maybe I could turn this situation into one where my shop would get even more business — since I wasn't sure all these people interested in my store were buying anything. I'd been putting off scheduling another of my talks on animal superstitions until the suspicion around me was removed. I'd have to schedule one soon.

But it wouldn't be the next night, I learned when Martha came over to me with a big, happy grin on her face. "I'm so glad you cleared yourself of murder, like you did with me. Good girl!" She sounded as if she was talking to a pup, but I knew how much she loved animals, so that was fine.

"Yes, I guess I did," I replied.

"Well, our dear mayor is planning to reassure us and the visitors to Destiny that all's well in our town of superstitions. Word is out that he's throwing a new Welcome tomorrow night."

Bevin Dermot was known for using any opportunity he could find, or create, to talk to people in Destiny about our wonderful town and its superstitions, so I wasn't surprised. I only wondered which superstitions he would work into his talk. I decided I wouldn't be surprised if he happened to mention that things happen in threes. If so, Destiny shouldn't have another murder in . . . well, forever.

I felt my fingers cross fervently about that.

The rest of the day passed quickly and, yes, the Lucky Dog actually did a lot of business, since word had apparently gotten out that its manager had been the recipient of some pretty good luck that day.

I wasn't about to argue with that.

I was somewhat surprised when Justin arrived at seven o'clock that evening as I was in the process of closing up. I hadn't heard from him since he'd dropped me off back here late that morning, and I had no doubt that he was busy.

That could happen to a police chief in a small town when an arrest was made in a murder case.

Martha was still in the shop, but our assistants had already left.

"Hi, Justin," I heard her call while I was putting a few things away in the storeroom. I hurried out and smiled to see the two of them hugging, once again like mother and son. I didn't interrupt them.

When their embrace ended, though, I approached Justin. "How are things?" I asked. He was bound to realize I was inquiring about whether all seemed to be going well in the arrest and future prosecution of Brad.

I'd thought often that afternoon about Lorraine, and I hoped she and her kids would return to Destiny. The Wish-on-a-Star hadn't been open for business today, but it would surely be a good thing to continue to have that children's shop with its superstition-related merchandise open in this town.

"Things are going well. I can't talk much about it, as you know, but so far I think we're putting together a good, solid case against our murder suspect — thanks to you." To my surprise, he bent down and kissed me.

Not that I was surprised that he kissed me, but in public? And particularly in front of Martha?

"Let's keep the heat level down around here," my boss and friend said with a laugh. "Why don't you two head out for dinner?"

We hadn't talked about that at all. I looked up at Justin, then toward Martha. "Sounds good to me, if Justin wants to, but why don't you come with us?"

"Oh, I don't think I'd like to be a third wheel tonight. But you should bring your dogs along." She looked toward Pluckie, who was sitting eagerly by the counter where she was tethered.

"Okay." I drew the word out a bit, especially when I saw the two other humans in the room exchange smiles that seemed to convey something I didn't understand.

Justin accompanied Martha upstairs while I finished preparing the shop to close. Then we were ready to go.

"My car's right outside," Justin said. "You and Pluckie can come with me and we'll pick up Killer to join us, okay?"

"Sure."

In the car, we decided to head to Ojai so we could eat dinner at Randie's, a nice restaurant with a pleasant patio where we'd eaten before. We picked up Killer and headed out there. I was surprised when the server on the patio, who'd taken care of us before, exchanged glances with Justin before placing champagne glasses in front of us.

The dinner was delicious, consisting of prime rib that we shared with both dogs. The conversation didn't even touch on murders or Justin's job, which I liked a lot.

But there was something in his demeanor that I didn't quite understand. Or did I?

We headed back to Destiny, but instead of going straight into town, Justin said, "How about if we pretend tonight that we're on a tour?"

"What do you mean?"

"I have an urge to go see the place where those Forty-Niners actually saw the end of the rainbow that caused them to find gold — and found Destiny."

"Really?" I could have said no, that the drive at night on that narrow winding road could be particularly treacherous.

On the other hand, it would definitely be scenic. And I knew Justin and his driving. I trusted everything about him.

"Really," he answered.

"Let's do it."

He drove slowly up that road where no other cars were present. The dogs seemed nice and calm in the backseat behind us. The car's headlights lit the guardrail ahead of us, and every once in a while, as we turned, I could see the lights of Destiny below us. The sky was a bit overcast, although a quarter moon peeked out from behind the clouds now and then. When a larger break arrived in the clouds and I happened to see my first star — or planet, as the case might be — I chanted "Star light, star bright, first star I see tonight, I wish I may, I wish I might, have the wish I wish tonight." And of course I crossed my fingers before glancing toward Justin.

What did I wish? Let's just say it had to do with him.

Maybe he guessed that. I didn't know. He was watching the road ahead, not me, but he was smiling.

We soon reached the parking lot where tour buses stopped, and so did Justin. He parked and dashed around to my side of the car, opening my door. We opened the back door and grabbed our dogs' leashes before heading toward the railing where we could see a marvelous vista of mountain shadows around us and the lights of Destiny below.

Then Justin stepped back and took my hand.

His voice was a little hoarse and a lot emotional as he said, "I've been considering this for a while, Rory. And not being able to spend as much time with you as I wanted only made me feel more determined. Now that we're together . . . well . . ."

He knelt down, as I'd kind of anticipated — and hoped for. Both dogs flanked him but just stood there, as if they were trained to be part of what was to come.

"Aurora Belinda Chasen," he said, using my full name, so I knew he was serious. He pulled a small box out of his pocket, opened it to reveal a ring that gleamed in the moonlight, and held it out to me. "Will you marry me?"

Lots of thoughts cascaded through my mind. Oh, yes, I'd been hoping for this, although maybe not this soon. He'd told me he loved me — and I hadn't yet let him know it was reciprocal.

I'd lost a prior fiancé due to superstitions — but had found Justin as a result of superstitions, too.

And in fact, I'd fallen recently while going upstairs. It had possibly been an omen.

A wedding was to occur in my family — mine!

I took a deep breath, reached down to pull him to his feet, and said, "Yes, Justin Halbertson, I'll marry you."

And as we kissed, I thought fleetingly that I'd better start researching more superstitions about engagements, weddings, and marriage.

ABOUT THE AUTHOR

Linda O. Johnston (Los Angeles, CA) has published forty-four romance and mystery novels, including the Pet Rescue Mystery series and the Kendra Ballantyne, Pet-Sitter Mystery series for Berkley Prime Crime, and the Superstition Mysteries and the Barkery & Biscuits Mysteries for Midnight Ink.